A PIECE OF MY HEART

Mick and Kate thought they were falling in love. Kate hadn't been just the girl next door. She'd been Mick's life, and he hers. When an unforeseen force draws them apart they're left with wounds that refuse to heal. Now, ten years on, Mick's father's will should have been straightforward, except his addendum was like ice water in Mick's face. It's essential that Mick and Kate work together to save his family's farm. Mick doesn't count on his new manager being accused of murder, and Kate doesn't expect a dangerously seductive woman from Dublin to claim Mick is the father of her child.

A PIECE OF MY HEART

A Piece Of My Heart

by

Kemberlee Shortland

Magna Large Print Books
Long Preston, North Yorkshire,
BD23 4ND, England.

British Library Cataloguing in Publication Data.

Shortland, Kemberlee
    A piece of my heart.

    A catalogue record of this book is
    available from the British Library

    ISBN   978-0-7505-4061-2

First published in Great Britain in 2014 by Tirgearr Publishing

Copyright © 2014 Kemberlee Shortland

Cover illustration © Tirgearr Publishing

The moral right of the author has been asserted

Published in Large Print 2015 by arrangement with
Tirgearr Publishing

Magna Large Print is an imprint of Library Magna Books Ltd.

Printed and bound in Great Britain by
T.J. (International) Ltd., Cornwall, PL28 8RW

DEDICATION

Always for Peter
My own Irishman

ACKNOWLEDGEMENTS

I want to give a special acknowledgement to the two beautiful creatures which inspired this story – Daisie and Poppy, our two Border Collies who are the two dogs featured on this cover.

It's unfortunate that in this day and age, animal cruelty is still a problem in societies all around the world. Places where working breeds are still used for the task they have been bred into for decades, dogs like Border Collies are often still treated like farm equipment. Dogs no longer needed or puppies unwanted from day one are dispatched with little care or thought.

It's with mixed feelings I mention this, because had two such farmers not taken such callous actions to try disposing of unwanted puppies, we would not have the amazing, intelligent, and fun-loving dogs we have today.

Our Daisie originally came to us as Molly and was the inspiration for this story's Molly, and Poppy was the inspiration for Jess. And as Daisie nears her twelfth birthday and Poppy having just turned ten, I look back at the starts they both had in their lives and am so thankful and grateful to have had this time with them, and hope more years are to come.

I want to thank the magical rock goddess, Kim Killian of the Killion Group – http://thekilliongroupinc.com – who agreed to my unusual request. She did an amazing job at incorporating the original image of Daisie and Poppy into this stunning cover.

A special thanks goes out to friend, Chris Williams of Zoeica Images – http://zoieca.com and http://www.zoeicaimages.net – for donating one of his stunning images of an Irish stone circle to this cover.

And finally, a big thanks to my editor, Christine, for her unwavering dedication to this series. Her advice is always sound, and her gentle nature through the process helps keep me grounded.

Chapter One

Solicitor's office, Galway City
September

'What are you doing here?'

'Nice to see you too, Mick.' She opened one eye to look at him.

He stood just inside the solicitor's office door. He'd expected Kate at the funeral service yesterday, but he couldn't see any reason for her to be here today.

He scowled in her direction then strode to reception. The clerk behind the desk turned a harried glance his way, continuing to sort folders beside her computer. 'Can I help you?' she asked, not bothering to stop what she was doing.

'Michael Spillane to see Tighe Lynch,' he grumbled.

Finally looking up, the clerk said, 'He's expecting you. I'll let him know you're here.'

As the clerk reached for the intercom, he turned back to Kate. If this hadn't been his father's solicitor's office and if today hadn't been the reading of his father's will, he would have appreciated the sight of her in her smart dark blue suit, white blouse with the Irish lace trim, and matching blue pumps. She sat calmly, her head against the wall behind her, eyes closed. She bent her shapely legs under her and crossed them

11

at the ankle, her hands folded in her lap.

Her emerald eyes hid beneath lids edged with thick dark lashes. He knew the exact shade of them, since he'd looked into them so often in the past. They were eyes no man could forget.

Her normally unruly black hair was pulled back in a twist and away from her heart-shaped face.

When they were younger, he used to love it when she left her hair down. The tight curls of it bounced over her shoulders like springs when she ran. He'd seen her like that once last year when he'd been home during Christmas. They'd been invited to join the Conneelys, but he'd convinced his father not to go. He couldn't bear being in the same room with her for so long, but she'd delivered food and he'd suffered anyway.

He recalled how he'd stiffened just watching her walk across the farmyard that day. As he did now. He mentally shook himself. This wasn't the time or place to get an erection. The business at hand was the will and what she was doing here now. Not the fact that just looking at her could make him hard.

Clearing his throat, he repeated, 'You didn't answer my question. What are you doing here?'

Her eyes fluttered open. The look she gave him made his heart skip a beat. His groin tightened again watching her tongue smooth its way over her lips. She had no idea just how erotic that simple act was. She was about to speak when a door opened behind him. Both of them spun to face Tighe Lynch.

'Mickleen,' Tighe exclaimed, using the common endearment and thrusting his hand into his.

'Welcome home, lad. I just wish it were under different circumstances. I can't tell you how much Donal will be missed.'

Mick could only tip his head at the man's kindness. Words were still too hard to come by.

Tighe grasped Kate by her shoulders as she stood to greet him and kissed her on both cheeks. 'Kate. Lovely as ever. Won't you both step into my office?'

Not one to stand on ceremony, Mick strode through the door ahead of Kate and Tighe, and went right into the solicitor's office. He knew where it was. Was it really only a little more than two years ago he'd been here to discuss his mother's will?

His scowl deepened when Kate walked through the office door ahead of Tighe. He got the perfect look at her shapely bum as she was forced to step between him and the desk to the seat beside him. He shifted in his seat, crossing his legs and pulling his coat around him to hide his erection. He kept his mind on wondering why she was at the reading of his father's will to keep his libido under control.

Surely, she'd earned a regular wage for the time she spent cleaning his father's house and cooking his meals. She was hired help and would have been paid accordingly. So there should be no reason why she should be here today. Unless there was something the solicitor knew and wasn't telling them. Yet.

'I thought this was just a formality, Tighe. Why is she here?' He couldn't even say her name. Just the feel of it in his mouth would leave him

13

tongue-tied.

Tighe stopped him with an upheld hand. 'If you'll both bear with me, I will explain.' The solicitor turned to a folder on his desk and opened it, extracting two documents. Holding one before him, he said, 'This is your father's will, Michael. It's all very straightforward. In it, the farm, the stock, the land – almost everything is left to you.'

'Almost?'

'We'll get to that, lad.'

Tighe looked at Kate and held up the second document. 'This is the addendum to the will.'

'Addendum?' she asked.

'An addendum means that instead of making up a whole new will, Dad just changed the original one.' Mick, not looking at her, directed his statement to the solicitor and waited for the shoe to drop.

Leave it to his father to make this more difficult on him than it already was. Wasn't it bad enough Mick couldn't get rid of the tremendous feeling of guilt for not spending more time with him? He had never wanted to believe, or admit, his father was that sick. Sure, Kate called him regularly with updates. He heard everything she'd said, but why the hell hadn't he listened to her!

'Changed the will?' she asked. 'Is that right, Mr Lynch?'

'In a manner of speaking,' Tighe replied. 'It means he added something into the original will.'

'When was this?' Mick asked.

'If you'll allow me, I'll read what Donal has bequeathed. If you have any questions, we can go from there. Right?'

14

Both Mick and Kate nodded agreement. Tighe read the will as it stood and then the addendum. Mick couldn't believe what he was hearing. 'That bastard!' he muttered. Out of the corner of his eye he saw the wide glares both Kate and Tighe gave him at the curse.

'Mr Lynch.' Kate's voice came on a whisper. 'What does this mean? I don't understand.' Her eyes were big as she now clutched the arms of her chair, knuckles as white as her face. Gone was the cool Kate he'd seen in the waiting room. In a matter of minutes, she'd gone from radiant to ashen. He was pretty sure he wasn't looking too good right about now, either.

'Yes, can you explain it in plain English?' he asked. *Why do will readings always have to be so damn dramatic?*

'In plain English, your father left everything to you, Michael. However, the addendum states that if you try selling the farm, I have instructions to give everything to Kate.'

'Everything?' whispered Kate, shaking her head.

'That's insane,' muttered Mick.

Tighe sat back in his tucked leather chair and clasped his fingers together on the desk. 'Your father was quite sane at the time, lad. He knew exactly what he was doing.'

'Knew what he was doing? He's giving the farm to her. That's sane?' He flung his arm toward Kate as he bellowed. She flinched. Good. Her weakness meant she wouldn't fight him when he contested the will. And he meant to.

'He was well within his rights, Michael. But Kate gets everything only if you try to sell.'

15

'What am I going to do with a bloody farm?' It was a rhetorical question. He raked his trembling fingers through his hair.

Silence settled around the office. It was a moment before he realized Tighe was staring at him. 'Ah, no, Tighe. There's more, isn't there?'

'Your father gave Kate full custody of Molly. It was his opinion that since she raised the dog because he couldn't, Kate should have her.'

'Bollocks!' he spat, ignoring Kate's sharp intake of breath. 'I gave him that dog. She's part of the farm. By rights, she's mine.'

'You two will have to work out where the dog lives, but Molly is Kate's dog now.'

Mick threw himself back in the chair. 'What if I contest the whole thing?'

'Try, lad. It won't get you anywhere. Your father was determined to give Kate something for everything she's done for your family.'

'But, Mr Lynch, I haven't done anything,' Kate finally spoke. 'I only kept his house and made a meal or two. That was nothing less than I'd have done for my own family.'

Tighe looked at her with seriousness and understanding. 'Kate, you were an important part of Donal's last years and he was grateful to you. He told me everything you did for him, and for Mary when she was dying from the cancer. And without so much as a euro in payment. Don't be so modest, girleen. The world needs more lasses such as yourself.'

'Yeah, right.' Mick couldn't imagine Kate putting her life on hold for so long without a cent in payment.

16

Tighe turned to Mick, exasperation written all over his face. 'Everything's completely documented, Michael. Kate hasn't accepted a cent for everything she's done the past few years. She took complete care of both of your parents in their final years.' The glare Tighe shot him was clearly meant to cut him down to size – and it worked. Suitably berated, he slunk back in his seat. 'You should be thanking her, not doubting her.'

He glanced at Kate, her face pink from Tighe's comments, but she didn't say anything. The only telling sign of her emotion was the tear rolling down her cheek and the quiver of her chin. He had a sudden desire to kiss that tear away and still her trembling. Instead, he mentally slapped himself to remind him what was happening. He was going to lose the farm. He'd already lost the dog.

'I know this must be very hard for you, lass,' the lawyer continued. 'Donal told me often enough how he and Mary loved you like a daughter.'

Kate sniffled heavily. Her voice was a mere whisper and she spoke through trembling lips, the same lips Mick still longed to kiss. 'He always told me that, but I thought it was just because he missed Mick so much. I never realized he meant it. And now it's too late to tell him I loved him, too.'

She buried her face in her palms, bringing Tighe from behind his desk. He withdrew a hankie from his breast pocket and handed it to her, patting her on the shoulder. 'He knew, dear. Actions often speak louder than words.'

17

She dabbed at the corners of her eyes. 'I – I'm sorry. He was such a lovely man and I miss him so.'

Mick was caught between anger at what his father had done and the urge to push Tighe aside and comfort Kate himself.

What was he to do about his father's wishes? He could contest, but Tighe said he didn't stand a chance. Supposedly, his father had been sane when he wrote the will, and the addendum.

What was Mick going to do with the farm? Farm life wasn't for him. His life was in Dublin. He had a great job there in the museum. It was the ideal situation to use his history degree. He had friends and a new flat. He couldn't just up and leave it all behind. He wouldn't. There had to be another way. If there were any way out of this, he'd find it.

Mick cleared his throat. Tighe looked up. 'Are we done here then?'

'Aye, Michael, as soon as you sign these forms. Just a formality.' Tighe explained the final paperwork that closed the file.

Signature in place, Mick rose and begrudgingly lifted his hand to Tighe's. 'Thank you, Tighe. I think.' He turned and left the office, not bothering to look at Kate. He couldn't. By all rights, her grief should be his. If he'd only listened to her... Now, instead of grief, guilt overwhelmed him.

Kate stepped up to the park bench in front of the solicitor's office on Eyre Square where Mick was sitting. His feet were on the bench seat with his bum hanging off the backrest. He was bent over with his elbows resting on his knees, his dark curly hair falling over his eyes, and a cigarette smoldering between his fingers.

'Did you pick up that habit in Dublin?'

He cast her little more than a glance through the curls and took a long drag on his cigarette. She ignored his glare and sat on the opposite end of the bench. She extended her hand toward him, inclining her head at the cigarette. He hesitated for just a moment before giving it to her.

Fool.

She dropped it on the pavement in front of her and squashed it out.

'Hey!'

'Smoking doesn't suit you, Mick.' She bent to retrieve the butt and stuffed it into the cigarette box on the side of the bin next to her.

'What I do is no concern of yours.'

She crossed her legs and arms, then shook her head back and forth, watching the people in the park. 'You don't get it, do you? Your father just died because he'd spent a lifetime smoking them fags. Yet, here you sit with one hanging out of your mouth, and right from the reading of his will. What did they teach you at that fancy school of yours, anyway?'

She looked up at him as she spoke. His moss-colored eyes darkened at her comment.

For a moment, they stared at each other. He didn't bother to brush the hair out of his eyes. She had to suppress the urge to reach up and do it herself.

Since he'd walked into the solicitor's office in his tailored charcoal suit, her heart had pounded in her chest. His dark hair was full of wavy curls that framed his face. His gaze bore into her, heating her in the pit of her belly, and threatened to steal her breath. She relented and backed down, looking away.

There was something in his eyes she couldn't read. When she was fifteen, she thought she could see into his soul through his eyes. That was when she thought there was something more between them than friendship. She'd loved him as a friend. Possibly even more, but certainly never as a brother.

Then something happened. She never knew what drew him away. She'd even sent him notes asking him to meet her at the stone circle, which had been their secret place growing up. The circle was on the property lines of both Conneely and Fairhill farms. They spent countless hours there together. Growing up and growing close. But he'd never come to meet her.

In time, she stopped trying. She didn't want to be a clingy female begging for his attention. He'd told her once to mind her own business, so she had.

That didn't mean the sight of him didn't tear out her heart. She lived for years with an ache she couldn't name. It was only when Mick moved to Dublin that she'd been able to get on with her life. There'd been no chance of meeting him in the village or seeing him again. His life was in Dublin now, and she could get on with hers in Connemara. With his absence, she'd tried to let her heart heal.

Since his move, she hadn't seen him except on

the very rare occasion, like holidays and the funeral yesterday when he'd stood as far away from her as possible. And today. The sight of him stole her breath. As always, there had been that brief instant where she expected him to open to her. Instead, the anger in his eyes snapped her back to reality quick enough.

Looking into his eyes now, she could almost see him as she had when she'd been fifteen–full of hope and expectations. He must have sensed her scrutiny and erected a wall between them, challenging her to get through it. Her heart lurched, and the feelings she'd thought buried deep inside her surfaced almost instantly.

She turned away before she made a fool of herself. There was no denying what she felt. God help her, even through all the heartache and his retreat from her, she still loved him.

So deep in her revelation, she almost missed what he said next.

'I suppose you'd also deny a man a pint as well.' There it was again, the bitterness he seemed to throw at her for no reason.

Well, she wouldn't let him hurt her again. She might still love him, but not enough to let him walk over her. And that's just what he'd done the last ten years.

She picked at a non-existent speck on her skirt then slowly stood before turning toward him. She needed time before she could face him. When she finally did, she wished she had a few more moments, because now that she looked back into his challenging eyes, she wanted to turn and run. But she stood her ground. She wouldn't let him intimidate her. There was too much at stake since the will had been read.

She had to find a way to help Mick keep his farm.

Looking into his eyes, she knew she was right. Anything they had between each other was just the result of growing up in farms that were side by side, and the fact their fathers had been close friends. Nothing more.

Was it hatred she saw in his gaze, or jealousy? Whatever it was, she would ignore it. She would help him find a way to keep the farm then be out of his life forever.

'No, Mick,' she finally said, letting herself breathe again. 'As a matter of fact, I'll buy it for you. Come on.' She turned on her heel and strode across the park without looking back.

Chapter Two

Okay, so she was running after all, even if it was disguised as a brisk walk through Galway City to its medieval heart. When she finally stopped, she found herself on the other side of the city, in front of The Quays Bar. The pub's colorful blue exterior, with red trim and bright window boxes, did nothing to lighten her dark mood.

A winded Mick came up behind her as she reached for the door. 'Could ye not walk any faster, woman!' His Connemara brogue came through in his voice.

'I could, but then I'd be through me first pint and still be waiting on the like of ye,' she mimicked. Not waiting to see if he stood on ceremony, she pulled the door open and stepped through.

It wasn't lunch hour yet, so The Quays was quiet. Several small bars were scattered around the pub on two different levels, with tables tucked into corners, snugs, and any other cubbyhole that would take them. A few tourists occupied the tables near the front windows, and what looked like a couple of regulars sat at the Gothic bar. Portraits of legendary patrons lined the walls in the oldest section of the pub. And the original hearths were ablaze with traditional peat fires.

By far, The Quays' most striking feature was the church-like decor, which included intricate woodwork details, Gothic-style faux windows, a pipe organ against the back wall, and a pulpit in front of the stage where live music could be heard nightly.

She continued on to the back in the old section of the pub and slid into a snug behind the main bar.

A waitress stepped over as Mick slid into a seat across from her. 'Two pints of the black,' he said. The waitress nodded and went off to fill the order.

'I guess since you ordered for me, you can pay for me, too.'

'Smooth, Conneely. And here I thought you'd invited me for a pint.'

'I had until you took charge. Can I assume you'll be taking charge of the issue of the farm as well?' No sense in putting off the subject. If he got mad at her, one of two things was liable to happen. One, he'd find a way to make the will stand in his favor. Or two, he'd get mad enough to leave, which would give her the chance to relax again and sort through her reawakened feelings for him.

And she'd have the two pints he'd ordered to herself. Both outcomes would be most welcome. The vision of a pint in each hand nearly made her smile. Nearly. But the look in Mick's eyes as he stared at her stopped her.

'What?' she asked, with more irritation in her voice than necessary.

'What, what?'

'You're staring.'

'Am I?' He leaned back, still staring at her, but seeming to relax a bit.

'Aye. Why?'

'Trying to figure you out, I guess.'

She was taken aback by his statement. What was there to figure out? 'Care to explain?'

He fidgeted a moment. The waitress's arrival with their pints gave him a few moments reprieve while he fished a few euro out of his wallet to pay for their drinks.

'Will there be anything else?' the waitress asked.

Mick looked back to her, waiting for her answer. 'Nothing, thanks.' He tipped the woman then slid his wallet back into his back pocket.

She ignored the waitress. Her gaze was locked on Mick. The simple motion of raising his hips off the seat to maneuver the wallet into place forced his shirt to draw tight over his chest. His muscles splayed across the fabric. Forcing herself to look away, she raised the pint to her lips and took a long sip, welcoming the bitter taste of the stout.

When she looked back, Mick was staring at her again. She lifted an eyebrow at him in question.

After drawing on his own pint, he finally obliged her. 'So, tell me, what are you up to?'

She sat back and crossed her arms over her chest. 'I don't know what you mean.'

He leaned his arms on the table and wove his fingers together, his gaze penetrating her. His challenging posture made her more anxious than she already was. She crossed her legs under the table automatically, as if preparing to be attacked. Her foot bounced restlessly.

'What are you about? Why would my father leave you the farm, let alone put you in the will at all? I don't understand.'

'That makes two of us then, Mick, because until I got the letter yesterday from Mr Lynch, I had no idea your father put me in his will.'

'Didn't you?'

There was no mistaking the doubt in his voice. She drew her eyebrows together. 'What are you insinuating?'

He sat back again, but his gaze never left hers 'Nothing. Nothing at all. Just asking why my father would leave everything to a virtual stranger.'

'I'm not a virtual stranger, and you know it. I've spent the last five years of my life caring for your parents while you fecked off to Dublin. I practically lived in that house. You should have been there.' How dare he call her a stranger! He should have been the one who cared for his parents. If anyone was the stranger, it was him.

She'd only seen him a handful of times. Even when he was home, he wasn't; leaving her to care for his parents during holidays when they most wanted to see him. 'You should have been there for them,' she repeated, this time her voice a mere whisper.

Before she could stop it, a tear stole down her cheek. She squeezed her eyes shut, trying to stop it. She roughly swiped at the tear and pulled the pint to her lips again in an effort to calm the quiver in her chin. All the while, he kept staring at her.

After a moment, he backed down. 'You're probably right.'

'Probably?'

'Okay, you are right. But I have a job. I couldn't just leave every time you called and expect it to be there waiting for me when I got back.'

Kate huffed and shook her head. 'You don't get it, Mick. Your parents were dying. You should

26

have been there for them. No job is worth keeping if it means losing your parents. Without them, you have nothing left but a lonely, empty farm.'

'Which you will own if I try selling it.'

'Aye. So, I suspect you better find a way to keep it.'

'What am I going to do with it? I never wanted the farm. Why do you think I went to Dublin? Farm life is not for me. It never has been.'

'I never knew that to be an issue with you until you went off to university.'

'Well, it had been. That's probably why Dad wrote up that ridiculous addendum.'

'What's ridiculous about it? Donal worked the farm until he couldn't work anymore. Like his father before him, and his before him. Fairhill has been in your family for six generations. It was one of the few farms that didn't succumb to the famine. When your family couldn't pay the rent, the landlord let them remain because the Spillanes helped feed the starving, by teaching the people to fish and to eat something besides potatoes. There's more history on the farm, Mick, than your self-centered desires will let you see.'

He flinched at her words as if she'd slapped his face. Well, good. He needed to cop himself on.

He didn't know much of the history of the place he'd once called home. Had he stayed to take care of his parents, he would have been the one to hear the stories Donal told, not her.

'You seem to know an awful lot about the place.'

'Donal and I spent a lot of time together.'

'It's no wonder my father left you the farm.'

'No, Mick. He left it to you. Don't sell it and

it's yours for life.'

'But I don't want it.'

'Then you're in a right state, because I don't want it either. But I won't hesitate to honor your father's wishes if you try to sell.' She took the last swallow of her pint and put the glass down with a little more force than necessary, slamming down on the table like a gavel.

He went quiet for a moment as he looked around the pub, his expression unreadable. When he spoke again, his voice sounded more resigned. 'So, where does that leave us, then?'

'Not us. You. You need to find a way to keep the farm, and your precious career in Dublin, it would seem.'

Frustration seemed to tighten Mick's features. 'Where do I start?'

She smiled wryly. 'Are you asking me for help, Mick?'

'Looks that way, doesn't it, Kate?'

She couldn't help notice the use of her name. It reminded her of how much she liked the sound of it coming off his lips. She shook herself to keep her thoughts on track. 'You tell me what the first thing should be. You're the one with the degree.'

'In literary history.'

'And your point? Did they teach you nothing else at that fancy school besides Peig Sayers?'

Mick inhaled deeply, then released the breath slowly. 'I suppose I should go over the accounts to see what Dad owed and who owed him.'

'That would be a good start. The accounts are in his desk in the sitting room. I can also tell you he owed no one and no one owed him.'

'How do you know?'

'Because I spent the last two years with him since your mum died. I kept his accounts as well as cooked his meals, cleaned his house, and–'

'Okay, I get it,' he cut in. 'Is there any business going on the farm at all now?'

The discussion was moving in a more positive direction. Good. There were a few things she'd love to tell him about the abandonment of his parents in their time of need, but this wasn't the time or the place. She doubted there was a time and place for what she wanted to say. Not that it would serve any purpose, except create more tension between them. She didn't want that. She just wanted to help him find a way to keep the farm so she could get on with her life.

She'd once been accepted into Galway General Hospital as a palliative care nurse, but she'd put the job on hold when Mary Spillane fell ill. She wondered if she could get the job again.

'There are about a hundred head of sheep. Donal stopped most business around the time your mother was diagnosed with cancer. Once he finally acknowledged he had emphysema, he soon became confined to the house. Everything but cash business ceased. Anything he sold was paid for in cash. Anything he bought was paid for in cash.

'Your father couldn't get around the farm un-assisted, so he was pretty much housebound, unless Dad went over and got him up in the trac-tor to take him around the farm. Even though he couldn't get about on his own, he still appreciated Dad taking him around the place to oversee it. It

29

made him feel like he was still part of the goings-on.'

'Do you know if the farm is paid off? Are there any debts to the bank?' His voice took on a businesslike tone.

She shook her head. 'Donal made sure everything was paid up so there wouldn't be any debt on his death.'

He cocked a brow at her statement. 'You say that with such casualness.'

'What? Death? I've been facing it every day for five years. Both of your parents knew they were dying, so there was no use in skirting the subject around them. Some delicacy, yes, but there was no denial about their health. At least, not by them or me.'

He grunted. 'If Dad was housebound, how could he manage a handful of sheep?'

'That would bring us to the next issue. Molly.'

'Ah, right.' Mick sat back. 'The dog. What about her? I'm assuming if I can manage to keep the farm, Molly stays, too.'

'You know what they say about assuming, Mick.'

'Will this be another argument?'

'I didn't know we were arguing in the first place.'

'Okay, let's talk about the dog. She's been working sheep for fun and pleasure?' he bit.

'There you go again. I thought we were discussing the farm like a couple adults. Nothing will be accomplished with your snide comments.'

There were no apologies forthcoming, so she continued. 'Molly has been working the sheep for a couple reasons. First and foremost, so she can get trained as a proper sheepdog. Collies are working dogs and need a job to be happy. Also, your father wanted to keep some business going on the farm to feel part of it, so he and I struck a deal.'

'I knew there was something going on.'

'Nothing was going on, Mick. Jazuz!' *Jesus, Mary and Joseph, he's exasperating.* 'I trained Molly to work the sheep. Plain and simple. Occasionally, someone would buy a lamb or ewe when the flock got too big. And we had to cull the rams. Molly is a good sheepdog, but she needs to work. I intend to take her back to our farm so she can work a few head there. She and I get on well together. Since your father left her to me outright, I will honor the gift.'

'The dog wasn't his to give you,' he told her matter-of-factly. 'Molly's mine.'

'Molly was your father's dog. You gave her to him when your mum passed. Now she's my dog.' She looked him straight in the eye and dared him to challenge her.

After a moment, once he'd managed to calm down, he continued. 'If Molly has been working sheep on … the farm … then I assume there are sheep still there.'

'Aye, there are. As I said, about a hundred.'

'If you take Molly off the farm, then I'll have to get another sheepdog to manage them.'

'I suppose you're right, if you're planning to keep the place a working farm. You'll need a shepherd, too. Dogs aren't self-motivated. Alternatively, you could sell the sheep and stop all business. If you do that, then what will happen to the farm?'

'Nothing, I suppose.' He probably hadn't

thought beyond his last sentence.

A knot twisted in her stomach. 'You can't let the farm fall into ruin, Mick. That would be a fate worse than selling it.'

'Can we compromise, then?'

'Depends on what you have in mind.'

'Leave Molly on the farm. You can keep coming over to work with her there. She's grown up on the farm. There's no use in removing her just because Dad isn't there anymore.'

She tried to ignore the hitch in his voice. 'Not if you're going to let the farm fall into ruin.'

'If Molly stays on the farm to work the sheep, then there's no reason for the farm to fall into ruin.'

'So you plan on staying and running the farm?'

He shook his head, a hint of a smile curving his lips. 'Nooo.'

She sat back again and refolded her arms. 'So what you're saying is that you want Molly to stay on the farm, you want me to go over and work her, but you aren't staying on and you expect the farm to pay its own way. Is that right?'

She could practically see the wheels turning in Mick's mind as he sorted through this. 'Well, yeah, I guess. If you're there–'

'No,' she said flatly.

Mick seemed taken aback. 'No?'

'I'm not going to keep going over there as I had – as if I lived there – to do your job.'

'I thought that's what you wanted.'

'No, Mick. What I want is for you to find a way to keep the farm from falling into ruin. I intend to see if I can get my job back at the hospital. I won't have time to run your farm and work at the same time. You're practically asking me to move in and run the farm for you.'

'I'll pay you to run the farm. You can keep anything you make off the sheep.'

'Why should I when I can take over the farm free and clear if you try to sell it?' Good Lord, how could he assume such a thing? She didn't want to be beholden to him for anything anymore. Now that his parents were gone, God rest their souls, she could get on with her life. 'No, Mick. This is your responsibility.'

'So leave Molly on the farm and go over on your days off to work her.'

She sighed deeply, then looked into his eyes. 'What good would that do her? Aside from being alone the whole time, who will feed her? She needs human interaction. She needs constant training. She'll only get that by moving her to Conneely Farm.'

'Well, help me out then, because I obviously don't know what you expect me to do.' Mick threw his hands in the air in exasperation.

She stared at him. Possible solutions tumbled around in her mind and crashed into her mix of emotions. Did he really think she'd agree to his outrageous proposal?

She took a deep breath. 'Why don't I just take Molly home with me until you figure it out? I'll get Dad over to help move the sheep and we'll work them at our place. When you decide what you want to do, let me know and we'll talk.'

She started to gather her things before sliding out of her seat. She was stilled by his hand on hers. The heat of it shot through her like a flash of lightning, and she spun to face him.

His eyes had softened. 'Wait,' he said softly.

'For what?' For a moment, they gazed at each other. She wasn't sure what she saw, but it looked a lot like pleading.

Finally, 'There has to be a solution. I just can't see it for myself.'

She sighed. 'Why don't you head back to the farm? Sleep on it. Think things through. Maybe you'll find an answer in a day or two. I don't expect you to make any decisions right now. Your father's just died. You've received a huge shock over the will. Things are confusing for you right now. Give it a few days, then–'

'Then, what?'

'Ring me and we'll talk about them.' She moved her hand from under his, the warmth of his touch evaporating, and slid out of the snug.

'Kate, I haven't been to the farm yet.'

She froze, unable to hide her surprise.

'I took a room at a hotel up on Eyre Square.'

She eased back into her seat. She kept her gaze locked with his, searching for an answer. He lowered his gaze to his fingers, which were fidgeting with a spare coaster on the table. When he finally looked back at her, his eyes were filled with pain. She understood then that guilt haunted him.

Slowly, she reached over and placed her fingers on top of his. He let the coaster fall to the table and took her hand in his. His gaze rose to their entwined hands. His thumb rubbed the backs of her fingers.

After a moment, he met her gaze. The last ten

years seemed to have never happened and they were back to being the best of friends; the best of friends who'd always shared their thoughts and feelings. But in a blink, the reality of the situation brought her back to the present. Nothing had changed between them since he'd pulled away from her ten years ago. Her heart ached to comfort him, but she reined in her emotions. She would treat him with as much distance as he treated her.

'I haven't been able to go.'

Her other hand came up to pat his. 'It's okay, Mick. I understand.'

'I just can't go alone. I drove by when I got in from Dublin, but–'

She thought about what she was going to say next before she actually spoke. She wanted to be sure she was doing the right thing. By all rights, she should let him sort through his feelings. After all, he's the one who got himself into this mess. He should get himself out. It was the look in his eyes now that changed her mind. For a moment, just a split second, she thought she could see into his soul again.

'Do you want me to go with you?'

He gazed up at her then. 'I–'

'I was going over, anyway,' she lied, cutting him off. She stood again and pulled him up with her. If he was going, it had better be now or he'd never go.

'Kate–'

She squeezed his hand before releasing it. 'Come on, then.'

Chapter Three

Mick found her waiting outside the pub when he exited. 'Really, Kate, I can make it on my own. I just need–'

'Time?'

'Maybe.' Now that he was outside, the fresh air hit him. The warmth of the pub had dulled his senses. Sitting with her, he started relaxing when what he really wanted to do was tell her in no uncertain terms what his intentions were for the farm. But once she started questioning him, he found he wasn't so sure.

True, he hadn't been out to the farm since he got the call that his father had died. He'd hoped to get the place sold without having to go back. There were too many memories there, good and bad, and he didn't fancy revisiting them.

Now that the will had been read, and after talking to Kate and hearing her intentions, he had to think carefully about his next step. If he couldn't sell the property, then he had to find a way to keep it. Moving back to run it himself wasn't an option. If he knew Kate, she was serious about his not letting the farm fall into ruin. He didn't want to see the farm fail. He just didn't want to be the one running it.

Maybe he should let her take him out to the farm. Perhaps together they could find a solution. Then he could go back to Dublin.

'Shall I drive or you?' he asked.

'I'll follow you. My car is parked just there in the car park.'

He glanced up at The Quays car park sign and nodded. 'I'm up on the Square.'

'Grand. I'll give you a lift up then follow you out.'

She turned and headed into the car park. Would she never just slow down for a minute so a man could catch his breath?

He followed her up three flights of stairs and across the car park. When they reached her car, he froze. Surely she didn't intend for him to get into this soup can on wheels.

'What?' she asked sharply, drawing his gaze.

'This yours?'

She looked over the car. 'Yeah. Is there a problem?'

'It's a Mini.'

'And your point?' She folded her arms across her breasts and lifted an eyebrow.

'None. I just thought you'd be driving something a little more–'

'A little more what, Mick?'

'I don't know. After all the money my parents paid you, I expected you might be driving–'

'A Mercedes? A BMW perhaps?'

'Well, yeah. Or at least a new Mini.' His father must have been keeping the few head of sheep just to pay her for her services. She had to have a tidy bank balance by now.

'You thought wrong, Mick. Remember what Tighe said? I didn't take a cent from your father. Now, get in.' She pulled the door open, slid in,

37

then reached over and flipped the lock on his side.

He drew his fingers through his hair, exhaled sharply, then climbed in beside her. She was right about what Tighe said. He'd been so upset in the office, the fact had barely registered.

The drive back to Eyre Square took a few minutes as she zipped through lunchtime traffic clogging the streets. The car was tighter than he expected. Each time she shifted gears, she brushed his thigh. The first time she apologized and said his leg was in the way. He'd moved it, but now she seemed to be touching him on purpose. Or was his leg just gravitating in her direction on its own?

Her fragrance filled the closed-in car and contradicted the professional outfit she wore. He'd expected something floral, something feminine, not this heady, musky scent. It gave her an air of mystery that suited her. He had been too agitated in the solicitor's office to notice much, and the pub had too many of its own stale odors. But here in her tiny car, her scent swirled around, intoxicating him.

He glanced over and watched her negotiate the traffic. He remembered her hair the last time he saw her. He'd been visiting his father over Easter. He hadn't expected to see her there. His father's appearance had shocked him. He sat in his old chair, staring at the TV with his oxygen tank beside him, the tubes connected to help him breathe. Mick's heart had ached at the pale complexion on the man's face, the look of exhaustion, and the sound of him struggling to breathe.

Then he'd caught sight of Kate standing at the

door to the kitchen. She wore a pair of snug-fitting old jeans tucked into a well-worn pair of green Wellies, and a cream colored Aran jumper. Her dark hair was down around her shoulders, curling tightly in ringlets that framed her heart-shaped face. For an instant before she saw him, she looked totally relaxed. Her cheeks were flushed from being outside. By the look of her Wellies, she must have been in the garden. She clutched a bunch of fresh carrots. At that moment, she was the most beautiful woman he'd ever seen.

When she saw him, she stiffened, and the smile creasing her lips flattened. Her features hardened instantly. Still, she looked beautiful. She exchanged a brief greeting with him then he returned his attention to his father. But the sight of her had clenched his heart in a different way, and he wasn't sure what it meant.

He had that same clenching now sitting beside her in the Mini. He longed to reach up and pull her hair out of its twist, so it could spill over her shoulders as it had that day in the kitchen. He shifted in his seat at the tightening in his groin.

The sound of her voice pulled him out of his thoughts. 'Which one is it?' she asked as she pulled onto Eyre Square.

He pointed to a dark blue Honda with a rear spoiler and alloy wheels. 'There.'

Kate pulled up behind the car and pulled on the handbrake. 'I never figured you for a boy racer, Mick.' She smiled at him then and he had a sudden urge to kiss her.

'And I never figured you for a rally driver,' he countered, unlatching the safety belt. He had to

39

get out of the car. He'd seen Kate only a handful of times in the last six months, but each time she confused and muddled his mind.

'My driving isn't that bad.'

'I was making a joke about the Mini, not your driving.'

'It gets me around.'

He grunted and got out of the car. The fresh air hit him again, snapping him into alertness. What was it about being around Kate that put his mind into a fog?

He slammed the door and walked around to the driver's side of his car. He opened the door and slid in.

Fastening the seatbelt, his thoughts came back to the discussion in the pub. He had to find a way to keep both the farm and his job in Dublin. He hoped Kate would help him find a way, because he had no ideas of his own. Tighe's reading of the will had stunned him. If he had known what his father intended, he might have been able to prevent it.

Behind him, Kate had backed her car up to give him room to pull out. He thrust the key in the ignition and started the engine. He signaled and reversed. Soon, they were both on the N59 heading into Connemara.

Mick pulled off the main road and passed between two overgrown fuchsias to join the connecting road between Conneely Farm and Fairhill Farm. The flowers hung heavy with scarlet buds, their scent filtering in through the car vents and sparking something familiar inside him.

He followed the long winding road across the

hillside toward the house. As he neared, he slowed. The farmyard, surrounded by an old stable house, the barn, chicken coop and other outbuildings, came into view.

He pulled to a stop in front of the house and cut the motor. He sat a moment to compose himself. The sudden revelation that his father wouldn't be here to greet him this time stole his breath. His heart raced. He gazed around the farmyard as ghosts of his past came to life.

The house had been painted just before he left for university. Yellow had been his mother's favorite color. He'd never noticed it before, but now the paint definitely showed its age.

Under every window, where his mother had spent so much time tending the little patches of earth, flowers bloomed. Even now he could picture her placing the colorful bedding flowers in the dark brown earth. The window boxes also burst with color, both on the ground floor windows and the bedroom windows upstairs. Mick credited Kate with having kept them in bloom since his mother's passing. He knew she'd done this for his father.

The yard, though free from clutter, showed the obvious signs of many decades of use. The barn had been whitewashed around the same time the house had been painted. He and his father had seen to it. The once bright yellow door, like the house, was faded and stood half opened. Someone had backed in the tractor. Probably Kate's father, Liam. Beside the house, a dozen chickens wandered outside their little stone coop, pecking at the ground.

From across the yard, past the old slaughter-house, sheds, and turf store, Molly galloped to-ward the parked cars. The dog skidded to a halt at Kate's feet and flopped herself on her back, wig-gling uncontrollably, waiting for Kate to scratch her belly.

He hadn't noticed Kate pulling up next to him or getting out of the car, but he was now mesmer-ized, watching the pair. Her voice drifted through the closed windows of his Honda. The dog seemed to talk back to Kate with her snuffles and grunts of pleasure.

He slid out from behind the wheel and closed the door behind him. Molly shot to her feet, immediately alert, but stayed protectively beside Kate. He stepped up to the two and put his hand down for Molly to sniff. When it seemed Molly had accepted him, he patted her head.

'I don't have keys for the house.' He'd never had keys when he was growing up. He'd never needed them. His parents were always home. Now that he thought about it, he couldn't remember his par-ents ever spending time away from the farm. Not even to take a holiday.

'I've got keys.' She turned to the front door and twisted the handle. The door swung open. 'We still never lock our doors this far out in the coun-try, but I'm sure you'll want to lock up when you leave for Dublin.'

He nodded, then followed her inside. Once the door was closed, all he could do was stand there and stare into the empty room. Somehow, it seemed smaller than he remembered. Or maybe it was that his father had always been larger than life, and any room he was in had to stretch and expand to fit him. Without him in the sitting room, it felt as if the room squeezed in on Mick.

He expected, even now, to see his father sitting in his chair before the telly, wheezing through the tubes that helped him breathe. But the chair was empty, the telly was off, and the ever-present oxygen tank gone. The air seemed to hang thick with memories. Heavier still was the guilt weighing him down. Would that feeling ever leave?

'Are you all right, Mick?' Her voice filtered into his mind as he turned to see the concerned look on her face.

'Yeah, why?' He sounded a bit more defensive than was necessary.

'You've gone pale.'

He waved off her observance. The room was exactly as he remembered it as a child, and every other visit since he'd left for university. The great stone hearth, with its thick oak mantel, dominated the room. The opening to the hearth was so large that as a child he could walk right into it without having to crouch. Stone shelves built into the insides had once held cooking implements. A turf fire would have been used for cooking. A big iron pot would have hung from a big hook suspended over the flames. Or a trivet would have been set within the coals to hold a baking pot for making bread. Bits of the glowing embers would be placed on the lid to balance the cooking temperature.

He remembered his mother baking bread like that when he was very young, and his father and he would get out an old churn to make the butter. Not because they had to, but to remind him of

43

what it was like for his ancestors. His mother always told him never to forget his roots. Something in Kate's words in the pub told him she probably knew more about his roots than he did.

Suddenly, sunlight flooded through the windows. It brightened the room, shining the brightest on his father's empty chair. The only telltale sign that his father had used the chair for so many years was the imprint left by his dad's backside in the seat cushion and the worn spots that his mother's hand-crocheted doilies still covered.

His mother had sat in her own chair beside his father's, a crochet hook in hand. Back then, both chairs had faced the hearth. His father would have been listening to the wireless, usually a G.A.A. match, while his mother's hands flew over her work. How his father loved Gaelic football.

Mick, himself, would have been lying on his belly in front of the fire, reading one of his many books or doing his homework. Memories flooded through him, making his chest ache. He had to remind himself to breathe. That had been a happy time in his life. A time before—

'Mick!' Her raised voice shocked him out of his thoughts. 'I'm making tea. Will you have a cuppa?' She was ignorant of his thoughts. Ignorant that she was the cause of his ten year-long heartache.

He gazed into her eyes, trying to find an answer to a long-asked question in his own mind. How could she have done it to him? But the answer wasn't forthcoming, so he simply nodded in reply and turned toward the stairs.

He took the steps by twos until he reached the landing, where he stood looking at two doors. The door in front of him belonged to his parents' room. The door to his right was his old room. Both doors stood open, calling to him. He chose his own. He couldn't face his parents' room. Not yet.

His bedroom hadn't changed since he'd left. His mother didn't see the point, as there were no other children to move into it, and he didn't seem inclined to move home and change it himself. He didn't know what he expected to find up here now, but something pulled him up the stairs.

His single bed sat under the window. He remembered moving it there himself so he could see the moon and stars at night. It still had the same spread on it. It was a much-faded green now, but he remembered a time when the color had matched Kate's eyes.

He turned his gaze to the small bookcase near the head of the bed. Most of the books were Irish classics from the likes of Synge, O'Sullivan, Macken, Joyce, and Keane, and some literary classics by Hemingway, Poe, Shelley, Stevenson, and Steinbeck. He'd loved reading as long as he could remember. His tastes had always been eclectic.

He sat on the edge of his bed and ran his fingers over the worn spines. He had read each book–most of them many times over.

His finger came to rest on one particular book and his heart started to race. 'The Works of Lord Byron.' He pulled it off the shelf. He knew which page he was looking for, but the book fell open automatically. He went right to the passage he could recite from memory because he'd read it so often.

She walks in beauty, like the night
Of cloudless climes and starry skies;
And all that's best of dark and bright
Meet in her aspect and her eyes.

There was a strip of small pictures of Kate and him that had been taken at a shop kiosk. He wondered if she still had the second photo strip they'd made. He'd tucked his between the pages like a pressed flower and gazed into the eyes of the fifteen-year-old girl he'd thought he was falling in love with. If possible, in the ten years since those photos were taken, Kate had grown more beautiful.

Next, he flipped to the first page of the book. Opposite an engraving of the poet himself was a simple line and declaration:

'You will always be my best friend!
All my love, Kate, xoxo'

Those simple words were worn thin on the page. His fingers, then as now, traced the lines Kate had written. He remembered the day she'd given him the book.

They were walking home from school together, as usual, and cut a path through Fairhill's pastures. The climb up the hillside to the ancient stone circle was sheltered from view by gorse.

As adolescents, the stone circle was their secret place to escape chores at home. It was a castle or Celtic fort, depending on which game they were playing. As teenagers, it was a place that had quickly grown to be a much more private place, where they could talk – about what they'd read, school, or the places they wanted to see in the world. It was their place to dream.

On this particular day, he'd taken Kate to the circle as an excuse to spend more time with her. He didn't understand it then, but more than friendship had blossomed between them.

He'd been surprised when she pulled a package out of her coat pocket and handed it to him. She didn't say anything. Just handed it to him. The plain paper wrapping seemed to shine in the dim light of the day. His fingers shook taking it from her.

He was thrilled with the gift. She'd obviously bought the book in a used bookstore, most likely Kenny's in Galway City, as it was an old copy that dated back to the turn of the century. The pages were delicate and yellowing around the edges, and the typeset was old-fashioned. It had character, this book, and he loved it.

This was his sixteenth birthday. She was the only one who knew what pleasure he would get from receiving a book as a gift, even one of poetry. He was so thrilled with the gift, he leant over to quickly kiss her on the cheek. Only she'd looked up at him just then and his lips touched hers.

The flush that rushed across her skin must have echoed his. Both slowly grinned like eejits on a bog trot when they realized what had happened. Their first kiss. It was then he realized their relationship had changed forever.

They were no longer children, but heading quickly into adulthood. The firmness in his trousers that day was enough to tell him that. More so was the twisting in his chest every time he thought of her, every time she was around, and every time he read through this book. Knowing she'd given it to him, that her delicate fingers had touched the pages, was enough to increase his heart rate.

A movement across the room startled him. He looked up to see the object of his adolescent desire step through the door. A look of worry etched across her face.

'I was calling you.'

He moved to replace the book on the shelf. 'Sorry, I didn't hear you. I was–'

'Here, let's have a look at that.' She sat beside him and took the book before he could protest. 'Byron. I gave this to you, sure.'

There was no need for Mick to reply. They both knew she had. Her cheeks pinkened. *She must remember the day as well.*

He watched her flip through the book then stop at one of the passages. She cleared her throat, then read the passage softly with feeling.

You call me still your life.–Oh! change the word–
Life is as transient as the inconstant sigh:
Say rather I'm your soul; more just that name,
For, like the soul, my love can never die.

The words struck deep in his soul as much now as they had the first time he'd heard her read them so long ago. He remembered how he had felt for her back then and knew he'd always care for her. Back then, she'd been his life and he hers. Her handwritten vow was forever etched on the first page of the book, and he'd never forget that special day at the stone circle.

She sat so close to him he could smell her skin, unadorned by manmade perfumes. Sitting close to her in her Mini earlier in the city, he'd thought she wore perfume. He now realized it was only the fragrance of her soap mingling with her body's unique scent. The combination of the two intoxicated him.

His gaze slipped down her body, his heating in response.

She'd slipped off her shoes downstairs, which probably accounted for his not hearing her on the stairs. Her slim feet curved up to narrow ankles and tapered calves. Her knees were the last he saw of her shapely legs before they disappeared under her prim dark skirt.

Her blouse had been pulled free of the confining waistband. She looked as if she was just in from work, home for the evening and relaxing before slipping into something more comfortable. For some reason, the thought of her coming home to him warmed him.

His gaze came back to her mouth as she finished the poem. Her lips moved as she distinctly pronounced each word of the passage. What would those lips feel like on his skin – better yet, wrapped around his arousal? That thought made him stiffen even more.

She'd let her hair down earlier, probably while she was down in the kitchen. It spilled over her shoulders and haloed her heart-shaped face. The sun filtering through the window netting sparked red lights of fire in the dark curls.

On impulse, he reached up and took a curl between his fingers and rubbed it between them. It was so much softer than it looked. He brought it to his nose and inhaled deeply, closing his eyes at the scent of it. It smelled like the Irish rain.

As he opened his eyes, Kate had half turned to glance at him as she came to the end of the passage. 'My love can never die.' Wariness played across her features. He drew himself closer until her breath touched his cheek. He smelled the sweet tea she'd been drinking in the kitchen.

Unable to resist, he closed the space between them. Her eyes fluttered, unsure, until his lips met hers. He squeezed his eyes shut as fire shot through him.

Instinctively, he sought her heat. He moved his mouth over hers with deliberation. At first she hesitated, but she didn't pull away. She relaxed as he nipped and tugged, encouraging him to demand more with each movement. When he touched the tip of his tongue to her upper lip, she didn't fight him, so he deepened his kiss.

They were both apprehensive, tasting each other this way for the first time. When he touched his tongue to hers, she hesitated but leaned into him, returning his kiss.

Kate seemed as unsure as he, but she made no indication she wanted to stop. Their tongues coiled repeatedly, and longing squeezed Mick from his chest clear to his groin.

Wrapping his arm around her waist, he pulled her closer. Her hand clasped his shoulder, her fingers pressing into his muscles.

When she moaned, it echoed through her ribcage, up into her throat to pass through her lips and into his mouth. He swallowed it blissfully and thrust his tongue into her mouth again to suckle her, tease her, taste her. Oh, the taste of her about undid him.

He slid his hand up her back and wound his fingers through her hair to her scalp. Holding her against him, he lowered her to the bed.

Chapter Four

What was he doing to her? Kate's mind reeled as Mick's mouth plundered hers. She was powerless against him; not that she wanted him to stop, mind.

At the same time, she didn't want him to continue. It was wrong. She knew it was wrong, but she couldn't stop him. She couldn't stop herself, for that matter.

Emotions washed through her. She'd dreamed of this and wondered what Mick's kiss would be like, how it would affect her, how he would taste. She'd wanted him since she was old enough to know what wanting was. Now that she was in his arms, she wanted to make her dreams a reality, regardless of his motives.

The realization that Donal had just died was at the back of her mind, but his essence was still in the house. She half expected him to walk through the door and chastise them for what they were doing under his roof. She knew he wouldn't, but it didn't calm the anxiety that they would still be caught. Hadn't she and Mick been strangers for the last ten years? Could a simple kiss wipe away all the tears she'd shed over him?

As much as she knew she should stop this, she couldn't. She'd wanted him too long. His masculine warmth pressed against her. His touch felt natural. She lay in the crook of his arm on his narrow single bed while his other hand roamed over her body.

Normally, she would have been self-conscious. She wasn't fat, but she was fuller in places that rounded out her figure and made it harder to find clothes that fit properly. Her bottom was the part of her she liked the least and tried to hide whenever possible in oversized shirts and jackets.

Mick made her forget her self-consciousness. He made her feel sexy. She wanted him to keep touching her. He stroked the soft mound of her belly, then moved along her hip to her thigh to pull her even closer and against his erection. She couldn't keep her moan of pleasure to herself. He soothed the longing that ten years of aching couldn't erase.

His caress moved up again, across her hip, along her waist to her ribcage and under her blouse. His fingers pressed into her flesh, not quite scratching her skin, but not delicate either.

When he cupped her breast, she couldn't breathe. She'd never been touched like this. When he stroked the taut nipple pressing through her lacy bra, she sucked in her breath, forcing oxygen into her lungs.

She didn't know when it happened or how, but Mick had unbuttoned her blouse. Cool air wafted over her stomach. He returned his attention to her breasts, first one, then the other, gently squeezing them and rolling the nipples between finger and thumb. The rough texture of the lace as it rubbed against her skin heightened her arousal. She arched involuntarily into his palm.

He pulled the straps just off her shoulders, ran his fingers down to the cup, then dipped his fingers underneath the lace to her nipple to flick it back and forth. Soon, he had freed the breast and held the mound in his hand.

He trailed hot kisses along her jawline and down her throat to the well at her collarbone. He dipped lower still, where he pulled her erect nipple into his mouth.

She dug her nails into his back through his shirt, arching against him. She'd never been made love to before and it was gloriously delicious. The flash of electricity that shot through her was intense, and she was in no hurry to have it end any time soon. Her body was alive with desire, and everywhere he touched her was like fire on her already heated flesh.

While he drove her wild with his tongue, his hand strayed back to her stomach again, then down her hip to her thigh where he held her against his more than obvious erection. He slid his hand under her skirt, parting her legs as he moved. It was slow and sweet torture.

When his palm cupped her, her eyes shot open. He silenced her protest with another deep kiss. At once she fell into compliance.

Just then, a car horn sounded in the yard. Molly barked. Mick's head snapped up and he looked out the window.

'Shit!' He threw himself off the bed.

She leapt from the bed after him. Her blouse almost fell off her shoulders, and a flush of shame shot through her so hot she thought she was poor Joan of Arc on the martyr's post. What had she done? What had she allowed Mick to do to her?

He turned, his bulge still very much in evidence. 'I'll see to whoever it is, then come back to finish what we started.'

'Oh, no, we won't. How dare you–'

'How dare me?' He cut her off. 'You weren't exactly screaming "no".'

Her cheeks burned. What could she say? He was right. 'Maybe so, but–'

'But what?'

She turned him by the shoulders and pushed him toward the bedroom door. 'Oh! Just get down there and see who it is while I do something about the state of me. We can forget this ever happened.'

She flew into the bathroom and slammed the door. Pressing her back to the door, she tried to calm her racing heart. Then she caught her reflection in the mirror.

'Oh, no,' she moaned. She looked like a woman who had just hopped out of bed. And literally, she had. She couldn't go downstairs in this condition. She quickly removed her blouse and pulled a hand cloth from the stack from under the sink. She soaked it in cold water then wrung it out before scrubbing her face with it. She didn't stop there. She bathed all the places Mick's lips had scorched her. No matter how much she washed, she couldn't scrub away the feel of him. Her skin still burned everywhere he'd touched her.

What a fool she was to let him get away with this. What a fool to let herself enjoy it so much she couldn't justify pushing him away, as would have been appropriate. He'd made her lose herself. Like it was possible to forget the last ten years and pick up where they'd left off.

He knew she was vulnerable right now. The

death of his father had hit her hard. He had to know that. Did he hope to seduce her into giving up ownership of the farm if he tried to sell?

Well, whatever his motives, she wouldn't let it happen. She would honor Donal's last wishes, regardless how she felt about Mick. No matter how he tried to seduce her.

She grabbed an old brush kept under the sink and ran it through her hair. The curls were thoroughly tangled, thanks to Mick. She ended up ripping at her scalp to bring the mass under control again.

She wasn't sure if it was the pain of the rough brushing or the thought of what had just happened that brought tears to her eyes, but they fell just the same. She threw the brush into the sink, pulled the cool hand cloth to her face, and let the tears come in racking sobs.

When Kate descended the stairs, she was mortified to find her father, Liam, in the sitting room, having a cup of tea with Mick.

'Da!'

'Kate,' came his deep voice. 'Ye're lookin' absolutely flushed, girl.'

Heat flooded her face at his observation. Could he tell what had happened?

'We just came from the reading of the will, Mr Conneely,' Mick cut in, saving her from disgrace. 'Kate was rather upset by it.'

Her father took a sip from his cup. 'Is that so?'

'Aye, Da. I told you I was going into the city this morning. I had an interview at the hospital and then I was going to the reading. I'm sure I told you.'

He seemed to think about it. 'I'm sure you did, pet. Don't just stand there looking stricken, girl. Get yourself some tea and join us.'

She nodded and went into the kitchen. She heard the men talking through the doorway.

'I thought the will was just a formality.'

'I thought it was, too. I was surprised to see Kate there when I arrived. Turns out my father had a strange sense of humor in his last days.'

'What do you mean? Did the will say something extraordinary?' That was her father. Right to the point. She was actually surprised by the tone of his voice. Was it possible that his closest friend hadn't told him about putting her in the will?

'Aye. He's giving everything to Kate, as it turns out.'

'What?' her father gasped.

She needed to get back in there.

'Only if you try to sell, Mick.'

She set her cup on the table, then sat on the sofa beside her father. Mick sat in his mother's chair. Donal's chair remained empty.

Her father looked at her, waiting for an explanation.

'Mick inherited everything.'

'Except the dog,' Mick reminded her.

'Except Molly. But if he tries to sell, everything reverts to me.' She lifted her cup and sipped the hot tea. The bitterness hit her in the back of the throat and threatened to wash the taste of Mick from her mouth. She quickly set the cup aside. Even after all the names she'd just called him, she wasn't sure she wanted to let him go so quickly.

'Mr Conneely, did you know my father was

doing this?'

Her father shook his head. 'He said he'd put Kate into the will, but he didn't say what he was giving her. I never asked. Just assumed it was a little something for helping out around the place.'

Silence filled the room. No one seemed to know what to say. The ticking of the mantle clock echoed off the walls like a Lambeg Drum.

'So,' her father finally said, looking back and forth between them, 'what will you do, son?'

A slight twitch at the corners of Mick's eyes told Kate her father's endearment had struck a chord. It wouldn't have been noticeable to anyone but her, because she knew him so well, but it was there just the same.

'I'm not sure. Obviously, it's in my best advantage to keep the farm, but I've no interest in it.' Mick slunk back against the chair, balancing his mug on the armrest.

'Sounds to me like you're in a spot of bother,' her father said.

'We've been trying to think of a way for Mick to keep the farm, Da,' Kate chimed in. If two heads were better than one, certainty three were better still. 'Mick has no interest in moving home to manage the farm himself, and I'd rather enforce the will myself than let it fall into ruin.'

'Uh-huh, a spot of bother, boy.'

'Da, do you have any ideas that would help Mick keep the farm and allow him to return to Dublin? There has to be something he can do.'

Her father set his mug on the table. He placed his elbows on his knees, steepled his fingers and brought them to his lips as he thought, as if he

58

was praying.

'Hmmm–' Liam muttered as he thought. When he looked up, she wasn't sure what he'd say. Her breath caught in her chest anticipating his words. 'Is there any harm with Kate continuing on here?'

Immediately, she spoke up. She didn't have to think as the words tumbled out. 'No, that's not an option. I'm going back to nursing. Sure, and I might have that position in Galway City. Besides, what would I do around here with themselves gone, and all? No, I don't think that's an option at all, Da. And even if I did, I might as well have inherited the place altogether.'

'Hmm, you've a point, girl.'

'I've already suggested as much, Mr Conneely. There really isn't anything she could do here, anyway. How much tidying can an empty house need? And if she's only here to work the dog – Molly I mean – she can just as easily do it at home.'

'Do you want to get the business going again?' he asked Mick.

'If the place can make some money, then aye, it wouldn't do any harm. As long as it can be done with me in Dublin.'

'So, why don't you hire a manager?'

Kate shot a look at Mick, whose eyes widened with sudden clarity. Neither of them had thought beyond themselves, and she saw he liked this option. She was hesitant, but there was nothing she would be able to do about his decision. He'd be able to keep the farm, return to Dublin, and get on with his life.

She would be the only one affected. For the last five years, she'd spent nearly every day here on the farm. No longer obligated to return, she would have to find a new life for herself. Wasn't that what she wanted?

Going back to nursing seemed the logical route to go, since it was her formal training. Though deep down, she wasn't sure anymore that it was what she wanted to do with her life. Caring for the Spillanes had taken its toll, and she wasn't sure she could go through it all again.

'Kate?' Mick's voice cut through her thoughts.

She looked up to find both men looking at her. 'Sorry, I was thinking.'

'I asked what you thought of your father's idea.'

'I suppose it would work. What about Molly?' No matter what happened with the farm, the dog was hers now and Molly's best interest was also an issue.

'If there's a manager on the premises, there's no reason why she can't stay on here. She's familiar with the farm and the land. She'll be needed to tend the flock,' Mick told her. 'Obviously, the decision's yours if you'll take her home or leave her here, but you can always come over whenever you want to see her.'

'Aye,' was all she could say as she thought about her options.

'And it might not be a bad idea if you did stop in occasionally to look in on the place, to be sure everything's in order. Maybe to put a few things away for me if I decide to come back to check up on the place,' Mick further suggested.

While it wasn't her responsibility anymore, the

idea of being in the Spillane home appealed to her. She'd grown so used to the place, and the idea of no longer needing to come over felt like a door in her life had slammed closed in her face. She'd developed such a strong relationship with the Spillanes, the place felt like home to her, and she didn't like the idea of never returning now that they were gone.

Continuing an occasional visit would allow her to keep an eye on Molly, if nothing else.

'Well?' Liam pressed.

Kate looked between the men. The decision was hers. It was a viable option. There was no disputing it. Everyone got what they wanted. Or did they?

What did she expect Mick to do? He didn't want to move home. She couldn't force him, but did she really want him living back next door? She'd be in the same position she'd been in ten years ago. His stunt upstairs earlier had reignited her desire for him. She didn't think she could handle it. Worse, with him so close and trying it on with her time and again, toying with her feelings.

Damn him for doing this to her. Damn her for letting him.

'Earth to Kate,' called Mick. Her head snapped up. 'What's the decision?'

'Fine,' she snapped. 'I'm all for it. Let's do it.' This was the right decision. Mick would be on the other side of the country where he wanted to be. With him so far away, there was hope she could learn to live without him. Again.

Mick turned to her father. 'Right. We have a solution. The next question is where do we find someone willing to manage this place?'

'I might know a man. I'll call him this evening after tea and see what he has to say,' offered Liam.

'Fantastic,' said Mick.

Liam stood to leave and looked to Kate. 'Shall I wait for you, pet?'

'No, Da. I'll be along shortly. I'll just tidy up here and be on my way.' She wanted a final word with Mick before she told him goodbye.

'Right, so.' Liam grabbed his hat from a table beside the door and turned back to Mick. 'Deirdre is putting the tea out soon, if you want to join us.'

'I appreciate the invitation, Mr Conneely, but I think I'll head back to Galway until you've contacted your man about the job.'

'If you change your mind, Mick, just call in. No need to phone ahead. You're more than welcome. You're good as family, son.'

'Thank you, sir. I appreciate that.'

At the door, Liam took Mick's hand in his own and looked him in the eye. Her father glanced her way, then back to Mick. His gaze spoke volumes, she was sure, but not being a man she had no idea what her father was trying to convey to Mick. By the look on Mick's face, there was an understanding.

Finally, Liam just said, 'Mind yourself,' and was gone.

As soon as her father left, she shot into the kitchen and began tidying up from the tea. She heard Mick step into the room. He stopped in the doorway and watched her work. His gaze burned into her.

'What do you really think of the idea, Kate?'

Without turning to face him, she asked, 'What idea?'

'The one about hiring a manager.' To her surprise, Mick went into the sitting room then returned with the three dirty mugs and slipped them into the sink. From the corner of her eye, she saw him leaned back against the countertop, crossing his arms as he stood casually beside her.

Damn! Why did it still feel so natural to do something as mundane as wash the dishes while he stood, chatting as if nothing had happened upstairs – as if the last ten years hadn't happened?

'I said it was fine.' She didn't bother to disguise her annoyance.

'You said that before. You don't sound keen on the idea, though. I want to know what you really think.'

Kate turned to pick up a tea towel and began drying what she'd just washed. Her hands shook. She hoped she didn't drop Mary's crockery. Mary had told her it had been passed down in the family for three generations. Did Mick know?

'The one thing you may not remember about me, Mick, is that I always say what I feel, and mean what I say. And I said it was fine. What do you want me to say?' Why couldn't he drop the subject and go back to whatever he was doing upstairs?

No. Scratch that. She wanted him to go back to what he was doing before she went up looking for him. She didn't want to find herself on his bed again.

Mick was forced to move when she reached up to open the press behind him to put away the

63

cups. He startled her by grasping her wrist and forcing her to look at him.

'Kate, can we talk about this, please?'

'There really isn't anything to talk about. It's a good idea. It's obviously the only solution. I'm surprised one of us hadn't thought about it earlier, but I'm glad we've found an option.' She slipped free of his grip and stepped away to put the milk back in the fridge.

'Will you leave Molly on the farm?'

At first, she didn't say anything. She would rather take the dog home with her. At the same time, Molly was familiar with Fairhill Farm. And, with a manager, there was no reason why the dog should have to move. She knew the land here, knew the flock.

Finally, she said, 'Aye. She can stay.' Then she turned to Mick and locked gazes with him. 'With a manager here, Molly will be able to work the flock with him. I'll go out with them a few times until she's comfortable taking direction from him, then I'll leave them to it. I'll come over now and again to see how she's getting on.' Then she added, 'And while I'm here, I can check up on the place.'

He nodded his agreement. 'I'm impressed.'

'About what?'

'It didn't take you long to work everything out.'

'What do you expect me to do, Mick? It's the only solution, since you don't want to move home. I'll do what I can to make the transition go smoothly. It's hard enough on Molly since your da died.' He winced at the mention of his father's death. 'If I just up and leave and a stranger comes in to work Molly, there's no telling what would happen with her. I want this to be easy on her. Since we've finally found a way to make this arrangement work, I'd like to see it done right.

'And so that we're on the same page, if I feel Molly needs to be removed from the farm, I will do it.'

'Fair enough, Kate.'

She nodded sharply to end the discussion, then looked around the kitchen to be sure she hadn't missed anything. Nothing appeared amiss. Never mind the tension snapping in the air that passed between them.

'Well, since everything is tidy, I'll be on my way.' She started past Mick, but he grasped her by the upper arm, stopping her in her tracks. He wasn't forcing her to stop, but at the same time she wasn't trying to pull away from him, either. Damn her body for responding to him so quickly. The faster he found a manager and got himself back to Dublin, the sooner she could get her life back on track.

'Kate.' His voice was low, almost a whisper. Still she wouldn't look at him. 'Are you sure you have to go so soon?'

She remained silent. He hoped she was thinking about staying. Then she turned. What he thought he'd see in her eyes wasn't there.

'Aye, I do, Mick. We've nothing left to say,' she told him in her no uncertain terms voice, her gaze serious.

'What about finishing what we started upstairs, then?' he chanced.

That's when her expression changed. Her lovely

65

dark brows drew together and he swore he saw flames in her eyes. And not the good kind.

'Aye, perhaps there is something left to say, after all.' She yanked her arm out of his grasp and stepped back into the kitchen. 'How dare you try to seduce me? Especially when my nerves are so on edge as they are. Your father's just died. I've just got a huge shock with the will reading. And then you try taking advantage of me?' Her voice rose with each accusation.

'I don't know what foolishness is whirling around in your head, Michael Spillane, but the last thing you'll be getting out of me is a consent to sell this farm. I'll do everything within my power to stop you. Your father worked too hard to keep a roof over your head. And his father before him, and his before him.

'I might be naïve about all that carry on upstairs, and I might have enjoyed it,' she admitted with obvious alarm, 'but I'll not let you take advantage of me. And I'll not allow you to coerce me into giving up the farm.'

All he could do was let her rail at him. She was on a roll. There was no denying it. He dodged the finger she poked at him. The fire in her eyes could have burned him if he dared to meet her gaze.

When at last it seemed she'd run out of steam, she shoved past him and stormed into the sitting room. She was leaving without even giving him a chance to reply.

He caught up with her at the door. His hand came to rest on hers on the door latch. Before he could open his mouth to speak, she whirled around and pushed him away.

He threw his hands up in the air to defend himself. 'Whoa, Kate. I just want to talk to you. I can't do that if you leave.'

She threw her arms together in front of her and narrowed her eyes. 'And what if I'm done talking to you?'

'That's grand, because it's my turn to say something. You've had your rail. Now let me get a word in edgewise.'

Women!

After a moment's silence, the two of them locked in what would have looked like a staring contest to the average person, Kate lifted an eyebrow. 'Well, then?'

He leaned heavily on one leg and tossed a hand onto his hip. He ran his other fingers through his hair. This was more difficult than he thought it would be. 'I...' he started, but couldn't get much farther than that. He knew what he wanted to say, but couldn't seem to get it out.

'I, what? I'm not going to stand here all day. I've things to do.'

'What I want to say is...' She lifted her brow at him again. He took a deep breath. 'I wanted to say you're right. I'm sorry.'

He could tell that his apology wasn't what she expected to hear. 'Sorry?'

'Yes, I'm sorry.'

'And what would you be sorry for? Be specific, because I have a long memory.'

'I've no doubt that you do.'

'Then tell me what you're sorry for so I can leave.'

67

He flicked a glance at the stairs. 'I'm sorry about what happened above. Well...' He grinned uncontrollably.

'Well, what?'

'I'm sorry what happened above upset you. I'm not sorry I kissed you, though. We both enjoyed it and you know it.'

'Whether I enjoyed it or not is irrelevant. What is relevant is what it has to do with the farm and what you're willing to do to keep it.'

Mick stiffened at her accusation. 'What we did had nothing to do with the farm. It just happened. I didn't plan it.'

'Didn't you?' He thought he heard a bit of hesitance in her voice.

He sat on the arm of his father's chair. She acted as if what had happened between them only affected her. For him, from the moment his lips touched hers, it seemed the last ten years had been wiped away and they were back at the stone circle again sharing that first kiss. Only this time, he wanted to show her what his adolescence didn't know how to show her then. When she hadn't protested, indeed when she seemed eager, he found kissing her and touching her felt as natural as breathing.

How could he tell her that now? Did he want to? The memory of what happened ten years ago found its way back into his thoughts.

'No, Kate. I didn't plan it,' he said calmly. 'I told you coming back here was hard for me. Everywhere I look, I see Mum and Dad. And seeing you walk around the house with so much ease isn't easy.

'You caught me off guard upstairs. It just happened. I don't know how else to explain it. It just ... happened.' By the look on her face, she didn't seem inclined to believe him, but she continued looking at him, as if willing him to continue.

'Did I enjoy it? Of course. I'd be a damn fool to say I didn't. You did, too. If you didn't, you would have pulled away. As you said yourself, you say what you mean. I assume your actions are the same. You wouldn't do something if you didn't want to. Am I wrong?'

She re-crossed her arms in front of her, averting her gaze. Everything in her body language told him he was right.

'Is there something wrong with two consenting adults turning to each other in their time of need to comfort each other?'

She gazed at him again. Her voice softer than before. 'Yes, Mick. There is. I won't have sex for the sake of it. It means something to me. If you want to appease your guilty conscience, you'll have to find another way. I'll not be used in that manner.'

'Are you telling me you've never had sex just for the sake of it?'

'No, I haven't.'

'Don't tell me you're the last virgin in Connemara.' That was apparently the wrong thing to say, because the look on her face stung him worse than if she'd slapped him.

She was already in her Mini and speeding down the driveway by the time he got to the door.

Damn his mouth!

Chapter Five

After locking up, Mick found himself back in Galway City. It had grown dark by the time he arrived, so he went to a pub near his hotel to forget the day's events. It had been a long day at that.

As he sat at the bar in An Pucán Bar, the city's oldest and most traditional pub, Mick tried making some rhyme or reason for how the day had gone. The reading of the will should have gone smoothly. Legally speaking, it probably had. But both Kate and he had gotten one hell of a shock when Tighe read the addendum.

What had his father been thinking?

In all fairness, it could have turned out worse. At least she was willing to help him find a way to keep the farm so he didn't have to be there to see to the everyday running of it.

He was grateful to Liam for the suggestion of hiring a manager. It was so easy and seemed to be the answer to everything. Why hadn't he thought of it himself?

If it was such an easy solution, why was he in such a state now? He should be happy everything was going in a positive direction. All he needed to do was to find someone who wanted to live and work on the farm. That couldn't be too difficult. Could it?

If it wasn't the farm that had him sitting alone

in a pub, soaking his injured pride in a glass of Ireland's finest whiskey, then what was it?

Injured pride? Was it really? It probably was. Did he really think Kate would have sex with him just for the sake of release? She wasn't that kind of person and he knew it. Or did he? It had been ten years since they had the kind of relationship where he would have known for sure.

Her announcement that sex meant something to her shouldn't have shocked him. She had been raised in a traditional Irish family. Sex before marriage was a sin. For all he knew, she had probably rushed right to church to confess what happened today.

He probably should be confessing right alongside her. In a manner of speaking, he was. He was telling his tale of woe to a glass of John Jameson at this very moment.

He held the glass before him and watched the backbar lights reflect through the amber liquid. Yes, he much preferred this type of confession, he thought, tossing back the measure. The fire had long gone out of the whiskey, as it does after tossing back three or four of them, but each drink pulled him closer to the fog he sought.

After the first few drinks, the bartender had been kind enough just to leave the bottle.

The numbness settling over his body failed to reach his mind. That's what he'd hoped to numb. Instead, the whiskey brought some clarity to his thoughts.

He was wrong to have asked Kate to stay for a repeat of what they'd shared in his room. He knew it as much now as he had then. Her parting words and glare had been a painful reminder.

His mind drifted back to her in his arms. How rapidly she heated under his touch, the quickening in her breath – kissing her erased years of bad memories from his mind. It was as if she was meant to be there all along.

If he weren't so stubborn, the last ten years would have been very different. Where would his life have led had their relationship been allowed to continue as it was? They had been close. He would have to be a fool not to see it. If only...

From his vantage point at the bar, Mick saw most of the pub. He glanced around and tried pulling his thoughts away from Kate.

An Pucán's patrons were those from the *gaeltacht,* one of the few remaining Irish speaking areas in Ireland, where the native language hadn't been allowed to die out over the centuries. He had to pay careful attention to the conversations around him in order to understand them. Living in Dublin had taken its toll on his memory for the language he'd grown up with. There was all manner of discussion going on. And everyone was oblivious to his troubles.

Many here were from all walks of Irish country life. Others were tourists who'd come in to listen to the live traditional music. What they got here was the real thing, not the tarted-up stuff they played for tourists in the city center. There were no 'Irish Eyes' or 'Danny Boys' here. This was the music made for the Irish.

As he poured himself another measure, someone pushed past and sat down beside him on a recently vacated stool. He hoped it was someone

72

of the female persuasion who would help him forget those fleeting moments with Kate. When he looked up though, the face he saw was definitely not feminine.

The man sitting beside him was dark as the devil. His hair was wild about his head and well-tanned face, and showed some graying around the temples. His clothing was as unkempt as the rest of him.

The man hailed the bartender, but either the bartender ignored him or didn't see him for all the people around the bar. He grumbled when the bartender passed him a second time. Was it really so busy in the pub? Mick thought, looking around. It didn't appear to be.

After a third call, which was also ignored, Mick thought he saw the bartender sneer at the man. Mick wasn't sure, but he thought he heard the man growl under his breath. Was a fight about to break out? Bollocks! He didn't need to be the innocent bystander who was sent to hospital as the result of an errant punch.

To keep the peace, he reached over the bar and pulled a glass from the stack he'd seen the bartender stow away earlier, and poured a measure from his bottle into it. He then shoved it toward the man beside him.

The man turned, obviously surprised, and it was then that Mick saw his eyes. They were as dark as the rest of him; the irises black as night. The only brightness about him was the white of his eyes that glared through bushy dark brows that vee'd in a scowl.

He shook off the odd feeling the man gave him,

accounting it to the number of measures he'd consumed and not the man himself, and lifted his glass in salute. The man hesitated, but not for long. After clinking their glasses, they both tossed back their whiskey in one gulp.

He chuckled at the face the man made. He remembered the initial fire that seared his own throat with the first shot. 'It gets easier after a few.'

'Aye, and don't I know it,' came the man's deep voice, raspy through the fumes fogging his throat. He reached out a beefy hand and shook Mick's. 'Flann Flannery.'

A breath caught in Mick's chest at the familiar sounding name. He well-knew there were hundreds of Flannerys in Ireland, but he would forever be transported back to a time better left forgotten.

'Michael Spillane,' he finally replied.

Mick poured them another drink, emptying the bottle. They clinked their glasses again and tossed the measures back. Flann sucked in his breath. 'Aye, and doesn't the second go down a might smoother, so it does.'

Mick chuckled. Then realizing that the bottle was empty, he called to the bartender. To Mick's surprise, the bartender cast him a look he could only understand as refusal, before he went back to polishing his glasses at the other end of the bar.

'What the–' Mick started. 'Oy, mate,' he called to the bartender.

He got the man's attention again by waving the bottle to indicate it was empty and he wanted another. After a moment when the bartender seemed to be considering what do to, he finally approached them. The bartender stopped in front of them, but didn't say anything as he looked from Mick to Flann then back to Mick again, with challenge in his eyes.

'We seem to be out of whiskey. Would you bring us another bottle?' Mick suggested as he pulled some money out of his wallet.

'Don't you think you've had enough ... sir?' The bartender hesitated before adding the last.

'Shouldn't I be the one to determine that?' asked Mick.

The bartender considered. He looked back to Flann briefly, then to Mick. 'One more, then it's done you are.' He took a bottle from the backbar, poured a measure into his glass, then set it back on the bar, none too lightly either, as a bit sloshed over the side of the glass.

'And one for my friend here,' Mick pressed.

'I'll not be serving the likes of him.' Mick looked to Flann, whose already dark features had grown darker. The crease between his brows deepened. His scowl was imposing.

He didn't know what the bartender had against Flann, but he didn't like the man's attitude. So he pushed his drink to Flann and said, 'Well then, I'll serve him. And now I seem to be in need of that last drink you promised me.'

Mick met the bartender's challenging glare with one of his own, unspoken messages flying between them, before the bartender relented and poured him another drink. 'When you're done with this one, it will be out with you.'

The man turned on his heel and returned to

the other end of the bar, where he nodded to a man at the door with an even more imposing glare than Flann's. The bouncer.

Fortunately, they were left in peace, but Mick knew he'd have to leave once he was done with his drink. In truth, the day had been way too long to end it getting knocked around by a bald-headed muscle-bound bully.

He stared into his glass, his thoughts bouncing between Kate and his father.

'Women!' Flann exclaimed.

Mick's head shot up. 'How did you know?'

'Sure, and aren't they the reason pubs were invented?' Flann chuckled. Mick chuckled along with him. 'It's either a woman or you've come from a funeral.'

Mick huffed. 'You should market that talent of yours.'

Flann chuckled again.

After a moment, he continued, 'My father passed away the other day. His will was read today.'

Flann sighed. 'And you were cut out of it.'

Mick grunted. 'Might as well have been.' He proceeded to tell him the contents of the will.

'And what does your lady friend have to say about all this? Is she trying to get the farm? Is this where your woman trouble comes in?'

Mick shook his head. 'No, Kate has actually been very supportive of me finding a way to keep the place.'

'Well, that's all right, so.' Flann nodded. 'So, what's the problem with her, then?'

'She's upset because I kissed her. No. She was

upset because I kissed her and she liked it.' Mick grinned, unable to deny how much he had enjoyed it, too. Had her father not shown up when he did, they would've done the deed this afternoon.

It was probably for the best Liam had arrived when he had. In reality, while he hoped they both would have found pleasure, Kate wasn't the kind of woman to have casual sex. Hadn't she said as much before she stormed out of the house? And she hadn't denied being a virgin. Had they slept together, he didn't know if he could live with the responsibility of having taken that from her and then returned to Dublin.

Flann grunted. 'They all like it, but didn't the church convince them it was a sin? The bastards,' he muttered.

'Aye, the bastards,' Mick agreed, but only half-heartedly. He couldn't really fault the church. It was Kate's upbringing and her own set of morals.

'So, where does that leave you now?' Flann continued.

'Who knows? I haven't really talked to her in ten years until today. I don't know what possessed me to kiss her.' Mick shook his head once more, then ran his fingers through his hair. His gaze moved from his glass to the backbar, but he wasn't seeing it at all. His thoughts drifted back to Kate and the angry look she'd left him with this afternoon. He'd have to find her to apologize.

'You were possessed by the same thing we're all possessed with when our lad gets near a beautiful woman.' Flann elbowed him annoyingly in the side.

Mick chuffed weakly at the comment.

When Flann's chuckles subsided, he continued, 'What I meant was, where does that leave you with the farm? Are you selling, and give your wan a run to get it from you? Or will you just hand it over to her and walk away?'

He turned to Flann and studied him. He hadn't really looked at the man after he sat down. He didn't know what had compelled him to offer him a drink in the first place. He wasn't normally so generous with his whiskey, not that he drank much. He justified the libation tonight because this had been one day in hell he didn't want to live through again anytime soon. And he'd poured the man a drink in order to quiet him down. The last thing he wanted while he was working on getting numb was some rabble-rouser getting into a fight with the bartender.

Flann was a sizable man. Not as tall as he was wide. He remembered the man's beefy hands from their earlier handshake. There was strength and power in those hands. A workman's hands. And by the deep creases in the man's dark features, the man had worked outdoors most of his life. But there was something familiar about him he couldn't put his finger on.

'We've decided to compromise.'

'Compromise with a woman? Lad, you've been bitten, you have.' Flann chuckled again.

'The only compromise we've made is over the farm. We're hiring a manager.'

'A manager you say?' This seemed to pique the man's interest, as Flann's right eyebrow lifted noticeably.

'Aye. He'll live on the farm and work the sheep so I can go back to Dublin.'

'And what about yer wan?'

He shrugged. 'She'll go back to her own place, I suspect. I don't know. I don't really care. I just want this whole ordeal over with so I can get on with my life.'

There was a silence between them. Mick spun his glass in his hands as he stared into the amber liquid. The numbness the previous measures had provided was starting to wear thin. He hadn't been ready to leave the pub yet. With this being his last drink, he was savoring the aroma before tossing it back.

Flann shifted in his seat and turned to face Mick. He looked up into the man's black eyes. 'Well, isn't it lucky you are tonight, boyo.'

He squinted as he tried to figure out what Flann meant by his comment.

'I'm just up from Limerick this very day and looking for a position just as you describe.' Flann's look was serious. If it hadn't been, Mick would have thought the man was joking. 'Isn't that ironic?'

'Indeed.'

Chapter Six

When Kate pulled into Fairhill Farm to take Molly out to the flock, she was surprised to see Mick's Honda parked in front of the house. More surprising was the small battered red van parked beside it.

She pulled in beside Mick's car and slid out from behind the wheel. The front door of the house stood open. She was heading in that direction when Molly barked across the yard.

Molly practically bowled her over as she skidded to a stop at Kate's feet. The dog could barely contain her excitement. Kate knelt in front of the dog to give her a good scratch behind the ears.

'Hey, Molly. How's my girl?' she crooned. Molly instantly flopped over on her back for a belly rub and wriggled uncontrollably.

Kate heard voices and looked up to see Mick walking across the yard. Beside him was a man with dark features, wearing familiar farmers' garb – a pair of dark trousers tucked into a pair of green Wellies, a jumper pulled on over a collared shirt, a battered sports coat, and an equally battered tweed cap. The entire outfit had definitely seen better days. She nearly laughed at the way the man's hair shot out from under his cap every which way. What stopped her was the glare he gave her.

His eyes looked the color of coal against his well-weathered skin that looked like dirty old leather. As he drew nearer, she got a closer look at his hair, which was every bit as greasy as it looked.

Where had Mick dug up this codger?

Molly got to her feet and trotted over to lie under a window box near the front door.

'Kate,' said Mick, as his way of greeting her.

'Mick,' she replied. She'd hoped to get over here to feed and work Molly before he decided to show up. She wasn't expecting to see him, and she certainly wasn't expecting to see anyone else.

'Aye, Mickie, now I see what you meant.'

Mickie? Kate arched an eyebrow and waited for an explanation not only for the comment, but also for the little endearment.

'Kate, this is Flann Flannery,' Mick said.

Flann extended a large hand in Kate's direction. The look in his eyes unnerved her and she was leery of putting her hand into his. She did, though, and quickly, just to get the introductions over with. When she tried pulling away, he tightened his grip longer than necessary, and much longer than she would have preferred.

She jerked her hand from his. She hoped it wasn't obvious when she rubbed her palm against her jeans.

'Mick, can I have a word with you, please?'

'Sure.'

'Alone.' She passed a glance toward Flann then back to Mick.

Mick turned to Flann. 'I think we're sorted here. Flann?'

'Aye, boy. I think we are. I'll just get my gear.' Flann briskly walked over to the van and hauled

81

open the back door. It groaned loudly, making her cringe from the sound.

Looking back at Mick, she folded her arms in front of her and waited for his explanation.

'What?' He pulled a cigarette from its pack and stuck it between his lips. Meeting her glare, he stopped, as if remembering what she'd done to the last cigarette he'd smoked in her presence. Wisely, he put it back in its pack and pocketed it.

'What, as in what the devil is going on here? Who is that ... man?' She jerked her head sharply toward Flann.

'He's my new manager,' Mick said matter-of-factly.

'Your what?'

'My new manager. He's going to live on the farm and take care of things for me while I'm in Dublin. Your da had a great idea. I'm surprised I didn't think of it myself.'

Kate held her tongue when Flann walked past them carrying his belongings toward a small barn that had been converted for a worker's apartment. When Mick left for university, they'd had to hire someone to help out around the place. John had been a devoted employee, but when Donal fell ill, he stopped most of the business and had no need for the help. John had understood.

Mick's voice shook Kate out of her thoughts. 'Wh-what?' she asked, looking toward him.

'I said, your da had a great idea to hire a manager.'

'Is that Da's man?'

Mick shook his head.

'I thought you were going to talk to Da's friend.

Where did this one come from? He's certainly a dodgy enough looking character.'

'I met him last night. He was looking for a manager's job. We talked and I'm satisfied he can do the job. And yes, I thought the same thing as you. That's another reason why he's perfect for the job. He'll keep the riff-raff away. I don't want to have to worry about anything while I'm in Dublin.

'I don't want to worry about you either,' he confessed. 'I would worry if you were on the farm alone. If anything were to happen to you, Flann would be here.'

'I think Da should come over and meet him at least. I don't like the looks of this Flann at all, at all, and I dare say he will want him checked out.' There was something about him that unnerved her, which was nothing like the unnerving Mick gave her.

When Flann walked past them once more to his van, he gave Kate a big wink. Her stomach turned.

'He's hired, Kate. I'm not going to let him go because you don't like the way he looks.' Mick crossed his arms in front of him, challenging her.

Well, her glare could be just as fierce as his. 'But, Mick, you know nothing about him. Where did you meet him?'

Mick didn't answer right away and that set her nerves on a more jagged edge. 'An Pucán.'

'At the pub?' She was dumbfounded. 'You met him at the pub? Oh, Mick!' What else could she say? Her heavy sigh showed her exasperation. 'Mick, we need to talk.'

Flann passed them one more time, tipping his

tweed cap at her as he went. Her stomach lurched again.

'Aye, we do,' he agreed.

'Not here, though. Can't we go inside?'

Mick nodded and followed her into the house.

As soon as the door closed behind them, Kate lit into him about his irresponsibility at hiring a man he knew nothing about. As she paced in front of him, he couldn't take his eyes off her. Her curly black hair was down today and bounced about her shoulders as her arms waved about in her rant. Her delicate brows were angrily drawn together and her beautiful full lips cut him to the quick.

He could only stare at her. She was gorgeous on a normal day. Today was something else altogether. Oh, how the color rose to her cheeks when she was riled! She had the appearance of just having come off the hills, where the wind whipped her hair into a frenzy and burnished her skin. He remembered days like that. When they were younger.

They'd spent many days and long afternoons up at that stone circle. The wind wasn't always kind to them up there, nor the rain. But they'd stayed just the same, because they were together and it was *their* place. The only difference between then and now was the anger etched in her face. It didn't mar her beauty, though. It only intensified it, making his insides ache.

'And another thing,' she went on. 'What are you smiling about? Can't you see how angry I am with you?' She finally stopped pacing to look at him. She was trying her damnedest to give him 'the eye'. It wasn't working – unless she wanted him to take her in his arms and kiss her senseless. It was damn tempting.

'I'm smiling at how beautiful you are when you're upset.'

'Ah, Mick. Can you not be serious for one minute? Have you not been listening to anything I've said?'

'I think your very own da heard you over on the farm.'

She gasped. He took the chance to take her by the arm and lead her to the kitchen where he'd make them a cup of tea.

The kettle took its time to boil, so he turned to face Kate. 'Look, Kate. Flann is already hired. I'm not going to let him go because your father hasn't met him. I talked to him last night and he seems to know what's what. He'll stay until he gives me a reason to get rid of him.'

Kate slumped against the kitchen table. She wasn't happy. If her words didn't tell it all, her glare certainly did.

'Now,' he continued. 'Sweet tea as usual?' He was rewarded with her nod and he set about to putting a drop of milk and a heaping spoonful of sugar in the steaming cup.

By the time he handed her the tea, some of the bluster had gone out of her. She was staring at him. 'What?' he asked.

'Doesn't he unnerve you?' She'd lowered her voice finally. He was thankful for that.

He considered for a moment. 'A little, perhaps. But you can't judge a book by its cover, nor a man by his hat.'

'I wasn't referring to his hat, Mick. Your man looks like an explosion in a hair factory.'

For a moment, they stared at each other. Mick wasn't sure if he should laugh or not, but the more he thought about her description of Flann, the less he could contain his mirth. He roared with laughter at the same time Kate let go with her own uncontrolled giggles.

When her tea sloshed onto the floor, she set the cup on the table beside her. She wrapped her arms around her stomach and doubled over as the tears streamed down her face.

Mick wasn't doing much better. He couldn't remember ever laughing so hard in all his life. Before they both knew it, they were holding each other up.

Awareness abruptly hit and their gazes met. The laughter eased, but they stood in each other's arms, grinning like fools.

Mick reached up and brushed the backs of his fingers across her cheek to smooth away her tears of laughter. Her smile faltered then and her eyes seemed to darken. Should he kiss her? Did he dare? More importantly, would she let him?

Slowly, as not to spook her, he eased his fingers from her cheek. He turned his hand to cup the side of her face. He slid his fingers along the curve of her jaw to the back of her neck and gently, slowly, cautiously, drew her to him. Her eyes never left his until the moment their lips met.

The explosion behind his eyelids staggered him. He'd meant to kiss her once to test the waters, but as soon as their mouths touched, it was as if the sudden flash of fire fused them together.

He teased her mouth open and stroked his tongue against hers. She never protested, but encouraged him by wrapping her arms around his neck. Her fingers ran through his hair and she sighed as he slanted his mouth over hers, first to the right, then the left, then back again.

When she pressed her breasts against him, she also pressed against his groin. He groaned into her mouth.

His hand found its way under her Aran jumper. The idea of the rough fabric against her delicate flesh excited him. Most people would have worn a shirt under the itchy wool, but not Kate.

She sighed when his hand slid higher along her ribcage and brushed the underside of her breast. He fingered the lacy bra she wore and ached to remove it. He curled his fingers gently around her. His thumb made contact with her erect nipple and stroked her until she panted into his mouth.

He trailed kisses across her cheek to a spot on her neck just behind her ear, then traced the curve of her ear with his tongue, gently pulling at her earlobe with his lips. She moaned, flexing to give him better access.

His free hand splayed the width of her lower back and he moved it up until he found the back strap of her bra. Following the contour of it around to the front, he caressed her other breast.

With both hands under her jumper now, he nearly had the thing off.

'Mick.' Her voice came out on a gasp.

'Aye, love,' he said, between kisses. He toyed with the hooks, wanting her breasts free of their confinement. He wanted to touch all of her.

She pulled away and met his gaze. Her eyes had darkened from a deep emerald to something he could only liken to green-black velvet. Her lids were heavy and her lashes tinged with moisture clinging from her recently shed tears of laughter.

God, she's beautiful. He lowered his lips to hers, but she put her hand on his chest and held him at a distance.

Kate opened her mouth to speak, but nothing came out. She had a hard time keeping her thoughts clear. She shouldn't allow Mick such liberties. But this might be the last time she'd see him.

She'd longed to know what it would be like to kiss him. Not an innocent peck on the cheek and certainly not the few innocent kisses they'd shared at the stone circle as teenagers. She'd dreamed about a kiss ... like this. One that stole her breath and robbed her of all thought. One that made her forget every value she'd lived by.

When she didn't speak, he kissed her again. He grasped her hips and pulled her against his groin. His gaze penetrated, darkening with passion.

'See what you're doing to me?'

She grasped his shoulders, but instead of pushing him away, she pulled him closer. This was wrong. But just this once, she longed for a taste of what she would never have.

When he nipped her breast through the lace cup of her bra, she sucked in her breath and flung back her head. Her body arched against him. He stroked her with his hardness. Something inside her pulsed with need. Weak and vulnerable, she ached for more.

He buried his fingers in her hair and held her to him, his breath hot against her cheek. With every slant of his lips on hers, he stole her breath. His tongue in her mouth stroked hers, and her body hummed with desire. Her chest tightened, and pressure built between her thighs.

If this was desire and uncontrolled passion, then she wanted more.

But wait. Mick was leaving. He'd hired a man to manage the farm so he could return to Dublin. The thick fog of arousal cleared from her head, and her eyes flashed open.

Soon he'd be gone. And she refused to give him what he wanted from her, no matter how much she wanted him.

'What's wrong, love?'

She didn't say anything, but she studied his face. She wanted to memorize this moment – his face impassioned, expectant, and – dare she imagine – full of love?

When she had this image burned into her memory, she said, 'I can't do this.'

He just looked at her for a long moment without speaking, then took a deep breath and pulled her into his embrace. God, how she wanted him. She'd never experienced such depth of feelings from any other man's kiss. Her body shivered with need, and her mind retreated to its earlier fog of desire.

He pulled away and looked at her. Was he searching for an answer of his own?

'Kate?' He dropped his hands to the tabletop,

one on either side of her and let his heated gaze roam over her face and body. He looked everywhere but into her eyes.

'I won't deny I like your touch,' she admitted. 'More than like it. But I can't do this. It's not right. You don't love me.' She nearly choked on her last sentence.

It seemed to catch him off guard, and he finally met her gaze. Could he love the woman she was today, or only the memory of the girl she used to be? There was no denying their physical attraction, but she needed the emotional one, too.

A day hadn't passed in the last ten years that she hadn't thought of him at least a dozen times. Now they were just strangers who shared a common past.

Mick took a deep breath and hung his head. She wished she knew what he was thinking. The silence of the kitchen was only intensified by the ticking of the small clock above the cooker.

When he lifted his gaze to hers, the seriousness of her words reflected in his eyes. She wanted love and he wasn't prepared to give it to her.

'You don't need love to feel pleasure.'

'I do.'

She wouldn't do a casual fling, and Mick resisted emotional intimacy. They'd reached an impasse.

'All right, Kate.'

'All right?' She frowned. 'What does that mean?'

'It means the only love I can give you is the kind I can make. I'll make love with you and to you, but that's all I can offer.'

'It's not enough.' Regret filled her voice, and her heart sank.

'I know.'

They looked into each other's eyes, silence settling between them. 'I think you should get off me now.'

'Aye, probably.'

'What are you grinning at? Get off me.'

'I can't.'

'Can't or won't?' Annoyance replaced passion. She pushed at his shoulders, but he didn't budge.

'Can't. You'll have to let go of me first.'

She followed his gaze as it lowered between them. She'd wrapped her legs around him, squeezing him against her. She gasped. When had she done such a thing?

'Oh, God.' She crossed herself for the blasphemy, letting her legs fall to the floor, then gave Mick a strong push. He stepped back and threw himself into a chair. She pulled herself off the table, her cheeks on fire with embarrassment.

She glared at him. 'What are you laughing at? I'm sure you think this is funny.'

'It's not funny at all, Kate. You've got me so hard I can barely stand. You're beautiful and I want you. It would be a lie to tell you otherwise,' he confessed. 'It's not funny in the least.'

Chapter Seven

She was still mortified with what she'd allowed Mick to do to her yesterday – again, no less. Hadn't she lambasted him for assuming she'd sleep with him because he wanted her to, but then to encourage him because of her own selfish desires, values be damned? It made no difference she'd thought about him every day, wondering what it would be like to kiss him so passionately and to feel his body against hers. The fact remained she wouldn't sleep with just anyone, no matter how he made her body feel. The man she gave herself to had to be 'the one'.

There had been a day when she'd thought she and Mick would make love together – years ago, before she'd set such high expectations of herself. In her mind, the timing had been perfect. Since the accidental kiss on his birthday, they'd shared a few kisses. They were very innocent, almost chaste. And nothing like those they'd shared yesterday. They were too young and inexperienced then to know about passion and sensuality. At the time, the moment seemed perfect. But something had changed between them before they got to the stone circle that particular day. She'd sensed it for a few days and could see it clearly in his eyes as they walked toward Fairhill Farm from where the bus had dropped them off.

Fairhill Farm was the first farm on the road.

Her family's was next. There were only the two farms on this road, so they were always the only two walking on it. It afforded them the privacy they so loved when together.

She had tried brushing off the feeling something wasn't right. He'd been reserved all day and had refused to hold her hand once they got off the bus. But by the time they got to the old stone circle, Mick seemed to have loosened up.

As they lay together watching the clouds passing over, he'd finally turned to her, looked into her eyes for a long time, then slowly leaned in to kiss her. She let him kiss her. Had wanted him to kiss her. She loved him. But it was over too fast.

She opened her eyes and saw his gaze had darkened. This was it. This would be the day that their relationship changed. Mick loved her. She knew that now. They'd get married, have a family, and live happily ever after. She was never as sure of anything in her whole life as she was just then. She could barely contain her anticipation.

Tentatively, he cupped her breast. The feeling of his trembling hand sent fire shooting through her veins. His fingers moved to the buttons on her school uniform blouse and popped the first one, then the next. His hand slipped under the fabric to touch her again. He was so gentle with her, but electricity shot through her like lightning, and she had squeezed her eyes shut at the sensation. A tiny whimper escaped her lips.

He suddenly pulled his hand free. When he didn't touch her again, she opened her eyes. The look he gave her was one she'd never seen. Back then, she couldn't explain it. Today, she would describe it as a mixture of desire and resentment.

'It's okay, Mick. You can touch me,' she'd whispered softly, trying to control the waver in her voice. She didn't want him to know she was scared, yet thrilled, at this moment in their lives.

It must have been the wrong thing to say because he'd fixed her with another look that she'd never seen: Hatred. He got to his feet then and left her alone and bewildered.

Not long afterwards, he stopped talking to her altogether.

Just because she'd thought about him every day since then, didn't mean she knew the man he was today. Going by how he had acted during his parents' illnesses, she wasn't sure she wanted to know the man he'd become.

Over the last five years, she'd run the gamut of emotions with Mick over his parents. More often than not she was angry with him, because he refused to listen to her pleas to come home. Or was frustrated because he wouldn't return her calls. And she hurt, because she'd remembered the kind of relationship they'd had growing up and now that relationship seemed as far away as the moon.

Now anger surged through her in a different direction. Flann had followed her out to the pasture. After the incident in the kitchen, she just wanted to be alone with Molly. Molly gave her unconditional love, and working the sheep gave Kate something to do to take her mind off her churning emotions.

As she followed the dog through the back gates with a small flock of sheep, Flann came up behind her.

'It's about time we got that dog trained.'

'Molly is already trained, Mr Flannery. It's you who's in need of training.'

She continued walking. He intimidated her. As long as she didn't have to stop, she wouldn't have to look into his eyes. She didn't like the way he made her feel. He brought out the worst in her. She certainly would never have insulted anyone else as she just had him.

The man chuckled at her insult. 'I'll follow you out just the same.'

'Suit yourself. Just stay out of my way.' She'd have rather Mick been here to act as a go-between, but it was better to get this over with as soon as possible. Molly needed to learn to work with this man, no matter how much she wished otherwise.

To his credit, he stood back and watched her work the dog. She was sure she felt his gaze more on her than on Molly, but she kept her focus averted and stayed to her task.

'Ye've a way about ye, Katie, ye do.'

Slowly, she turned to look up at him. The words he spoke could have meant anything, but not the way he looked her up and down. His gaze lingered over her breasts before coming back to her eyes. Then he winked, as if he knew something. She could only gape at him and wonder what he'd seen, or rather how much he had seen.

She shivered at the thought he'd been spying on them. He was such a disgusting man.

'I'll thank you to keep your comments to yourself, Mr Flannery.'

'Flann. Please. No need to remain so formal when we're so familiar with each other now.'

She'd tried ignoring his comment and got on with Molly's work. She familiarized him with her technique and got Molly used to working with a new trainer.

On the walk back to the house, Kate kept Molly between them. The further from him the better, as far as she was concerned.

'If I get the job at the hospital, I won't be coming here as often to work Molly.'

'Don't you worry, Katie. I'll keep the dog busy enough.'

'Just keep her to her normal routine. She doesn't need any more than that.'

'Mickie hired me to manage this farm and that's what I mean to do. We've a few sheep here and I mean to make the most of them.' The tone of his voice challenged her to contest him.

What was it about Flann? He really never did anything or said anything to make her think he was irresponsible, or even that he was a bad person. He'd handled Molly well enough, the job got done, and he'd kept his comments to himself about her once they were about their task. But something in her gut warned her to be cautious.

She met Mick back in the farmhouse kitchen.

'Everything all right with you and Flann?'

'Grand.' She went to straighten up the sitting room. Mick followed her. 'I'm leaving in the morning.'

'Grand.' She couldn't look at him. Saying goodbye the first time had been hard enough.

'Is that all you have to say?'

'What do you want me to say?' She pushed past him and went to straighten the cushions on the sofa. When she was done, she turned to Donal's chair to straighten the blanket hanging on the back. Mick grasped her by the wrist, which forced her to look up at him.

'Please, Kate.'

'Please, what? Tell me what you want to hear and I'll say it.'

'I don't know.'

He released her wrist and ran his fingers through his hair in frustration.

'I just don't want to leave like this.'

She balled her hands at her side and stared at him. 'Like what?'

He waved his arms in her direction. 'Like this. I'm trying to make this right and you're fighting me.'

'I'm not fighting you. I'm not doing anything with you. Now let me pass. I'm going home.' She pushed past him again, grabbed her coat off the peg, and went through the door, Mick on her heels. He reached for the door handle first. When he paused, she looked up at him. She wasn't sure if he was challenging her or vice versa, but their gazes held. Finally, he opened the door for her.

'Goodbye, Mick.' She eased in behind the wheel and slammed the door in his face. She turned the key and the old Mini roared to life. She reversed into the yard, then sped off down the driveway toward home, her heart breaking all over again. The physical feelings he awakened in her just compounded her ache.

As her Mini bounced along the connecting road joining Fairhill Farm with Conneely Farm, her thoughts drifted back to the kitchen and Mick.

97

She couldn't believe how long she'd spent with Flann out on the pasture. But even the warning bells he set off inside her didn't quell how Mick had made her feel. No matter how she tried refuting the facts, Mick had a way with his hands, and his mouth.

She'd almost given in to him. She hated to admit it, but she'd had a really difficult time pushing him away. She might have submitted to him when she was fifteen, but not today. Not ever. Mick was leaving the farm. He'd made that clear. If his words didn't convince her, hiring Flann had.

As much as she'd dreamed about it, there was no future with her and Mick. And if she was smart, she'd just take Molly home and try forgetting her childhood with Mick, the time she spent at the farm caring for his parents, and the last couple days when she'd allowed him to satisfy at least one of her fantasies – knowing what it felt like being kissed by him. To be kissed like that by him. And to imagine, for just a split second, what it might feel like to make love with him.

She groaned as her little car hit another bump in the road. Her already sensitive skin jolted against the abrasion of the rough wool of her jumper, reminding her of how Mick's hands had replaced the scratchy feeling of the wool with the softness of his fingers. His hands, once callused from working on the farm, now bore the smooth skin of a man who pushed pencils for a living. Not that he was soft man. She'd felt the strength in his grasp, though, and the gentleness. He may have lost the calluses, but he was still a strong and virile man. He probably worked out to maintain the muscles she felt beneath his shirt.

Her body hummed all the way home. No matter how hard she'd tried, she couldn't rid herself of the feeling of his hands and his mouth on her body. Not after spending time on the pasture with Molly. Not after working with Flann 'The Repulsive'. And not afterwards, when Mick confronted her in the sitting room.

Now, she barreled down the driveway of Conneely Farm and pulled into her regular parking space behind the house, threw the car into neutral, and pulled the hand brake before shutting off the motor. Tears welled up beneath her eyelids. She tried forcing herself to stop thinking about the last few days. It was just too overwhelming. And with the sensations remaining long after Mick's hands had left her body, she couldn't help but wonder if maybe she should have given in to him. Would she then be able to stop thinking of him every day of her life?

Probably not.

As much as she hated admitting it, she was still living in an adolescent's dream. She was twenty-five now. Mick had a new life, a life a hundred and fifty miles away. If the last five years of turmoil hadn't convinced him to come home, nothing would.

What was she waiting for, anyway? He wasn't interested in her. All he wanted was to get her into bed. No strings, no emotions, no promises. Just sex.

She wanted more. She'd wanted a life together, desire, and commitment. She wanted love, damn it! She deserved it all. She'd nursed a hopeless schoolgirl's dream for too long. Mick would never give her any of the things she craved. Yet she would always compare him to the man she finally married.

She would have to let her love for Mick die alongside his parents. She just needed to find a way to bring Molly home and get him to hire a part time housekeeper who would see to the house for the visits he'd never make.

The tears burst forth then in uncontrollable sobs, mourning the death of her dreams. She folded her arms across the steering wheel and buried her face in the thick wool of her jumper. The force of her body rocked the little car. She couldn't remember having ever cried so desperately. Not even when the boy she loved suddenly stopped loving her all those years ago and left her without so much as a look back or explanation.

She didn't know how long she cried or how it happened, but she found herself being hauled out of her Mini and into her father's warm arms. She hugged him and continued bawling. She felt like a baby, but right now she didn't care. She hurt so desperately and she needed to cry. Her father's comforting embrace helped her feel a little better, just as it had when she was a child.

Try as she might, she couldn't stop her tears. Her body shook until she was exhausted. When he stooped to pick her up and carry her into the house, she let him. She just wrapped her arms around him and buried her face in the crook of his neck and shoulder. The familiar scent of him calmed her.

Her mother gasped and her footsteps sounded

behind them as her da carried her up the narrow stairs to her room. He laid her gently on her bed then sat beside her as he smoothed her hair from her face.

When he spoke, it was in the voice he'd used many years ago when she was a child. Concern sounded in the timbre of it. 'What's this all about, pet?' He stroked her cheek.

How could she tell him? He didn't need to know his daughter dreamed of passion and love. And he certainly didn't need to know his daughter had let Mick do such things to her. She couldn't tell anyone, the humiliation of it too great. That realization brought the sobs again.

'Ah, shove over, Liam,' said her mother. Her father left her side and her mother sat down beside her. 'Leave us be, now. 'Tis women's talk we'll be after.' Her bedroom door closed just as her brother came down the hall.

'What's wrong with our Kate, Da?'

'I don't know, son, but your mother will sort it out.' And they were gone.

'Here now, child. Tell me what's after upsettin' you so,' her mother said in her soft Connemara brogue.

Kate rolled over to look up, her vision blurry from the onslaught of tears. 'Ah, Mam.' That was all she could get out before she sat up and insinuated herself into her mother's embrace. Her mother patted her on the back and shushed her until the sobs subsided. She rocked her back and forth until Kate was empty at last. Empty of tears and empty in her heart.

'Are you ready to talk to me now, dote?'

Hesitant to pull away from the warmth, Kate sat back and dragged a woolly sleeve across her face to wipe away the tears. Her mother smoothed the hairs from her face, where tears had glued them to her cheeks. The coolness of her hands soothed Kate.

'I'm such a fool, Mam.' What else could she say? It was the truth, after all.

'Would you be carin' to expand on that thought? If there's anything I'd be knowin' about me own daughter is she's no one's fool. So, tell me what's upset you. I can't remember a time since you were a wee thing you carried on so.' She took one of Kate's hands in hers, looked into her eyes, and waited patiently. Kate loved her mother, and her patience. Lord knew, Kate had tried it more than once.

'Where would you like me to begin?'

Her mother laughed lightly.

As much as Kate loved her mother, she wasn't ready to tell her about the compromising position Mick had gotten her into. Not just once, but twice, God help her. So, she gave her mother an answer she was sure to understand.

'I guess these last few weeks have caught up with me.'

'What do you mean?'

'I know Mr Spillane couldn't compare to Da, but he was family just the same. Watching him every day was hard. He was such a kind man and deserved better.' She pulled a tissue from the box on the side table.

'Aye, he did. But we can't change what the Good Lord has planned for any of us. We may not under-

102

stand why Donal was taken from this world; we just have to accept that there was a reason for it.'

'Twas cruel, Mam. Mrs. Spillane wasn't even cold in her grave when himself announced he was sick.'

'You've had a tough time of it, love. But you can be sure that Donal was thankful to have you there with him, both for Mary and himself.' Her mother patted Kate's hand.

'Mick should have been there,' Kate blurted.

Her mother nodded. 'Aye, love, he should have been. It's no use in beating yourself up over it. No one knows what's going on in that boy's head. But Donal appreciated having you there. You were a great help to him over the years.'

Kate remembered a long ago day that just seemed like yesterday. 'Mam, he said, "You're like the daughter I never had".'

'I'm sure you were. It's no wonder you're grieving like one. Don't forget Mick has suffered a tremendous loss, too. Men have a much different way of expressing their losses. Women cry. Men brood. One day, the brooding will come to an end and he'll grieve the same way you are now. God willing, there will be someone understanding there for him to help him through it.'

'Well, it won't be me. I've washed my hands of him.'

'Oh?' Her mother's brow lifted. There was a question behind that look.

'Aye. I've tried talking to him, but he's useless. He's been rude since I met him in Mr Lynch's office yesterday.'

'Your father was under the impression you two

were gettin' on fine yesterday when he was over to the farm.'

Kate grunted. 'Hardly. Civil in Da's company, maybe, but we weren't getting along. Just getting through the day.'

'Hmm—'

'Did Da tell you about the will? Mr Spillane wrote an addendum. Mick was so angry.' She couldn't blame him really, but he had brought it all on himself. He was lucky she was so supportive of his finding a way to keep the farm so he could scurry back to Dublin guilt-free.

'I'm sure he was quite shocked by his father's surprise.'

Kate thought back to the reading of the will. 'Oh, Mam. The look on his face when Tighe read the addendum... Angry doesn't begin to cover it. Incensed would come closer.

'I think his plan was to get the reading over with and put the place on the market as soon as possible then head back to Dublin.' Kate looked into her mother's eyes. 'I wouldn't put it past him to just auction off everything, his parents' belongings and all, and just have done with it.'

'Everyone has their own way of grieving and men are the worst at it. Some worse than others.'

'Aye, I'm sure you're right. I've no experience with men, so I wouldn't know.'

Her mother laughed. 'No experience with men, child? Sweetheart, don't forget you live with two of them. You've plenty of experience.' Her smile faded. 'Unless you're talkin' of the other experience.'

'Oh, no, Mam! I'm not talking about that kind.

104

I certainly wouldn't be knowing anything about that,' Kate assured her, even as the flush shot up her body. She couldn't look her mother in the eye. It was almost as if her mother could see right through her and knew what she'd let Mick do.

'Mmm-hmm,' Deirdre mumbled. Her mother's fingers on her chin pulled her around to face her. 'What's this blushing all about then? Eh?'

Kate barely met her mother's gaze, but caught the laughter in her eyes. 'Trust me, Mam. I'm still waitin'.'

Then her mother shocked her. 'Waitin' for what, child? You're twenty-five years old, Kate. You can certainly make your own decision when it comes to sex.'

Heat rose up Kate's cheeks. 'Please, Mam. Can't we talk about something else?' She tried looking away, but saw her mother was laughing at her unease with the topic. Deirdre had had 'the talk' with her when she started her menses years ago, so she didn't know where her mother was going with this side of the discussion.

'Kate, there's nothing to be ashamed of. While I'm glad you waited through your teen years to sleep with someone, I do recognize the fact that you've grown up. You're quite a woman, and one of her own mind.' She reached up and cupped Kate's face in her hand and smiled. 'You'll know when it's right. I've told you that before. But don't be thinkin' it will be the wedding night. It's not always.'

Kate looked into her mother's eyes and realization hit her. Her parents had had s-e-x before marriage. Her mouth dropped open into an O of surprise, her eyes snapping wide.

'Mam! You and Da – you two–' She couldn't finish her sentence when her mother nodded and continued laughing.

'That surprises you? I'm a woman, too, you know.' Her mother blushed at her confession.

'But, Mam–'

'But, what? I had to test him out. Make sure he was worth spending the rest of my life with.' She said this matter-of-factly. Kate knew her mother was having trouble keeping a straight face. Before they knew it, they were laughing together.

'Well,' said Kate between giggles, 'I guess we know the consensus, don't we.'

'Aye, we do. Never mind the fact that we had to get married rather quickly afterwards.'

'Did Granddad find out and get out the shotgun?'

Her mother shook her head. 'No, pet. It was so your brother could have a last name.' Kate's mouth dropped open again in astonishment. 'Fortunately for everyone involved, I loved your father with all my heart and he loved me the same in return.'

Kate started giggling again at the thought that her brother was the cause of their parents' hasty marriage.

'What are you laughing at now?'

'Just at all the times I thought Connor was such a bastard. Now you're telling me he really could have been!'

Kate was glad she'd had this talk with her mother. While she couldn't possibly tell her mother about what had almost happened between

106

her and Mick, at least not yet, she was happy to know she could when and if the time ever came.

'Right, so,' said her mother finally, getting up off the bedside. 'Get yourself cleaned up and come down for dinner.'

'I will, Mam. Thanks for the talk. I needed it.'

'Anytime.' Deirdre opened the door to leave and turned back to Kate with a question written in her eyes. 'By the way, why were you a fool?'

Kate had forgotten she'd said that. 'Because it took me ten years to grow up.'

Deirdre gave her a strange look, then left the room.

Downstairs, Kate walked into the kitchen just as everyone was sitting down to dinner. As soon as she stepped over the threshold, her family stopped talking.

'What?' She looked around and behind her to see what was wrong.

'You were fierce dramatic,' Connor said. Kate slid her eyes over him knowingly and grinned. Her mother cleared her throat then turned to finish ladling food onto plates.

'What?' Connor asked, suspicion in his voice. He looked between the two women. 'What?' His voice hitched up an octave.

Kate carried two plates to the table and set them in front of the men. She then found her seat as Deirdre came to the table with their plates. Connor kept his gaze on her as he dug into his meal. When Kate raised her brow at him and shot him 'the eye', he stopped eating immediately and waited for their mother to be seated so they could

107

say grace.

About halfway through the quiet meal, Kate said, 'Thank you for worrying.'

Liam took the opportunity to speak. Kate thought he must have been holding his breath the whole time. 'What happened up at the farm, Kate? Was all this about Mick?'

'She was just upset over Donal,' her mother said. Deirdre shot Kate a glance and a wink. This was a new side to her mother she hadn't seen before, a conspirator in a frilly floral apron.

'Aye, Da. Just a rough week,' she assured her father.

Her father mumbled something under his breath and went back to eating.

When the meal was over, Kate started clearing the plates but was halted by her father. 'I'm sending a man around to Mick tomorrow about that job, Kate. If you see him, you might mention it. He'll be over after tea.' Liam leaned back in his chair. He draped one arm over the high wooden back of it while he sipped at his tea with his other hand.

Kate wasn't quite sure how to go about telling her father what Mick had done, but it had to be told. 'That won't be necessary, Da.'

'What do you mean? Did Mick get some sense into his head and decide to stay put where he belongs?' Liam shot with a little more timbre than necessary.

'No, Da. He–'

'He what, Kate?' asked Connor.

'He hired someone already.' There. It was out. She tried moving quickly around the table to clear away the dirty dishes.

Her father was unnaturally quiet for a solid minute. She felt his eyes on her as she cleared the last plate. When she was done, she cast a glance at him and found his eyes boring into her.

'Sit for a minute,' he said.

Mick should have called her father to explain, instead of burdening her with the task.

When Liam finally spoke, he was obviously trying to maintain his temper. 'Tell me about what he did.'

'What's to tell, Da? You gave him sound advice to hire a manager so that's what he did.'

'I told him I'd send a man around to him.'

'Aye, you did. Apparently, he had someone else in mind.' If she ever saw Mick again, she'd give him what for. Why should she be the one interrogated? It wasn't even her farm, nor was she the one who hired Flann.

'Who did he hire? Is he local?'

'I don't know where he came from. His name is Flann. Flann Flannery.' Kate shivered as she said the man's name.

'What's wrong with him?'

'Nothing, why?'

'You don't normally react like that when you talk about people.'

Kate couldn't control the flush that heated her skin. 'I don't know where he's from. I don't like the looks of him, but,' she quoted Mick, 'you can't judge a person by the hat he wears. I worked Molly with him and he seems to know what he's on about. He'll probably work out fine. If I get the job at Galway Hospital, Molly will need someone

109

to work her.'

'Bring her home, Kate,' said Connor.

'I've already agreed to leave her on the farm. There's stock there and Flann will keep the farm going. Mick likes the idea that the place may turn a profit, even in his absence.' Kate wasn't sure of any of this herself. She could only go by what her eyes and ears told her. Her gut instinct was something else altogether.

Liam rose. 'I'm going over to talk with Mick.'

'I'm coming, too.' Connor quickly downed the last of his tea.

Kate laughed to herself. They were her knights in shining armor.

'He's gone.'

'What do you mean gone?' said both men in unison.

'Gone, as in left, absent, no longer there. He left this afternoon when I was done working Molly with Flann. I suggested he stay a while to make sure the man worked out, but he thought since Flann and I worked well enough today, that things would be fine,' she told him. 'Trust me. The first hint of mischief and I'll be on the phone with himself to get back here.'

Liam grabbed his coat off the wall peg by the back door, Connor following suit as if he were their father's shadow.

'Where are you going?' asked Deirdre.

'To Fairhill. Even if Mick's not there, I'll be meeting this Flann before the night's out.' The men slipped through the door and were gone. Kate stared at her mother. The tractor started up then headed off down the driveway.

110

Chapter Eight

'Bothersome, interfering, meddlesome busy-bodies,' Flann muttered to himself.

Liam and Connor Conneely had just left Fairhill Farm after interrogating him. What business was it of theirs to come over here and question him like the Gardai? 'None!' He answered his own question aloud, as he fairly slammed the teacup down on the table where he sat opposite the bed in the tiny apartment above one of the old barns.

It was bad enough he was going to have to deal with Spillane's woman. The last thing he needed was her men folk getting in his way, too.

The thought of Kate stopped Flann in his tracks as he stared at the single bed. Hmm – come to think of it, he just might enjoy having her around. He could teach her a thing or two that Spillane upstart never could.

He thought back to earlier in the day when he'd seen them there in the kitchen going at it like dogs in heat. It disgusted as well as excited him how she gave herself to Spillane. No self-respecting woman would throw herself at a man like that. Yet, watching her respond had made him crazy.

He watched them bent over the kitchen table and had to adjust himself in his loose trousers, but the instant his hand made contact with his willie, it sprang to life. It stiffened now just think-

111

ing about what those two had done on the other side of the glass.

Then he remembered how Kate pushed Spillane away from her. *The woman's a damn tease is what she is,* thought Flann. 'Always has been,' he added, aloud.

When she made motions to leave the house, he'd had to run back to his van and make himself look busy. The bitch had the nerve to look like nothing had just happened in the kitchen. She'd scowled at him as she passed, but he ignored it. He knew she didn't like him. She never had. He didn't care, though. She wasn't his concern. Managing this farm was, and he intended to turn a tasty profit. Soon.

For himself.

To get on with the job, he'd followed Kate to the back gate and told her he was going out with her to the pasture. He didn't give her a choice. He had to gain her trust, and that mangy dog's, to set his plans in motion. He was pleased with himself when she didn't argue. She was annoyed all right, but she let him follow along and eventually let him start working the dog.

Yes, his plans would come together, eventually. He just needed patience.

By the look on her face, he could tell she was uncomfortable with telling him her business, but her confession that she would only be out a few days a week lightened his mood a bit. He didn't need or want her around. Well, not for anything important. But her absence would help things run smoother.

He tilted the chair back against the wall so it

stood only on the back legs, his own legs dangling from the front as he thought to himself. Yes, this situation would work out nicely.

Flann spun a glance around the tiny room. He should be in the main house, he should. There was no one living there now. The least Spillane could have done was put him in an accommodation more fitting to his position on the farm. Not this – closet! There wasn't even a toilet in the room. He had to go next door to where someone had built a small bathroom. Spillane told him outright in the pub he hated the farm and an onsite manager would mean he didn't have to come back. So what was wrong with his staying in the main house? If he could keep the Conneely woman away permanently, he could move into the house and no one would be the wiser.

Now that it was sorted out, he had to wonder what he was going to do about the Conneely men. As long as he was pleasant to the woman and didn't give her any reason to question him, the men should leave him alone. Hmmm. How could he scare her off while staying pleasant with her so her men stayed away?

He got to his feet then and grabbed his jacket off the peg beside the door. He'd worry about the Conneelys later. Now that he had the farm to himself, there was no reason why he shouldn't get his bearings. There were barns to go through to check for inventory, there was machinery to inspect, and while he was at it, he'd check the lock on the back door to the farmhouse.

As he stepped through the door, he was met by Molly lying across the threshold. She looked up suddenly as the door swung wide. He'd almost tripped over her in his haste to get moving.

'Goddam dog,' he bit. The tip of his heavy boots connected with the dog's shoulder and she leapt away with a startled yip. As he closed the door, he watched her slink away into the shadows then went about his business.

The light on the answering machine was blinking when Mick stepped through his apartment door. The machine sat on the counter beside the fridge. He'd only been gone a few short days, but already there were over a dozen messages. His caller ID noted that many of them were from the same number.

'Gobnait,' he sighed.

She was nothing if not persistent. And he wasn't just talking about the phone calls. Gobnait had been like his shadow over the last few months. She was one of a small group of friends he occasionally went out with. He wouldn't call any of them best friends, or even close friends, but they'd shared more than their fair share of pints together and attended a few hurling matches at Croker.

Gobnait was a bit friendlier than the others. He'd taken her out without the group a time or two. She was just a friend and companion those times when he didn't want to be alone or with a bigger group. She'd made it clear she wanted more than he was prepared to give her, so even those times were rare and far between.

Looking at the flashing light on the machine, he hesitated to push the playback button. He didn't really want to know what she wanted. Not right now. The last thing he needed was for her to know he was back in the city. She'd be over like a shot. He wanted to be alone.

He walked into the bedroom and tossed his bag on the bed then shed his jacket, dropping it beside the bag. Looking around the small room, he saw everything was as it should be. Or rather, it was as he'd left it.

Mick had been thrilled when he'd finally gotten the apartment. It was small and not in a terribly good location, but it was all his, even if it was more than he could afford. And it was close enough to walk to work, his main reason for taking it above other places in better locations.

It had three rooms – one bedroom with an en suite bathroom, and the sitting room had a galley kitchen at the end. There were two windows in the place, the sitting room and bedroom, and both looked out to another building.

The building had originally been a warehouse of some sort, so the whole place had an industrial feeling about it with the red brick façade. The building had been gutted and restored as apartments. The red brick of the interior walls had been painted white to brighten what would otherwise have been a very dark set of rooms.

Once, when Mick happened to be home during the day, he couldn't help but notice the only sunlight actually reaching into the apartment was from a narrow stream that managed to make its way between the tightly built structures. And only when the sun was directly overhead. If he blinked, he'd miss it.

To counterbalance the lack of natural light, Mick

had decorated using pale beech wood furnishings with chrome details and neutral colored fabrics, and several lamps. He accented the sterile look with brightly colored abstract paintings and a few small area rugs. He'd gone for Feng Shui but ended up with Early Pigsty.

Admittedly, he wasn't the most tidy of people. This was confirmed as he looked around and saw his place in the same condition as when he'd left a few days ago. It was an absolute, utter, and complete kip. Calling it a pigsty would have been a compliment.

The bed linens were half-hanging off the bed, the sheets long in need of washing. From where he stood just inside the bedroom door, he saw the towels on the bathroom floor strewn beside the sports section from various weekend papers. Dirty clothes were everywhere.

He grimaced and stepped back into the sitting room. He intended to make himself something for dinner, but when he saw the state of the place, his stomach lurched. Pizza boxes littered the rug in the corner in front of the tiny telly, newspapers were strewn all over the sofa. And by the odor, he'd obviously neglected to empty the bin before leaving for Connemara.

He reluctantly turned toward the kitchen and was greeted by a tower of beer cans. He was happy to note all of his dishes and glassware were still in their respective places, so there wouldn't be any washing up to do. Being a bachelor meant he could eat his pizza straight from the box and could drink his beer right from the can.

He didn't know if it was just the long drive and

sitting in the car for the last four hours or if it was something else, but a sudden burst of energy hit him. He grabbed a roll of rubbish sacks from under the kitchen sink and set about to putting the apartment back to rights.

He hit play on the CD player and went to work, occasionally bopping to the Saw Doctors as he picked up the papers and pizza boxes and went about the business of making his place present-able.

Truth be told, the apartment mimicked his life more than he wanted to admit. While he'd never fancied himself a farmer like his father, the city didn't fit right, either. After university, Dublin just seemed as good a place to be as any other. And his friends, few as they were, had stayed in the city as well since they'd all gotten jobs there after graduation.

While he cleaned, his thoughts kept drifting back to Kate. He hadn't expected the reaction he had when he was near her.

He had to force himself to be annoyed with her presence in Tighe's office. In reality, he was almost glad to see her. She'd been the main link to his parents over the last five years. He understood why she was there the moment he walked through the door. It was only natural his father would want to leave Kate something, after all the time she'd spent on the farm. Of course, the addendum was a shock. He had expected his father to leave Kate money, not the whole bloody farm. Yes, he under-stood his father's reasoning. He didn't agree with it, but he understood.

If Kate were anyone else, he'd be well into a

117

legal battle over the land now. She'd worked with him from the first moment to help him find a way to keep the place. The only thing she'd fought him on was the issue of Molly. But she had been willing to leave the dog on the farm to work with the new manager. Fair dues to her.

This, and more, reminded Mick of what a pure heart the woman had. There wasn't an ounce of greed, selfishness, or bitterness in her. Her kindness, generosity, and yes, love, were all things he most cherished as they'd grown up together.

Was it just ironic the tune now playing from the CD was one with lyrics that said what was in his heart?

Heart beat like an earthy tremor
First love stays with you forever

The end lyric repeated over and over until he had to reach over to the player and push the button for the next song on the CD. This song made his thoughts go to places better left unexplored.

Mick tried pushing thoughts of Kate out of his mind. He shouldn't have kissed her. Never mind she looked like she needed a good and thorough kissing. He just shouldn't have been the one to do it. But damn if he wanted anyone else to. He couldn't figure out why he felt that way. He certainly wasn't going back, and that meant there would never be anything between them.

Shaking himself, he got back to work.

A short time later, the bed was made, sheets and towels were taking their turn in the tiny washer-dryer in the kitchen. And the beer cans, pizza boxes, and newspapers were in their respective sacks, ready for a trip to the recycle center. He grinned. The place actually looked habitable again.

The grin was quick to fade, though, as he picked up the phone to dial for pizza take-away. Before he finished dialing, he put the phone down and looked around. Something still wasn't right. Everything seemed to be where it was supposed to be. He pushed burglary out of his mind. Yet, something was missing. Or someone. It was an odd sense he just couldn't put his finger on.

Mick was so deep in thought, he nearly jumped out of his skin when the phone rang. His hand was still on the handset and the vibration of the ringing thrilled up his arm into his shoulders, which tensed in surprise.

He contemplated letting the machine pick it up, but decided against it. His thoughts started venturing into a direction he'd rather not go, and they had everything to do with Kate Conneely.

''Lo?' he greeted the caller, none too cheerily.

'Mick!' screeched the voice on the line. Gobnait. Mick sighed, rubbing his eyes. Should have checked caller ID first. He mentally kicked himself. 'Yous're back. Fine-illy. Is about bloody time.' Her voice was too bubbly. The sound of it annoyed him.

'Howya, Gob,' he said, greeting her with the traditional Dublin slang for hello. It still sounded funny with his Connemara accent.

'I'm only great. Is A1 I'yam.' Mick grimaced at her north inner city accent. He thought he'd gotten used to it, but a few days back in the west and he now found it grating. 'When did yous get in?'

'A bit ago,' he replied, staring at the sitting room window. The sun had gone down. The darkened window reflected the apartment back at him and aloneness settled on him with the sight.

'Mustn'ta bin too long ago. I bin drivin' by awl day and only jes saw da car. I'll be righ' up, yeah?' Before Mick could tell her not to bother, she'd disconnected her mobile phone and left him standing with the handset in his hand, beeping with the disconnect tone.

He gently put the handset back on the cradle. For an instant, he looked around to make sure everything was presentable then mentally slapped himself. What did he care if the place wasn't presentable for Gobnait? He hadn't invited her. And he certainly wasn't trying to impress her.

An instant later, the buzzer sounded at the front door to his building. Gobnait was ringing to be let in. He hit the button to release the door below, and put his own door on the latch so she could let herself in.

Just as he was turning to the fridge to see if there was anything to drink, Gobnait rushed through the door. She dropped her belongings as she crossed the room. She leapt into his arms and wrapped herself around him as he was turning toward her. She planted a sloppy kiss on his mouth. He was sure this was what it was like getting hit by a cyclone. He didn't even see her coming.

'Is gud to have yous home, Mick. Is bin dead boring since yous lef.' Mick couldn't help notice she kept her arms wrapped around him, as if she expected her exuberant kiss to be met with one of his own. *Ain't gonna happen.*

120

As nonchalantly as possible, he freed himself from her grasp. 'I'm not all that exciting, Gob.' He turned to look into the nearly empty fridge. 'I'd offer you something, but as you can see I haven't had time to get to the shops yet. I'm only just back this minute,' he lied.

Mick tried avoiding looking directly at her. If he could give her the hint he was preoccupied, she might leave.

He couldn't keep his head in the fridge all night, so he closed the door and turned back to see Gobnait's heavily mascara-lined eyes light up and her red painted lips curve into a toothy grin as she extracted a bottle of wine from the sack she held in her hand, wiggling it in the air. Her grin told him she'd been planning his welcome home. His gut twisted, but he forced a smile at her effort.

'Nice,' was all he could manage. Her perfume permeated his nostrils when she sailed past him. She pulled out a couple wine glasses and the bottle opener. She was a blaze of red as she moved around his tiny kitchen.

Her eyes sparkled as she held the bottle and opener out to him. 'Is the good stuff. I though' yous deserved it, yeah? Yous know? Considering things, like.'

Mick swallowed hard. Gobnait really did have a good heart, but her efforts were misdirected. He certainly never encouraged her affections.

'Thanks, Gob,' he managed. 'But I think I should eat something first. It's been a long day and I didn't eat before I left Connemara.'

'Not'a worry, luv. Gobnait's though' uh everything!' She tottered over to her previously deposited bags. As she bent over to retrieve the white plastic bags, Mick suddenly realized Gobnait was wearing a very short mini skirt. He got a full leg view, from red stiletto heel to the curve of her thong-clad bottom. She was dressed in red from toe to shoulder, including the sheer red hose covering her shapely legs.

'Jazus,' he exclaimed under his breath. What surprised him more than her outfit, or lack of, was the fact she did nothing for him physically. The outfit was erotic enough, but it was Kate he'd rather see in it.

He blinked. Where had that come from? He had to push Kate out of his mind. He wasn't going home so there was no use exploring the idea of trying to pick up with her. They had both moved on.

If that was true, then what was the harm in letting Gobnait ease his pain?

Gobnait returned to the kitchen, winking as she passed, and set the sacks on the countertop that divided the kitchen area with the rest of the room. Cartons and containers spilled out.

'Chi-nee'az, yeah?'

'It appears so.' He swallowed hard at the same time his belly growled. Okay, so he'd let her stay for just a while.

He pulled down a couple plates from the press then grabbed forks from the drawer. Gobnait piled food onto the plates and set them on the other side of the counter.

Once seated with their food and wine in front of them, Mick's thoughts began to roam. He was tired. The long drive home and cleaning the apartment had sapped him of any energy he had.

Images flashed in his mind as he ate – Kate in the solicitor's office in her prim suit, Kate in his bedroom and in the kitchen, with passion in her eyes. Kate in her Mini as she sped off after telling him goodbye. And Gobnait in her red mini skirt and very much available.

'Yous're awferly quiet, Mick. Yous alrigh'?'

Mick was glad to see some of her energy had subsided. When she was switched on, she was like an electric current snapping around a room. She was difficult to deal with until she finally wore herself out. He hoped she finally had, but doubted it. She was a little too convenient for the mood he was in right now.

'Sorry, Gob, just tired. It's a long drive from the west.' Mick stretched his arms over his head and forced a yawn, hinting at his exhaustion.

Gobnait sat back in her chair and sipped her wine, looking at him. 'I'd've taken da trayin.'

'I couldn't very well do that and leave my car in Galway now, could I?' His tone must have startled her, as silence fell between them again.

He quickly swallowed the last of his wine and moved to clear the dishes. Gobnait stilled him with her hand on his then poured more wine into his glass. She smiled at him again, nodded toward the sofa, and softly said, 'Relax, yeah?'

He picked up his wine glass, thus extricating himself from her grasp, and lifted the glass in a toast. 'To friends.' She paused before clinking her glass with his. He was sure she'd taken his meaning by the way her gaze lost some of its light.

He set his glass down again and rose to take the dishes to the sink. Once he'd cleared the counters of the debris and washed the dishes, which he left sitting in the drying rack, he turned back to Gobnait who watched him from her chair. He leaned against the counter, crossed his arms in front of him, and looked at her. Really looked at her this time.

Gobnait reminded Mick of a pixie. She was petite, full of energy, and usually flitting off to somewhere else before she'd alighted at the original destination. Some would call her a social butterfly. She was as generous with her affections as she was with her venom, though. He'd seen her in action. He didn't fancy being on the receiving end of Retribution a la Gobnait.

He raised an eyebrow at the state of her hair. She normally wore a sort of pageboy haircut that hugged her head. She bleached it a perfect white. But tonight she wore it in short spikes that had two distinct and strategically positioned devil's horns that had been sprayed red.

He didn't know how it had passed his notice, but she was dressed like a devil. She wore a tightly-laced red bustier that pushed her small breasts up to almost spilling over. Hadn't she worn something over her shoulders when she'd flung herself at him earlier? She'd removed it while he was tidying up, baring her shoulders. The creamy sweep of them tapered down to slim arms and delicate fingers tipped with long red nails.

Just then a smile curved her lips as she brought the wine glass to them. Coyly now, she looked up at him through her heavy lashes and softly asked,

'Wha' are yous starin' a'?' Had she thought he was staring at her in that way?

He caught himself. 'I was just wondering where your tail is. Those horns really work for you.'

Gobnait tittered. Did women really titter anymore?

'Like i'? I was feelin' a liddle divilish tonigh', yeah?' she said mischievously.

'How can you eat so much and still fit into that ... get-up?'

She put her glass down and sat up straight, tugging at the bottom of the bustier, which caused the top of it to lower and expose more of her breasts. 'I didn' eat that much.' She pouted, some of her coyness gone out of her now in mock protest.

'You ate as much as I did.'

'Well, ta be hones', is qui'e tigh' enyway,' she told him, turning on the seductress now. 'I suppose is a good thing I brough' something more comfertible, like, ta slip inta.' Her eyes met his now. Serious.

It had been a while since she'd tried to pull this stunt with him. Did she assume since she'd met him on his return, and taken care of the dinner and the drink, that he owed her something more?

Gobnait had been another one of Mick's mistakes. His mistake with Gobnait was that he'd slept with her. Just once. But apparently it was enough.

Not that he remembered. He could only go by what she'd told him the next morning when they'd woken up in bed together. All he could remember from the night before was going out with the gang for pints. The next thing he knew, he woke up in bed with a very naked Gobnait wrapped around him.

She rose from her chair now and stepped around the counter to stand before him.

He swallowed hard for the second time. 'Did your mother let you out of the house dressed like that?'

She put her hand on his arms and looked up into his eyes through mascara-caked lashes. 'Mam don' dress me anymore, Mick.' She pressed herself against him. He grasped the counter behind him. Her body pressed flat against his and her hands snaked their way up his belly to his chest. 'Bu' yous could undress me. Yeah?' she whispered, batting her lashes.

Mick forced himself to breathe deeply. 'There's not much there, in case you haven't noticed.'

Her hands worked their way up around his neck and pulled him closer. 'Then i' won' take long den, will i'?'

When her lips met his, Mick expected a flash of light behind his lids, tightness in his chest, a tingling in his groin. Between her outfit and her come-on, he expected something. He felt ... nothing. Absolutely nothing but the stiff fabric of her bustier and the rigid prodding of the belt at her waist poking at him uncomfortably as she rubbed against him.

Without touching her, his hands still gripping the countertop, he straightened, disengaging her lips from his. He looked down at her and could only think of Kate. When he'd kissed her, it had been erotic, enticing, explosive. Kissing Gobnait was like kissing ... a sister? It made him feel dirty and all he wanted to do was take a shower.

126

He used his body to push her away as he straightened. He towered over her, and the look she gave him, eyes wide and licking her lips, told him she thought all systems were go. She moved to unbutton his shirt. He clasped her hands in his and brought the backs of her fingers to his lips. He shut his eyes tight for a moment as he gathered his courage to tell her what was on his mind.

When he opened his eyes, Gobnait was watching him. There was such expectation in her eyes. He wouldn't call it love. Infatuation maybe. Lust, most certainly.

'Gobnait, this isn't a good idea.'

'Is the perfec' time. You're here. I'm here,' she told him softly. Disappointment edged her voice, even though she tried to cover it up.

'Yes, but I'm tired. My belly is full now, thanks to you.' He smiled lightly. 'All I want to do is just hang out for a while and watch some telly, then hit the sack. Alone.'

He kept his gaze on hers and knew that a thousand thoughts were whirling around in her head.

'Alrigh', Mick.'

'All right?' He was astounded by her capitulation.

'Yeah. I don' mind jus' cud'lin'.'

He fought to keep the shocked expression off his face. 'Gobnait...' The girl seemed to have missed it when he said he wanted to be alone.

'Come on, Mick.' She pouted in earnest now. 'Lemme stay. I'll be good. Promise.' She crossed herself as she said this.

Okay, so he'd let her stay just to get the evening over with. He couldn't just kick her out. Not after

127

she'd brought him dinner. He'd watch something short, then tell her it was time to leave.

He sighed and relented. Her smile lit up again and she rushed over to the sofa. She flipped off her stilettos to get comfortable and flipped the telly on with the remote. When Mick hesitated, she looked over the back of the sofa and smiled at him, patting the cushion beside her.

'Back in a minute,' he told her, as he headed through the bedroom to the loo. He closed the door and made sure to latch it. In her current mood, he wouldn't put it past Gobnait to try sneaking in.

Mick turned toward the sink. The small shaving light just illuminated the tiny room. He looked at himself in the mirror and tried figuring out what was going on in his head. And out in his sitting room.

Chapter Nine

Kate was thrilled she'd secured a job at Galway Hospital, albeit a part time one. She didn't quite know what to do with herself with so much free time on her hands now, but she enjoyed the work and finally made some friends her own age.

She kept her promise to Mick and stopped in at Fairhill Farm a couple times a week to ensure things were running smoothly. Her first few visits went as expected. She'd pull in and park, Molly would run to greet her. If Molly was in the pasture and saw Kate's Mini speeding along the common road, she'd race to the house to meet her. Kate thought this was cute but something she'd have to break soon, or Flann might take issue with the dog's behavior. It wasn't exactly acceptable for a sheepdog to leave the flock in the middle of work.

Once she'd taken Molly back out to the pasture, Kate would head into the house to dust a bit and make herself a cup of tea before heading out to feed the chickens.

Kate hadn't liked Flann from day one, but it wasn't long after Mick hired him that her suspicions grew. At first, she was unconcerned when chickens started disappearing. There were fox on the land so it was quite possible one could have gotten into the coop, even though she found no sign of damage to the pen and no feathers to indicate a struggle. The mystery was worrisome, but not as worrisome as Molly.

Molly's behavior became noticeably strange after a few weeks. When Kate showed up at the farm, she expected to see Molly at least once before she left. When she didn't see the dog, she went looking for her and found her penned in one of the barns. Kate opened the pen and called her outside, but Molly was leery of the affection. After a few more visits, Molly refused Kate's commands altogether. And she seemed to be gaining weight. Kate wondered if she was being worked as she should. The lack of work would put the weight on a collie quicker than overfeeding. If she could find Flann, she'd speak to him about this.

When her schedule at work changed, so did her visiting times to Fairhill. It was then she started seeing strange vehicles in the main yard. Flann wouldn't let her see who he was talking to as he ushered them to their vehicles to see them off. He'd cast her angry glances and stride off, oddly with Molly following behind him.

And so it went, until by the eighth week Kate had had enough. She would confront Flann and ask him what was going on. Mick hadn't so much as called her to check on the farm. Well, even if he didn't care, she did.

As her Mini sped down the common road between the farms, rain pelting the windscreen, Kate spotted Molly on the pasture with Flann and slowed. The dog was working perfectly, regardless of the inclement weather. Her attention was on the flock, not on Kate's car.

After parking in her usual spot in front of the house, she rushed through the rain to the backdoor. She wouldn't sully the sitting room with the mud on her shoes.

The instant she reached the back of the house, panic rose at the site of the damaged door. She quickly looked around to see if anyone else was on the farm. Seeing no one, she carefully pushed open the door and stepped inside the kitchen.

Instantly, she was hit by an unusual smell. She couldn't place it, as it wasn't so much a single odor, but a combination of odors ranging from sweat to grease to animal excrement. There was no one in the room now, but it was obvious someone had been, and quite possibly more than one person by the number of dishes in and around the sink – Mary's precious crockery. The hob had several greasy frying pans on it and there was mud caked on the floor.

She listened carefully for noises in the house. When she was satisfied she was alone, she decided to check the rest of the place.

Her heart was in her throat as she went through the litter-strewn sitting room and up the stairs. Mick's room had been ransacked, but it was obvious whatever the person was looking for wouldn't be found in a boy's room.

The connecting bathroom looked as if a mud bomb had exploded in it. Dirty towels littered the floor and there wasn't an inch of white tile showing through the filth.

When she stepped into Donal and Mary's room, Kate thought she'd be sick. The bed was a mess, there were clothes everywhere, and the closet had been riffled through aggressively, as had the chest of drawers.

A sob choked Kate and tears stung her eyes. What happened? It would have been one thing if the house had been robbed, but the absolute filth the person, or people, left in their wake was indescribable. It was as if a band of travelers had moved in and destroyed the place in their search for valuables.

With that thought in mind, she raced to a place only she knew about now that Donal was gone. She looked around carefully to be sure no one had come up after her then went to the far corner of the large rug sitting under Mary's dressing table. She lifted the edge and pulled up the loose floorboard. She sighed with relief when she saw the tiny box was still there. She removed it with the intention of taking it home with her.

To be sure it had been left untouched, she lifted the lid. Another relieved breath passed between her lips – the contents were still there. There wasn't a lot, but they were important items to Donal and Mary; a few pieces of jewelry, wedding photos, and their simple gold wedding bands. These were mementos Mick would want to have at some point in his life and Donal had entrusted her with them, regardless of how well she and Mick were getting along.

She wasn't sure how she made it back downstairs safely, with her shaking legs. She went into the kitchen where the phone was and dialed home.

'Mam,' she rushed. 'Is Da home?'

'No, love. He's out in the field. What's wrong?'

'I'm over at Fairhill. Someone has ransacked the place. And I think I know who.' She could barely

132

get the words out, she was so upset.

'Calm down, now. Tell me exactly what's happened. Have you talked to Flann?'

'No, Mam. He's out with the sheep. He saw me coming. I think he's still avoiding me.' Kate pulled the single remaining paper towel off the roll and dabbed her eyes with it. 'Can you call Da on his mobile and tell him to come over to help me sort this out?'

'Sure. Just give me a minute to collect my own one and I'll call him while you wait.' Kate heard her mother put the phone down to go in search of her mobile. Her mother was only gone a moment, but it seemed like forever.

'He's not answering. He's probably got the radio up too high in the tractor.'

'What am I going to do, Mam? The place is a mess.'

'Tell me everything.' She told her mother exactly what she'd seen from the moment she walked in the door. 'Well, it definitely sounds like someone's been living in the house. Are you sure it's Flann?'

'Aye. What do I do?' Kate pushed the palm of her hand against her forehead to quell a building headache, but it did no good.

'I'll leave a note for your father or Conn for when they come in and ask them to bring new locks. I'll come over to Fairhill and you and I'll put that house back to rights.' Her mother's voice remained calm as she spoke. Kate loved her mother's steely determination. She was always so calm in the face of an emergency. It helped to calm her. She hoped she would inherit some of that one day.

'Are you sure, Mam? I can tidy the place but, God help me, it'll take a month of holy days before it's truly clean again.' Her spirits sank, looking around at the state of the kitchen.

'That's why I'll come over to help. You can't possibly be expected to tackle that mess on your own. And if whoever has been living in the house comes back, there will be two of us to deal with.' It didn't take long for Kate to agree with her mother's logic. 'I'll be there in a few minutes. Close the doors and don't go anywhere.'

As promised, Deirdre was pulling into the driveway within minutes. Kate rushed out to greet her mother. She'd brought the tiny box with her and shoved it under the seat, then made her mother lock the doors. Her mother's odd look prompted an explanation. 'I knew where they kept the valuables.'

Kate walked her mother through the house. So unlike Deirdre, she was rendered speechless as she walked through the few rooms.

'See what I mean?'

Deirdre only nodded as she went to the next room. Kate watched her cross to the window in Donal and Mary's room and moved the curtain aside. 'Who's this coming with Molly?' she asked.

'Must be Flann back from the pasture. He probably stayed out there as long as he could to avoid me. Now that it's getting dark, he has to come in.'

'I'd like to meet this man.' Deirdre let the curtain drop back into place and turned back to Kate.

'I don't think that's such a good idea, Mam. He's not very pleasant.'

'If you're going to continue coming here, I want to know who we're dealing with. And that you're safe. Your father never tells me anything.' This fact obviously exasperated her mother.

Before Kate could stop her, her mother was heading out of the room and down the stairs. Once in the yard, the women spotted Flann coming through the back gate with Molly. Flann looked none too pleased to see either of them.

To make matters worse, the rain had started to come down full force. Kate wasn't bothered by it and neither was Deirdre, as she stomped across the yard, rain pelting her face. She knew her mother wanted as many answers as she did.

Kate called to Molly but the dog stayed with Flann, her coat dripping. She panted heavily and appeared to have been overworked by the way the poor dog's tongue lolled from the side of her mouth. Kate called Molly again and was surprised when Flann pointed to the barn and she waddled off in that direction.

'What the...?' Kate turned to her mother. 'Molly's never not come to me.'

'I'm sure there's a good explanation.'

'Aye, and I mean to get it.'

Flann stepped over to the women and tipped his grubby cap to them, splattering dirty water on Kate as he did so. 'Ladies.' The sour scent of him was heavy even in the damp air. He glanced between them. 'And what brings two fine ladies out of an evening such as this?'

Kate was disgusted how easily he turned on the charm.

'I'm Mrs Conneely. Kate's mother.' Deirdre

introduced herself before Kate could speak.

'Have you been in the house?' Kate blurted before she let her mother wrest the situation from her.

Flann turned to look directly at her. His gaze bore into her, making her nervous. She was sure that was his intent. If she were anyone else, and if she was alone, she probably would have scurried back to her car and driven off. Having her mother beside her boosted her courage, so she gave him a look of her own. It was one telling him she knew he'd been in the house and was waiting to see what his excuse was.

Silence fell between them for a moment and Kate saw him thinking about what he would tell them.

'Aye, 'twas meself all right,' he finally said, as if he had every right to be in there. Kate was surprised by his admission.

'What were you doing in the house? You know it's off limits. You have your quarters.'

'Aye, and I do. But wouldn't you know it? The cooker's on the blink in me own room. How was I to cook me dinner?' He stood with arms crossed and stared at her. His face dripped with rainwater. He was challenging her.

'Why didn't you call someone to repair it? I was here just two days ago. You could have mentioned it to me then. In just two days, the house has gone from a tidy and well-kept home to a disaster zone.'

'And why should I, when there's a perfectly good cooker in the house going unused?' He acted as if he had every right to it.

'What about the rest of it? You slept in their

136

bed. The place is a mess. You went through Donal and Mary's things. How could you? Is nothing sacred?' Tears welled up, but she refused to acknowledge them. She wouldn't let him see her cry.

For a moment, he didn't speak.

'I believe you were asked a direct question,' Deirdre interjected. Flann flashed his eyes in her direction. Before he could speak, Kate noticed the jacket and shoes and gasped.

'You bastard! You're wearing Donal's clothes?' She turned to her mother, anger raging through her. 'I can't believe the audacity of it, Mam. He's wearing Donal's clothes.' Before her mother could react, Kate launched herself at Flann and tore at him, trying to get the jacket off him. He fought her off, pushing her away from him with one hand. Her mother grabbed her by the arm and pulled her away at the same time. Kate fell against her, breathing heavily.

Just then, Molly appeared at the barn door. The shouting had alerted her to trouble. The dog stopped midway across the yard, watching. Her pricked ears twitched as she listened attentively.

Kate called the dog to her, but again Molly wouldn't come. Molly kept looking to Flann, shiverng noticeably in the heavy rain. He scowled at the dog, causing her to back up a step.

'What have you done to my dog?'

'I've done nothing to her. She obviously prefers my company to yours.' He pointed back to the barn and Molly reluctantly retreated. Kate watched her go, but could see her stop just inside the barn door, continuing to watch the fracas in the driveway.

'Molly is my dog and you better well remember that right now. She's only here because I let her stay. I can take her away just as easily.' Anger seethed through Kate.

Flann smiled wickedly. His voice was sickeningly sweet. 'Now, you won't want to be going and doing that now. You'd upset an expectant mother.'

Kate felt like she'd been punched in the stomach. 'She's pregnant? How – What – You bastard! What have you done?' She launched herself at the man again, but this time her mother held her firm.

'Kate,' her mother warned, holding fast. Deirdre's look was intent as she turned back at Flann. 'Why is Molly pregnant?'

'I was hired to run this farm. I assume yer man wants it to turn a profit. To do that means I need to increase the flock. I can't do that until I have a suitable dog to manage it. Maybe two.'

Kate cut him off. 'Molly is a perfectly good sheepdog and you know it. You don't need another dog.'

'Bloody bitches are hard to control. They're moody as sin, and when they're in heat, they attract every dog for miles. I bred her to the best dog I know. She'll throw sound pups.' As he spoke, his explanation rolled out so quickly over his thick accent Kate almost missed what he was telling her.

'Why didn't you just buy another dog? Why go through all of this for the sake of a dog you can't use right away?' Kate's anger fueled her determination to get to the bottom of this. She used her mother's presence to bolster her courage, foolish as it was to fight with him in the first place.

'No better trainer than to let the pup work beside a trained dog. He'll learn from his dam then go onto work the flock when he's ready,' he told her matter-of-factly. 'With luck, there'll be several dogs in her litter and we can train them up and sell them on for a tasty profit.'

'We are not dog breeders. I'll not allow you to use Molly in that way.' She straightened her back as she stood up to him.

'Maybe not, but there's no reason not to turn a profit by it.'

'And what of Molly?'

'If she gives us sound working dogs, we'll keep her. If not...' He shrugged, leaving the sentence open to interpretation.

'Then what?' Kate challenged.

'Then we'll get us another bitch,' he said the word with much venom in his voice, 'to get us the dogs we need for the work.'

'How dare you? Molly is my dog and she will not be tossed aside by the likes of you,' she bit. 'Molly is a perfectly sound working dog.'

'She won't do. I need a dog, not a bitch for the work. Bitches are only good for one thing.'

'And that is?'

'Supplying me with the dogs I need to run this farm proper. Now, if you'll excuse me, I've apparently a cold dinner to get to.'

The rain pelted down around them in fat droplets. They hit the ground and sounded like horses racing across the yard. She had blocked out the sound with her anger, but she was sure her racing heart matched the rhythm of the fall.

It pumped through her veins as surely as she felt the vibration of the rain hitting the ground beside her.

He tried leaving but Kate called after him.

'Wait right there. I'm not done with you yet.' She had to shout to be heard over the downpour.

Slowly, he turned back to them. With his face down-turned so the water would pour off his cap, he looked through his dark brows, the crease between his eyes deepening. His voice was low and deliberate, but full of malice. 'Watch yourself, Katie, love.' Venomous honey dripped from his every word. 'You don't want to get backed up against a wall again, do you? You leave me to my business and I'll leave you to yours.' He bore his gaze down on her. He was so close, Kate saw the red veins running through the whites of his eyes. His breath was warm and putrid.

She shook but wasn't sure if it was from her anger, the chill of the weather, or from the fear this man instilled in her. His comment sent shivers down her back, remembering a time better left forgotten. With as much rancor as he spat at her, she gave it back in equal measure.

'We'll play this game, Flann, but you'll need to understand the rules a little better. You will consult with me about everything that concerns my dog, and you will stay out of the Spillane's house. I expect to see the clothes you're wearing returned to me before I leave this evening. And if I so much as see you near the farmhouse again, I will have you hauled off by the Gardai for breaking and entering.'

When she was done, she stood with her arms

stiff at her sides, her hands in fists. She stared unblinking into his eyes, regardless of the rain hitting her face. His eyes were so black she saw her own reflection in them, even in the dim light of the stormy evening.

Her heart was in her throat.

Her mother grasped her by the upper arm as she leaned closer to him. 'Do I make myself clear, Mr Flannery?'

Flann continued staring at her. His only reaction to her threat was the scowl on his face. The rest of him was obliterated by the darkening sky as evening fell around them.

Then slowly, he looked behind her to her mother and said, 'I'd take your daughter home, missus, before she regrets tangling with the likes of me.'

Her mother gasped. Her unflappable mother had just been threatened with great effect.

'Kate, let's see to the cleaning of the house. Your father should be here any minute with the new locks.' Deirdre pulled at Kate's arm until she relented. As they walked back to the farmhouse, Kate heard Flann laughing. It took all of her willpower not to look back. He would know he got to her if she did.

Molly. What was she going to do about the dog now she was pregnant? Well, the first thing would be to call in the vet. She would do that in the morning. Once she explained the situation to Will, she was sure he'd come right over.

Once Molly was examined, Kate would know about when the pups were due. Maybe he'd even have a suggestion for capturing Molly so Kate could take her home. She didn't want to leave the dog here any longer than necessary. Flann was a demoralizing character, and the sooner she was done with him the better.

First things first, if she wanted to make a formal complaint, she knew she'd have to call the Gardai before she touched a thing in the house.

She supposed she'd have to call Mick and let him know what was happening. If he decided to come home to deal with this problem, he'd need a clean house to sleep in. She and her mother would see to that tonight. Hopefully, her father would bring new locks soon and repair the damage Flann had done breaking in.

Anger brewed in her anew when she walked through the house to the kitchen where she'd use the phone to call the Gardai. Her heart pounded in her chest again, but this time at the thought of talking to Mick. It had been eight weeks since he'd left. He'd not so much as sent her a text to see how things were going on the farm. It angered her to realize he'd left her in charge.

'What shall we tackle first, Kate?' her mother asked, as she began to roll up her sleeves and get to work.

'I'm going to ring the Gardai first. I want to make a formal complaint about the break-in. We can't touch a thing until they've been here. While we're waiting, I'm going to call Mick and tell him what his manager has been up to.'

Her head spun as she entered the kitchen for the second time that evening and saw the mess. The bin in the corner was overflowing and it was obvious now where the missing chickens had gone. Bones littered the floor and there were handfuls of feathers on the counter. She didn't know how she could have missed them before.

She gagged at the mess.

Turning back to her mother, she suggested, 'Maybe you can ring Da to see what's keeping him.'

'All right, pet. I'll be in the sitting room if you need me.'

As soon as her mother left the room, she rang the Gardai. They promised to be out straight away. While she waited, she'd ring Mick.

It was late when his mobile rang. Mick sat alone in a snug in the back of the Blues Tavern in Dublin. The snug was a darkened corner of the pub, with high walls around a small table intended for privacy. Privacy was just what he had.

He'd managed to dodge Gobnait by telling her he wasn't feeling well and didn't want her to catch whatever he had. But instead of staying home alone, he'd headed straight here for a pint with some of his mates he knew would be here. It wasn't long after his arrival when those same mates filtered out, which left him alone in the end. That was fine by him. They weren't very good company tonight, anyway.

Sitting there alone, he couldn't help thinking that since he returned from the farm his friends were avoiding him. They were standoffish, and he noticed they didn't call by the apartment much. If he wanted to see them, he had to make the first move.

Gobnait was persistent in her affection, but

143

even she was coming by irregularly. Maybe she was getting the hint he wasn't interested. It just seemed ironic they all chose the same time to alienate him.

He also wondered what was happening with his life. He wasn't enjoying his job; not that cataloging artifacts was exciting. He normally enjoyed it. And his thoughts kept drifting back to Kate.

He'd spent countless hours since returning to Dublin, thinking about Kate and what happened between them so long ago. The feel of her in his arms had given him a taste of what he was missing in his life and he wanted more. Just not from Gobnait. As long as he was in Dublin, it wouldn't be Kate, either.

He was so deep in thought that when his mobile went off it startled him. The bands were changing over now so he would be able to talk for a minute. He didn't like the idea of giving up his dark corner if he had to take his call outside for a bit of quiet. A group of people at the bar kept eyeing him to see when he was leaving.

''Lo?' He looked away from the group.

'It's Kate.' Two simple words made his heart pound. The object of his obsession was on the other end of the phone. He'd thought to call her a few times with the excuse of asking how the farm was doing, but had stopped himself every time.

It wasn't that he didn't want to know what was happening on the farm. It was that he didn't want to get the information from Kate. Their kisses were still fresh in his mind. The feel of her skin still lingered on the palms of his hands. Even though the memories were two months old now,

144

if he had her on the line, he doubted he'd be able to concentrate on whatever information she'd share with him.

He'd spoken with Flann a few times, though. According to him, everything was grand and going smoothly. He talked about turning a profit on the farm and increasing the flock to do so. Mick could only agree. Making a profit was always a good thing. Better still, he wasn't on the farm doing the work himself. That's what Flann was there for.

'Kate.'

'You've got to come home.' Her words tumbled out in a combination of Irish and English so quickly, he couldn't tell why she was so upset. Just as he started remembering the language he'd grown up with, she'd switch to English and he'd have to change his focus. Then she'd go back to Irish again and it was like she was speaking Greek.

'Whoa, Kate. Slow down. Pick a language, love. I can't understand you. Why is Molly in your family's way?' He ran his fingers through his hair and he tried making sense of what she was saying.

He heard her inhale deeply, as if trying to calm herself. 'No, Mick. Molly is in the family way. Flann bred her to another dog without my consent. I'm going to have Will come over tomorrow to examine her.'

'Did you ask him why he did this?'

'I did, indeed. He said he needed more dogs to work the farm.'

'I thought Molly was good at what she does.'

'She's brilliant at what she does. He's got some foolish notion that bitches aren't good for the

145

work, and wants dogs. He wants to use her as a breeding machine.' He heard her sniffle then. 'Oh, Mick, you have to come home. I don't think I can deal with this on my own.' She started crying now. He remembered the sound of her voice from when they were children. She'd never been able to hide it from him.

'Calm down, Kate. Why can't you handle this? Surely, it's just a small problem. Let her have the puppies, then get her fixed. You weren't going to breed her anyway – were you?'

'That's not the point. This is your farm. If it were mine, I could take serious action. I'd get Flann off the property. You should be lucky Da's here changing the locks for you.' She sniffled, then blew her nose, driving Mick to pull the phone from his ear.

'What do you mean he's changing the locks on the house?'

Something was happening on the farm and he needed to get the story from her as clearly as possible. If she was having the locks changed on the house, he wondered if she was taking over the farm. No, she wasn't doing that. If she were, then they wouldn't be having this conversation and she wouldn't have asked him to come home.

'That bastard you hired broke into your house. He's been living in it. The place is a wreck, and he's gone through everything.'

'Are you sure it was Flann? Did you talk to him?' He straightened in his seat and wished he had another pint in front of him. He might need it.

'I'm telling you Flann broke into your house,

Mick. He didn't deny it. He couldn't. He was wearing your father's clothes. He pried the backdoor open and made himself at home. The place looks like a monsoon hit it. There's food, mud, and feathers everywhere.'

'Feathers?' This had better be good.

'He's been eating your chickens. That's not the worst of it, Mick. He's turned Molly against me. I can deal with cleaning the house. Mam's here to help. And Da and Conn just arrived to change the locks. But this whole thing with Molly is really more than I can bear.'

For a moment, neither said anything. He tried digesting what she was telling him. 'It can't be all that bad.'

'You're not here. You can't see what I'm sitting in, what I have to deal with. Mick, he threatened me. I won't have him here, I'm telling you. I won't!'

'Kate, I can't talk to you if you keep screaming into the phone.'

The new band on stage was just starting to tune up. In a moment, he wouldn't hear anything she was saying.

'Listen, I have to go. I'll call you when I get home. I'm in town. Give me half an hour.' There was silence on the other end of the phone. 'Kate?'

'What?' she sniffed.

'Can I call you when I get home? Let's talk then. In a minute, the band here will start up and I won't be able to hear you. I'll have to call from home where it's quiet. Okay?' He waited for her to answer him. When she did, it was curt but an agreement. 'Okay, then. Thirty minutes. Try to

147

calm down. It'll be all right.'

Just then Gobnait walked through the door. If he was lucky, he'd be able to avoid her, but only if he moved fast. She knew this was their group's snug of choice, and she'd be heading this way as soon as she ordered a drink.

'I've got to go. I'll talk to you in a minute.' Before she could answer, he disconnected and slipped from the snug. Instantly, the group who'd been waiting rushed past him to grab it. The rush of bodies helped to disguise him as he slipped through the kitchen door behind the bar. He was greeted by Kieran Vaughan, one of the owners of the pub.

'Hey, Mick,' Kieran greeted him. The sandwich he'd ordered was in Kieran's hand. 'Couldn't wait for it, eh? Had to come looking?' Kieran chuckled.

Mick wasn't in a laughing mood. 'No, mate. Just got a call from home. I need to leave and I'm trying to avoid Gobnait. She just walked in and was heading my way. I don't think she saw me, though.'

'Well, you better duck out the back because here she comes now.' Mick ducked through the storage room door by mistake. It was too late to find the back door. Gobnait was on the other side of the door.

'Howya, Kieran,' she said in her thick Dublin accent. 'Seen Mick tonigh'?'

'I did. He was here with a few others then left.' Kieran was a champ. Mick owed him one.

'He say where he was goin'?' Gobnait asked. There was disappointment in her voice.

"Fraid not, love.' There was a pause, but Mick knew Gobnait was still there, thinking about her next move. 'Best I can do is offer you this sandwich if you're hungry. It's on the house.'

'No thanks. I've got to watch me figger.'

Kieran chuckled. 'Why not eat a little something and let some bloke watch your figure for you?'

Gobnait snorted. 'Why do you think I'm lookin' fer Mick?'

'Hmm–' was all Kieran said in reply.

A moment later, Gobnait was gone and Mick released a pent-up breath. He about jumped out of his skin, though, when a feminine voice came at him from behind.

'She seems a perfectly nice girl, Mick. I don't know why you're avoiding her,' the woman said sarcastically, yet ever so sweetly.

He spun around and nearly fell over a beer keg. 'Jazus, Eilis. You scared years off my life.'

She laughed lightly, stretched, then put her hand out to Mick. 'Help a really fat woman to her feet so she can get back to work, will ya?' He helped her stand, then kissed her cheek in greeting.

'Howya keeping? Looks like it's about any day now.' He nodded to her most prominent feature.

'A gentleman is not supposed to remark on the size of a pregnant woman. Isn't that right, Kieran?' She looked adoringly into Kieran's eyes when he opened the storage room door.

'I don't know what you're talking about, love. You're perfect to me.'

Mick was astounded by the love he saw flash between his friends. He could only dream of a

149

love like that. Oddly, as he watched Kieran move into the room to kiss Eilis, he could only think of how it felt to kiss Kate, and the love he'd thought they shared so long ago.

'Okay, you two, break it up. Look what happened last time you got carried away.' He pushed dramatically between them and stepped from the storage room. Kieran chuckled behind him.

'So you want this sandwich to go then, mate?' Kieran asked, still holding the plate in his hand.

'That'd be great.' He glanced through the kitchen door and was relieved when he didn't see Gobnait. Now, he just needed to get home and sort out Kate and what was happening on the farm.

'You look more upset than this business with Gobnait, Mick,' said Eilis. 'What's up?'

He looked back to her as she took the plate from Kieran so she could wrap the sandwich. Kieran picked up a couple other plates and scooted through the kitchen door to serve other patrons.

Mick could always talk to Eilis. She and Kieran already knew about the farm. They neither agreed nor disagreed with his decision, but they thought hiring a manager was a sound thing to do until he could decide what he wanted to do with the place. While he thought a manager was a permanent solution, Eilis thought he was just stalling for time until he decided what he really wanted.

She also told him he didn't fit in in Dublin – even though he didn't feel he belonged on the farm. She told him, 'You'll eventually know where you belong. Until then, you just need to keep an open mind.'

He laughed at her comments. 'Aw, Eilis, those comments are New Age,' he'd told her. 'Next, you're going to start wearing sandals and burning incense.' She'd laughed, too. But one night when he was home alone sitting in the dark with a pizza and the telly, he suddenly realized she was right.

Now, in the kitchen behind the bar, he told her about Kate's phone call.

'It's probably nothing that can't be sorted out over the phone.'

'I hope for your sake you're right. But take what she says seriously. After what you two have been through together, I don't see any reason why she'd lie or exaggerate things. I'm sure she's truly worried about what's happening there right now.

'And she's right. The farm is your responsibility. If there's something wrong, you really should see to it personally.' As usual, Eilis was right.

'Well, I better be getting on home then, so I can call her back. I don't want to be late.' He leaned down to kiss Eilis on the cheek again, pressed some coins into her hand for the sandwich then rushed out the back door.

Chapter Ten

Mick got home with two minutes to spare. He grabbed a fistful of paper towels on the way through the kitchen to mop the moisture from his face. He'd run all the way from the pub in the rain. He hadn't taken his car, as the pub was a few blocks away, and he'd intended on having a couple pints with the lads.

He dropped the sandwich on the counter then shed his jacket. He grabbed the phone and took it over to the sofa. He sat, kicked off his shoes, and pressed in the numbers for the farmhouse. The phone barely rang before it was picked up.

'Mick?'

'Aye, it's me,' he panted.

'What's wrong with you?'

'I ran home. I got stopped in the pub and had to run to make it home in time to call you. I said thirty minutes and here I am.'

'I'm impressed. An Irishman who keeps time.' So like her to calm herself through levity.

'Not really. I just didn't want you to be mad at me, too.' He leaned back and ran his fingers through his damp hair. 'So, tell me what's happening. You said Flann bred Molly without your consent? That was hardly right, was it?'

'No, Mick, it wasn't. And I don't agree with his reasoning for it, either. I told you I don't trust him and this is proof.' In the thirty minutes since

152

he'd talked to Kate, she had calmed significantly.

He hoped he'd be able to help her sort through this now. 'What else happened? Start from the beginning.'

She recounted the little things she'd seen happening over the last weeks leading up to today. She told him about her walk through the house and her confrontation with Flann in the middle of the farmyard in the pouring rain. And how the man even affected her mother. Mick knew how unflappable Deirdre was, so Flann really must have startled her.

Mick had to suppress a chuckle. He could just see Kate giving out to Flann. Once she got something in her head, no amount of Irish weather would keep her from getting her way. He had to remember it extended to him as well.

'I just couldn't believe it when I saw your man in your father's clothes,' she continued. 'I'm so disgusted I can't see straight.'

'Are you sure they're Dad's? Maybe they just shopped at the same store.'

'They're Donal's all right. I recognize the buttons on the jacket. I stitched them on myself last year.'

'Well, they are just clothes, Kate.'

'Just clothes?' Her voice hitched up an octave. 'Mick, they were your father's clothes. They were hanging in his wardrobe, in his bedroom, in his house. The doors were locked and Flann broke in and took them. That's not just theft. It's breaking and entering as well.'

Her anger was rising once more. He spoke softly to try to keep her calm. It would be the only way

153

to deal with the problem from where he sat.

'I understand, Kate. What I'm trying to say is, what am I supposed to do with the clothes? They don't do anyone any good hanging in a closet. Would you have me leave the house as a shrine to my parents?'

She didn't say anything for a moment. 'Well, it seems to me that's what you've done by locking up the house and leaving. I'm just the janitor who comes by to dust every now and again.'

Ouch! 'I deserved that. But can you see my point here? They're just clothes. I might have given them away to charity anyway. If Flann needs them, then let him have them. It's not like you saw him walking around with Dad's wedding band on. Or is there something you're not telling me?'

'I've told you everything. As far as I can tell, your parent's valuables were untouched. Only I knew where they were hidden,' she confessed.

'Dad had a hiding place and you didn't tell me?'

'He made me promise not to tell. He said I would know when the right time was to give it to you.'

When Mick didn't say anything, she continued. Her voice was softer now and what she said hit him in the heart.

'He loved you, Mick, even after the way you treated him. It was his way of looking after you.'

What could he say? Her news gave him a good set down. Even when he'd denied his father's illness, after all the times he refused to go home when Kate asked, his father had still put something away for him in case he needed it. He wondered if that money could have prolonged his father's life.

Guilt ripped through him and he had difficulty breathing. What had he done?

He took a deep breath so his emotions didn't overtake him.

'Mick?' she asked, when he didn't say anything.

'Yeah?' The wind had gone out of him.

Her voice was still soft when she spoke. It was the tone she used to reach inside him. He remembered it from their years together growing up. It was the voice she used when they were alone, usually up at the stone circle where they were free to speak from the heart.

'You okay?'

'Yeah.' He sighed. 'Just tired. Just ... I ... Can you tell me where the hiding place is now? I mean, does this constitute as a "need to know" situation?'

Kate hesitated. 'Sure, I can tell you. I'd rather show you. But I have the box now and we're taking it home with us. I don't want to leave it in the house in case Flann breaks in again. I promised Donal I'd keep it safe until you needed it.'

'It probably doesn't mean much, but... I appreciate it.' He really did, too.

'Do you, Mick?'

For just a moment, Kate sounded like the young girl he used to know, and instantly he wished he'd just pick up and go home as she was asking him to.

'Yeah,' he said softly.

He heard movement on her end of the phone, as if someone had come into the room where she was, and their moment was broken.

'So, now what?'

'I called the Gardai. I filed a report about this,' she told him. 'They were leaving just when you called.'

'That wasn't really necessary, was it?'

'I'd say it was. He knows he's not allowed in the house, but he broke in anyway. He's been living here for the last couple days at least. You should see the state of the place. It looks like animals have been fighting in every room.'

'Sounds like my old room.' He chuckled, trying to keep the mood of the conversation light.

'Oh, he went through your room, too, all right.' There was a smile in Kate's voice.

Mick groaned. He was glad he'd brought the book of Byron home with him. But he wondered now what else he should have brought back.

'Nice,' he said. 'Was probably an improvement.'

Kate laughed lightly at his sarcasm.

'Did they question Flann?'

'They tried. He wouldn't answer the door to his room, so I gave them the spare key to get in. He wasn't in there. They searched the barn and outbuildings, but it's like he's just vanished.'

'What about his van?'

'It's still parked in front of his place. He must have left by the back gate where we wouldn't have noticed. Molly is gone, too.'

'If the van is still there, I'm sure he'll be back. I'll call him and find out what's going on. Maybe he just went to the pub, or a mate dropped by up the back road to pick him up,' he suggested.

'Stop making excuses for him. He knows he's in the wrong and he scarpered off. I'm sure he'll be back, though. He's got a good deal here, with you being on the other side of the country. He wouldn't dare lose that. He'll be on his best behavior for a few days then he'll be back to his usual antics.'

'Well, keep me posted. So,' he continued, 'what's next?'

'My poor mam is upstairs now, trying to get the mud off the ceiling in the bathroom. How in sweet Jesus' name he got it up there, I'll never know. By the looks of things, it looks like the whole place will have to be repainted.'

He hated the thought of Kate's folks having to get involved in this.

'Why don't you get a maid service in?'

'That costs money and we're here. It will take most of the night to get this place back to normal again, if we can ever get the smell out of it, but it will get done. I'll see to it. I just wish you'd come home and deal with Flann. I'm telling you, I don't trust him. He went through everything.' She paused to take a deep breath.

Mick took the opportunity to cut in. The moment between them had been lost and her anger was creeping back. 'Well, I can't come home right now. I just got back. If I ask for more time off, they'll give me the boot at work, for sure. It sounds like you have everything under control and there's nothing else I'd be able to do if I were there. Let Flann have the clothes if he needs them. Your dad is changing the locks, so that should deter any future break-ins. I'll call Flann and remind him of his boundaries.'

'I don't think that will help.'

'Why not?'

'Why would he listen to you? You're a hundred and fifty miles away. If you're not coming home for this, he'll know he can get away with anything. It's obvious he thinks he's untouchable.'

'When you talked to Flann, did he tell you why he broke into the house?'

'Aye. He told me he broke in because his cooker in his flat was on the blink and wanted to cook his dinner,' she explained. 'Your chickens, by the way.' She reminded him.

'Chickens can be replaced. Why didn't he call for a repair?'

'I asked him the same thing. He told me there was no reason to when the one in the house was working and going unused. Da went up to take a look at Flann's cooker and the man refused to let Da in, if he was even there in the first place. After I let the guards in, Da went in to check the cooker. There's nothing wrong with it, Mick, so he's lied to me.'

'I'll call him as soon as I'm done talking to you and see what his story is. I'm sure there's a reasonable explanation.'

Kate huffed angrily. 'Yeah, to fleece you for everything you have.'

'Somehow, I doubt it. He seemed sound enough when I met him.'

'You met him in a pub, Mick. You had both been drinking and your judgment was impaired. You should have waited for Da's friend to come by. At least we know him. We don't know Flann. Hopefully, the guards will come up with something. I asked them to investigate him,' she added.

What could he say to that? Based on what she

was telling him, it seemed reasonable. Living in the house was against the agreement. He'd definitely call Flann on the indiscretion. But he wished Kate had left the guards out of it. She was determined, though, and he knew what she was like when she'd her mind set on something. It was better just to stand back and let her at it. Besides, she was looking out for the best interest of the farm.

'Have you nothing to say, Mick?'

'What do you want me to say?'

'What I want you to say and what you will say are two separate issues. I want you to say you'll come home and handle this. Since you won't, I have to,' she said matter-of-factly.

'And I appreciate it. I really do.'

'Well, just so we're clear here. If anything like this happens again, he's out of here. I will have the guards called in to extricate him if necessary.'

'All right,' he relented. He couldn't argue with her point. 'What will you do with Molly?'

'I'm calling Will in the morning and I'm going to have him out here to examine her. I want to know how far along she is, so I know when to expect the puppies. If I can get Molly to let me near her again, I will help her take care of the litter until they're old enough to go to homes. Then she'll go in for the snip.'

'Then what?'

'Then we'll see. I'd like to bring her home with me, but Flann has turned her against me.'

'He what?' Mick gasped.

'He turned her against me. She won't come to me and won't let me near her. I'll have to regain her trust before I can get her off the farm. She's been through as much as the rest of us have. I don't want to upset her anymore than necessary.'

He probably should go home, if for nothing else than to help clean the place, but by the time he got there, they'd be done and he'd have to come right back to Dublin again.

'Will you call me and let me know what Will says?'

There was a pause on the other end of the phone. 'What do you care?'

'I do care. I want to know what's happening with Molly. Genuinely.'

'Why? You never cared enough about your folks to ask questions?' Ouch! That was twice now she had been spot on.

'I deserved that, too. We're both tired. Can we just get through this and come to some agreements between us? You and me?' He really didn't want this to become a mud-slinging match. He knew how much he was in denial and he regretted it. But there was nothing he could do about it now except move on.

'What do you want, Mick?'

'Just tell me what you're going to do and let me know what Will says. I'll call Flann and have a word with him. And if the guards come up with anything on him, let me know.'

'All right.'

'And tell your folks I'll take care of the cost of the locks and for the help in putting the house back in order.'

'This isn't about money.'

'I know. But it's my house now, and if Flann has damaged anything needing replacement or repair, I don't want your folks thinking I expect them to pay for it.'

'It's okay. It won't cost much. It's just labor.'

'I appreciate it. You might not believe me, but I really do.'

'I believe you.'

There was another pause – near silence on Kate's end of the line. All he could hear was her breathing. He wished he were there with her. In another life he would have been there to reassure her, put his arm around her, and tell her the comforting things she wanted and needed to hear.

He supposed the discussion was over, but he didn't want to hang up yet. Hanging up meant severing the thin connection he had re-established with Kate. He'd done nothing but think of her since he returned to Dublin. He couldn't bring himself to call her, but now that she was on the line he was hesitant to let her go.

'It's good to hear your voice again, Kate,' he said finally.

She laughed lightly. 'You were just here a few weeks ago.'

'I know. And I'm sorry we parted on bad terms.'

'It's okay. We were both going through a hard time. We both suffered a loss of someone we cared a great deal about. Our emotions ran away with us.' Mick was sure she was right, but he seemed to remember they had both enjoyed the directions their emotions were taking them.

'I don't regret kissing you, Kate.' He heard her sharp intake of breath. 'I don't think you did, either.'

'Well, it was a mistake. And I don't make mistakes twice.'

'Hmm–'

'What, hmm?'

'I kissed you twice, so your statement is debatable. Unless you're telling me one of my kisses wasn't a mistake.'

'I have to go. I need to help get this house sorted. I don't want to be here all night.'

Mick chuckled heartily. 'Don't change the subject, love.'

'There is no subject.' Her annoyance rose once more, but only halfheartedly. 'It happened. It's over. The end. It was a mistake and it won't happen again.'

'Never say never.' His smile widened. She was just as easy to rile now as when she was younger.

'Goodbye, Mick.'

He didn't say anything for a moment. She wasn't upset. He knew that much. If she were, she'd have hung up on him.

When he still didn't say anything she said, 'Mick?'

'Yeah?' he answered softly.

'I'm hanging up now,' she threatened. Again, he didn't say anything. 'Mick, do you hear me?'

'Yeah.'

'What's wrong with you? I'm hanging up. The least you can do is say goodbye.'

'What if I don't want to hang up yet?'

'What? I don't have time for this. I have to clean your house.'

'I know. But I'm enjoying talking to you.'

Kate was obviously taken aback by his admission.

'Kate?'

'Yeah,' she replied, softly now.

'Do you remember when we used to play this game as kids?' When they were coming of age, they used to play the same phone game. They couldn't go to bed at night without wishing each other good night, and when it came time to hang up, neither wanted to.

It was barely audible, but she did reply. 'Yeah, I remember. That was a long time ago.'

'Yeah,' he replied, just as softly and full of regret.

'Goodnight, Mick.'

'Goodnight, love.' Then Mick was left with the phone in his hand and the disconnect signal blaring rudely in his ear.

Chapter Eleven

Will was very accommodating in rearranging his schedule so he and Kate could meet at Fairhill Farm in order for him to give Molly a check-up. But each day, Flann was suspiciously missing, or simply refused to come in from the pasture. After a week of this, Kate had had enough of Flann's carry-on.

As soon as she'd finished her tea, she phoned work to tell them she couldn't make it in – for the second time this week. Then she called Will. He agreed to meet her at home so they could drive over together. There was less of a chance Flann would avoid Will if he didn't see her coming.

Now, as she and Will sped along the common road between the farms, she was surprised to see the pasture empty. The sheep hadn't been moved from the back pasture and Flann and Molly were nowhere to be seen.

In the farmyard, Will honked to let Flann know he was there. They waited in the van because yesterday's storm hadn't let up. There were deep puddles around the farmyard and fat droplets hit the windscreen like stones.

While they waited to see if Flann would come out of hiding, they talked about what to do with Molly if they could get near her. Since Flann had kept Molly from her, there was no way of knowing how far along she was or even if she was healthy in her pregnancy. It was hard for Kate to believe, but it had been nearly nine weeks since she had last given Molly a proper cuddle. It broke Kate's heart every time she came to the farm and there was no Molly to greet her.

Suddenly, there was a sharp rap on the window on Will's side of the van. It startled them both, but Kate nearly leapt out of her skin. She was exhausted and edgy.

Will got out of the van, leaving the door cracked open, and introduced himself as the farm's vet. He told Flann he wanted to take a look at the sheep, and while he was there he'd give Molly her annual check-up, too.

'Your services are no longer needed here. I'd be obliged if you'd leave, as you're trespassing on private property.'

Kate should have known Flann would fight Will. When she gasped, Flann peered into the car, his already murky features darkening with anger.

'What the–' he exclaimed. The jerk of his head made rain water sluice off his cap.

She rushed out of the van and over to Will's side. Muddy water splashed up her clean pants and the heavy rain drenched her quickly, but she didn't care. She couldn't believe the audacity of the man.

'You have no right to deny Will to see to the flock,' she shouted over the heavy rainfall.

'I'm in charge of this farm and I say we don't need anyone meddling. It's off you go and I'm away to me business.' Anger seethed from the man.

'Yes, Flann, you're the manager, so manage. The flock is due their annual check-up and you'll

165

let Will see to his business. And while he's here, he's going to give Molly a check-up as well.'

Flann fumed at her. His eyes riveted to hers.

Will broke the silence. 'I won't be long. I just need to give the flock a quick once-over then I'll take a look at our expectant mother and be on my way.' He kept his voice calm.

Flann turned to Will. 'You'll do no such thing. I did not invite you here, but I'm inviting you to leave. The flock is fine.'

'And what about Molly?'

Flann faced her again. 'She's fine. Now, if you'll excuse me, I'll be about me own business. I recommend you both be about yours.'

'This is our business. I've every right to be on this farm as you, and I've asked Will to come over to check on Molly's condition. I mean to let him,' she told him firmly. 'Where is she, so we can get this over with? Then you can be to your business.'

He didn't speak. He just continued to stare at her, challenging her to question his authority.

'Really, Mr Flannery, this will only take a minute,' encouraged Will in his ever-patient tone.

'Take all the minutes you want with someone else's dog. I've got work to see to.' He turned to leave, but Kate halted him.

'I'll remind you that Molly is *my* dog. I demand you let us see her so she can get a proper health check.'

He flashed the same malicious look at her as the last night they'd argued. 'And I'll remind you, I manage this farm and all that's on it. That dog included.'

It was then Kate saw Molly sitting just inside

the main barn watching the commotion, just as she had the last night she'd argued with Flann.

'Here, Molly,' she called. The dog acted like she wanted to respond to her command, but when she saw Flann's scowl, she shied away into the recesses of the barn.

'See what I mean, Will? He's turned her against me. With him around, she won't let me near her.' Tears, mixed with the rain, coursed down her cheeks.

'Really, Mr Flannery. This is highly irregular. If you'll only let us see the dog, we'll be on our way,' Will encouraged.

'No.'

She had had enough. If Flann wouldn't bring the dog to them, she'd go to the dog. 'This is ridiculous,' Kate exclaimed, pushing past Flann.

'And where do you think you're going?'

Kate spun around. 'I'm getting my dog and taking her home. I've had enough of your carry-on.' She continued on her way to the barn. She saw Molly's white ruff reflecting in the darkness of the building's interior. The white tip of her tail whipped back and forth like a pendulum.

Kate yelped with surprise when a strong hand grabbed her by the wrist and spun her around. Flann hauled her up against him. She was met by his stench that nearly bowled her over. Terror ripped through her, as did the memory of the last time she'd been forcibly grabbed by someone against her will.

Flann's voice was barely audible, but full of venom. 'Get off me land.'

She didn't see him coming up behind Flann,

but Will was there with a hand on Flann's shoulder. 'Let her go.' This was the first time she'd ever heard anger in her friend's voice.

'And take that bastard with you,' Flann added, nodding to Will as he continued staring at her.

Kate shivered from head to toe, and it wasn't from the chill of the rain. Although suddenly very frightened, she'd be damned if she'd let him see it. 'How dare you?'

'I dare, all right.' He pulled her even closer. 'If you'd like to find out what else I dare, I'd be happy to show you.' He looked down at her breasts then back to her eyes, licking his lips. His look turned dangerously corporeal. 'I've seen what you have on offer.'

Kate gasped. 'You *were* watching!' His answer was to wiggle his tongue nastily at her. Thoroughly disgusted, she yanked her wrist out of his grasp and backed away. 'You bastard!'

She moved to Will's side. 'Let's get out of here.'

Flann laughed behind her as she and Will went back to the van.

'You okay?'

'I'm fine.' She looked back to see Flann walking toward the back gates, with Molly waddling heavily behind him. It was obvious she was having trouble keeping up with him. Kate's heart flipped in her chest.

Will must have seen them, too. 'Just by looking at her, I'd say she's due any day now.'

'Great,' was all she could say.

On arrival into work the next morning, Kate had been summoned to the Ward Sister's office. Sister

168

then sent her up to meet the hospital's disciplinary committee. She'd been working at the hospital for the last two months and had already been spoken to by Sister about her irregular hours. She had explained there was trouble at home, but didn't think it necessary to explain exactly what the trouble was. And now a formal complaint was being made.

This wasn't the kind of reputation she wanted to earn in the hospital. She'd wanted to be a nurse for as long as she could remember. For all intents and purposes, she had been one for the last five years caring for the Spillane's, but she hadn't worked in a hospital environment since her original training.

If it weren't for the trouble at Fairhill Farm, she'd be well on her way to establishing herself as an integral part of the hospital staff. Not being traipsed up to a formal reprimand.

Now, standing before the board, she was forced to tell them why she was unable to work the hours she'd been scheduled. She wanted to keep her troubles private; she didn't believe in talking about her problems with strangers. They wouldn't let her, so she pleaded they let her recount the most recent events. She hoped they'd have mercy on her and just send her out with her wrists slapped, and a clean record.

That wasn't to be the case.

'I'm sorry, Kate, but we're letting you go.'

'What do you mean you're letting me go?' she asked, incredulous. 'I thought this was just a formal reprimand. You can't be letting me go.' This couldn't be happening to her.

'I'm afraid so. When you took this position, you understood your responsibility. Sister assures me she's spoken with you on a number of occasions, but she's not satisfied that you're up to the job.'

'I am up for it. I love my work. Being a nurse is all I've ever wanted. I was at the top of my class and have excellent references,' she countered, unable to hide the panic in her voice.

She couldn't lose this job. It wasn't the money. It was that she was helping people in their time of need. She wanted to feel useful. She wanted to make a difference.

There was silence as the board conferred. 'What you say is true. However, you've not proven to us that a hospital environment is right for you,' the next board member told her. 'Have you considered private care, or any of the other nursing fields? They would leave your schedule open to cater to your own hours rather than the demanding ones of a hospital.'

She shook her head. 'No. I want to work in the hospital. I love my work here.'

'Unfortunately, your performance hasn't demonstrated that. This is for the best for all of us.'

'Please,' she pleaded.

'We're sorry.'

That was why she now found herself driving up the N59 on her way home.

As she drove back from Galway City, she'd bounced from hurt, to resentment, to anger with each bump in the road, and now she was just fed up.

She couldn't blame the hospital. She realized that once she'd calmed down, though it didn't lessen the hurt of the dismissal. She was so ashamed and sure her parents would be as well. How could she face them?

She blamed Mick for putting her in this position. That made her resentful and angry. She should have just told him no. She'd told herself over and over again she wasn't going to get involved, and yet she had. Again, it was all her fault.

Fed up? Yes, she was that all right – fed up with herself. As she drove, she mentally kicked herself about how she continually went back on her own word. It didn't make a lick of difference that her commitment had been made to herself and not someone else. Keeping her word was her own code of honor.

She laughed aloud. That was a crock. If that was true, why had she just been fired? She'd given her word to do her job as laid out, and she hadn't. Now she found herself driving home, still in her hospital uniform, and berating herself for her irresponsibility.

She couldn't go home yet, though. She was ashamed of what had happened and couldn't face her family. Not yet. Instead, she decided to give the Spillane farmhouse a quick once-over and ensure Flann had been staying out of the house. She refused to back down where he was concerned. She wouldn't let the shame she felt affect how she treated problems at Fairhill Farm.

Molly met her when she pulled into the farmyard. The rain had abated, but the dog's coat was soaked and muddy from her head clear down her front legs. Her backend was dry. She wondered what the dog had gotten into.

Molly didn't come right to her, but it was obvious the dog was distressed. Given the dogs behavior over the last few weeks, Kate found Molly's appearance startling. She looked around the yard. Flann was nowhere in sight. Something was definitely wrong. Molly hadn't been out of Flann's reach in weeks.

As she approached Molly, the dog cautiously stepped back. 'Hey, Molly,' she greeted softly. 'How's my girl?' She hardly expected the dog to reply, but hoped her soft voice'd remind Molly that she was her friend and could be trusted.

She lowered to her knees in the middle of the farmyard, regardless of the muddy gravel and her starched white uniform, and spoke in soothing tones. Molly seemed to listen to her, cocking her head to one side then the other, but continued keeping her distance. Kate's heart pounded but continued to try coaxing Molly to come to her.

When it was obvious Molly didn't trust her, the dam broke. Tears streamed down her cheeks. She'd refused to cry in front of the disciplinary board and refused to cry once she was in her car. This was too much, though, and she couldn't stop her tears once they started. The sky was full of dark clouds, but there was no falling rain to disguise them.

She buried her face in her palms. What was happening to her life? What was happening on the farm? And what was she going to do about it?

Right now Molly was the only thing that mattered. Once the dog was off the farm, she could find her balance again and get on with life. First, she had to find a way to get Molly away from

Flann. If the dog refused to come to her when the man wasn't around, how was she going to get her in the car?

Just then, there was a head in her lap. She peeked through her fingers to find Molly stretched out in front of her. Only the dog's snout rested in the crevice of her thighs. Kate's heart flipped with hope.

She choked back a sob and very slowly lowered a hand to stroke Molly's nose. She wiped the tears from her cheeks with the sleeve of her jumper and looked around the yard again. Flann was still oddly absent. If she could gain Molly's trust now, she could get her into the car and get her off the farm. She'd take her home, then call Mick and give him a piece of her mind. And she'd tell him to find someone else to dust his bloody house.

Molly let her stroke her muzzle, then her head. 'Oh, Molly, girl, what's happening to us?'

Carefully, as not to startle Molly, Kate grasped the dog's collar and moved to stand. There was a much better chance of getting the dog into the car now. Molly snapped back suddenly and out of Kate's grasp.

'Come on, girl. Let's go home,' she crooned. 'Come.' Molly ignored the command and backed toward the barn door, then sat.

Kate stood and watched her. Then Molly snuffled and strode to the corner of the barn. She turned, sat and looked back to Kate. Was it her imagination or did she see expectation in the dog's eyes, and maybe a bit of panic?

Molly snuffled again, spun a tight circle and sat again, whining.

173

She's agitated.

As she stepped forward, Molly repeated her spin and snuffle. 'What's wrong, Molly?' she asked again, this time lowering the timbre of her voice to reflect her concern.

Molly shot around the corner of the barn. When Kate didn't follow immediately, the dog came back around the building and barked once, watching to see if Kate was following.

When she started forward again, Molly disappeared around the building once more. She broke out into a jog to catch up with the dog. Molly was trying to tell her something. Had something happened to Flann? If something had, she thought, there would be a big moral dilemma – would she help him or leave him in God's hands? Was her dislike of the man so strong as to turn her back on him if he were injured?

She followed Molly behind the barn and between some of the old outbuildings. They passed the building where Flann's quarters were and continued through the oldest part of the farm proper. She lost sight of Molly as she disappeared behind the ruins of a stone building, the origins of which were unknown, but was probably one of the original structures on the farm.

She rounded the building and stopped dead in her tracks. Molly was standing on her hind legs and balancing herself against an old stone water trough. It was about six feet long, four feet wide and four feet deep. She shivered, thinking the trough looked like a coffin.

She noted it was half full of rainwater; no doubt from the latest heavy rains, and Molly was trying to pull a dirty sack from the water's murky depths.

She couldn't get the sack over the rim. It was catching on the stone ledge. She kept losing her grip, which caused the sack to drop back into the water.

A quick glance around told Kate that Molly had been at this for some time. Her exhaustion and frustration were now evident. Water splashes dampened the earth around the trough and Kate assumed this was what had dampened the dog's coat.

Stepping up, she asked, 'What's this, Molly?'

The dog leapt back and whined. She wanted the sack out of the water for some reason. If this were a test, she would quite happily take it. She'd do anything to gain the dog's trust again.

Molly spun excited circles as Kate reached into the trough to withdraw the sack. Molly whined and shot forward as the sack came toward the top of the trough.

There was something heavy in it, so Kate used both hands to remove the sack from the water and dropped it with a clunk on the ground. Molly pawed the sack frantically, as if she were trying to dig a hole in it.

Kate tried untying the sack. It was made from woven plastic, the kind of sack used to bag fertilizer, and had been tied with baling wire.

She wondered, as she worked the wire loose with one of her keys, just what was in the sack requiring it to be bound in such a way and then flung into a trough half full of water in the far reaches of the farmyard.

Her questions were answered the instant she

got the sack open and tipped out the contents. She sat back in horror and fought to stifle a scream of horror.

Puppies!

Kate was struck dumb as all of her basic nursing training went out of her head. What was she supposed to do?

'Think, Kate, think, you big eejit!' she chanted, her heart pounding in her ears.

Molly's whining caught her attention then. The dog was frantically licking her babies.

'Oh, Molly,' she cried, tears coming again. 'They're dead.' She tried pulling Molly away from the little bodies, but released her when she growled and snapped.

Kate looked at the scene before her and it suddenly registered what she saw. The newborn puppies had been murdered. The weight in the sack was stones. The puppies had been tossed on top of them, and then the sack tied with baling wire, and the whole lot tossed into a trough in the back of the farm where no one would find them. Only Flann hadn't counted on the frantic mother risking her own well-being to save her young.

'Oh, Molly,' Kate choked, her heart breaking in a million pieces and her tears blurring the sight before her. This was so tragic. She couldn't find the words to soothe her dear friend, nor herself. She felt so helpless.

A tiny squeak broke through her despair. She forced her vision to clear, wiping the tears from her eyes, and focusing on the sounds around her. Suddenly, there was absolute clarity. She heard Molly licking her pups, the sound of sheep bleating in the pasture, the breeze rustling through the trees, her own heart pounding.

There it was again. Kate looked closer and recognized what she'd heard – a puppy's weak yip! In one fluid motion, she was up, had her jumper off, and was running with the tiny puppy in her arms. She had to get it warm and get some food into it, if it were to survive.

She reached the house before she realized she was holding her breath. 'Breathe, Kate, breathe.'

Thankfully, the new locks had kept Flann out. She pulled her keys from her pocket and slipped through the door, making sure to let Molly in behind her.

She hit the stairs by twos and rushed for the bathroom. Fresh towels were folded under the sink, and she pulled all of them out. She took the pup back down to the sitting room, set the bundle in Donal's old chair, and built a fire in the hearth. Molly stood on her hind legs, propping herself on the chair, and went back to licking the pup's face.

'Light, damn you,' she cursed the sods of turf. The stuff was difficult to light on the best of days and now all she could do was get it smoldering.

Kate sat back, frustrated, and forced herself to calm down and remember what her brother had taught her about setting fires when he'd gone through his pyromania stage.

She pulled the sods out of the fire and cleared an area to work. In went kindling, stacked around a fire lighter and with enough gaps for the fire to breathe. Next she made a pyramid with sods around the kindling and set a lighted match to the fire starter.

Within minutes the kindling was blazing and the smoke off the turf was traveling up the flue, as it should.

Releasing a pent-up breath, she turned back to Molly and her pup. There was an old sheepskin over the back of Donal's chair that she hauled to the floor in front of the hearth, but not too close. She bundled the towels around it and encouraged Molly to get into the makeshift nest. Once she was lying down, Kate placed the puppy against Molly's belly and guided its tiny lips to one of Molly's milk swollen teats.

At first the pup refused to suckle. Molly's own instincts kicked in and she licked the pup's face to encourage nursing. A droplet of mother's milk seeped from the teat and the pup came alert. Kate let out a gasp of delight as the puppy made little suckling noises and began feeding.

A moment later, Kate was on the phone to Will. And within half an hour he was sitting beside her on the sofa watching Molly nurse her pup.

She told him about her day, how she'd lost her job at the hospital, then coming to the farm to find Molly frantic, and then finding the puppies.

'There were others?'

'Yes. There were four in all. I thought they were dead. I couldn't get Molly to stop licking them. She was desperate,' she told him, not taking her eyes off Molly.

'It's a good thing she has such good instincts. She probably saved this little one's life.'

Kate nodded. 'I'm sure you're right.'

'Where are the rest of the pups?'

Reluctantly, she stood. 'I'll show you.'

Chapter Twelve

Will buried the puppies behind the ruined building. Kate couldn't bring herself to touch them and didn't know why. So he'd sent her back to the house to watch after Molly and her pup while he tended to the task.

Will. He was such a wonderful and gentle man. She really cared for him. He was a great friend. And he was single, as her mother continually reminded her. She loved Will, but not in the way a woman loves a man. Her love for Will was as a brother rather than what she imagined it would be as a lover. At this stage in her life, she doubted she would ever find out what a lover's love was like.

Maybe she should consider Will. He'd asked her out enough times, so she knew there was interest on his part. Over their years together, maybe she could learn to love him as she should.

Guilt struck her then as Mick's kisses flashed through her mind. She had no idea why she felt guilty thinking about Will. Mick was nothing to her but a distant memory from youth. She could have a future with Will, if she wanted it. There was no future with Mick. He wasn't even here, for goodness sake.

Well, he will be soon if I have anything to say about it.

Will had taken the opportunity to give Molly a

quick health check to be sure she hadn't had any trouble whelping, then had checked the flock while he was there. Everything seemed to be fine. He had other appointments to keep, but said he would call her later to check on the pup.

She was alone in the house. The doors were locked, so she rang home and told her mother what had happened. She planned to stay the night at Fairhill to keep an eye on the dogs. She had no idea where Flann was. He'd been suspiciously absent all day. But she assured her mother she'd be okay then punched in Mick's number.

Her heart was pumping hard in her chest. What would she say to Mick when, and if, he picked up? How was one to describe what she had gone through in the last few hours?

When the answering machine at Mick's house picked up, she knew he wasn't home so she tried his mobile. The phone rang several times and she was about to hang up when he finally answered.

''Lo,' he whispered.

'It's Kate.' She heard someone singing in the background and wondered if Mick had the radio in his car up too loud.

'Hold on. The act is about over.'

The woman's voice coming through the line was unlike anything she'd heard before – smooth, sultry, and potent. Kate wondered what kind of pub had that kind of entertainment. It wasn't jazz, rock and roll, or any of the usual kinds of music she'd recognize. And it certainly wasn't traditional.

It was over too soon, though, when Mick came back on the line a moment later. 'Sorry about that. Eilis was on stage and the place was like a tomb listening to her.'

'She has a lovely voice. I don't think I've ever heard that kind of music before.'

'Eilis sings the blues.'

'Her voice is really powerful. I could tell even on the phone.' She was stalling and she knew it.

'Come to Dublin, Kate, and I'll introduce you to her. She's a friend of mine.' His voice was light and encouraging, but her eyebrow raised. What kind of friend was this Eilis? As if to answer the question that was only in her mind, Mick said, 'She and Kieran own the Blues Tavern. There's live music every night. They both perform when prodded.'

Heat warmed Kate's cheeks. She'd been jealous and couldn't understand why. 'Thanks, Mick. I appreciate the offer, but I don't see Dublin in my future.' She'd never been to Dublin City. The size of it scared her. Galway City was the biggest city she'd ever been in and that was quite big enough, thank you very much.

'You'll love it. There's a lot to do here.'

'I'm sure there is.'

'Come on, Kate. Live a little. Get on the train. I'll meet you on this end and show you around.'

Remembering she was without a job now, she said, 'I can't afford it, Mick.'

'It won't cost you anything. You can stay at my place and I'll be your escort.'

'No, Mick, really. I can't afford it. I lost my job today.' She hadn't really meant to tell him, but the old feelings came creeping back again as they talked, and she couldn't stop the words from tumbling out.

'What? What happened?'

181

'I've been taking too much time off and they didn't think I was dedicated to the job, so they let me go.' She tried to sound nonchalant, but it wasn't working. Her heart clenched, remembering the looks on the faces of the disciplinary committee that morning.

'I'm so sorry, Kate. I know you wanted that job. What happened? Why have you been taking so much time off? You just started there a couple months ago.' She didn't know why, but she assumed Mick didn't care about her life. Yet, he remembered when she took the job.

'Well, that's why I'm calling. You really need to come home.' No time like the present. Here was the opening she needed. She had to tell him.

She looked out the window. It was dark now and it had started raining again. She really didn't want to move Molly and her pup now she was sure the poor wee thing was going to live. They had both been through a harrowing time.

'Can I call you when I get home? Another band is about to go on and I won't be able to hear you. I'll be there in a couple hours.'

She heard annoyance in his voice. 'No, Mick. I need to tell you what's happened. It really can't wait.'

There was silence on the other end of the line for what seemed minutes. 'Mick? We need to talk. Please.' Before she could control them, the tears came again. 'Please,' she squeaked. 'I can't do this alone. I need you.' There. She said it.

'Kate, what's wrong?' Concern edged his words. 'Wait a minute. Let me find somewhere quiet to talk. Where are you? I'll call you back.'

She told him then hung up. The phone rang almost instantly. He explained he had gone into Kieran's office in the pub so they could talk privately and he could hear everything she had to say.

'You won't believe what your man is after doing now. I couldn't believe it when I saw it. It was so horrible.' She sobbed into the phone. She thought she was drained, but just looking at the pup and knowing it could have died along with its siblings tore her heart out. Knowing a human being could be so cruel to do a thing like this to a helpless animal crushed her.

'Kate, I know you don't like Flann. I'm sorry for that, but he's the manager. He's doing what he sees fit to keep that farm running.'

'Does that include murder, Mick?'

Silence. She knew she'd gotten him then.

'What are you talking about?' His voice lowered now. He knew she was serious.

'After I lost my job this morning, I came back to the farm. Molly was in the yard. Flann was gone.'

'Gone? What do you mean gone?'

'He's not here. I haven't seen him all day. All I know is Molly was alone in the yard and frantic. She got me to follow her to the back of the farmyard, behind that old stone building in the far back. She was trying to get a sack out of a water trough but she couldn't, so I did. And, my God, there were puppies in it.' The words spilled out.

'Wait, Kate. Slow down. Take a deep breath and start from the beginning.'

Mick couldn't believe what he heard. Flann had

gone too far. 'Are you sure it was Flann's doing? I mean, you said he wasn't there.'

'I'm sure, Mick. Why else would Molly have been alone in the yard today? She hasn't been allowed to be away from the man in weeks. Then I drive in today and it's like she's waiting for me.' He heard the agitation in her voice.

'No one else knows the farm like he does. Besides you and me, that is. No one else would have known about that trough. It's so out of the way. If it wasn't for Molly, I'm sure this would never have been known for years.'

'I-I don't know what to say, love.' His head spun with thoughts of the things he'd like to do to the bastard when he got his hands on him.

'Say you'll come home, Mick. Please.'

He didn't have to think about. He didn't know if it was the sound of her crying, her pleading that she needed him, or what Flann had done, but he was going home.

'Aye. I'll come home.' He ran his fingers through his hair and let out a long, slow breath to calm down. 'I'll leave tonight.'

He heard Kate sniffle into the phone. 'Thank you. I-I don't know what else to do.'

'You can't do anything more than you have, Kate. I shouldn't have put you in this position, and now it's come to this. I take the blame for it.'

'The only person to blame is Flann. You thought he was okay because he made you believe he was the right man for the job. I've seen a different side of him.'

'I know that now. I feel awful that this has happened,' he said.

'Well, when you get home, we can sort this out.'

'We?'

There was a pause on the line. 'Yes, I suppose we will.'

Mick liked the sound of that. We.

He thought he would feel some apprehension about going back to the farm. He normally did. The thought he would be seeing Kate again made his heart beat quicker.

'I'll have to stop at the flat for a few things, but it won't take long. I should be home in about three hours.'

'I'll be here.' To his surprise, he found he liked the idea of Kate waiting for him.

'It'll be late. I can see you tomorrow.'

'Dad changed the locks after the break-in so I'll have to let you in.'

'You could hide the key.'

'I'd rather not take the chance. I was planning on staying over, anyway – to keep an eye on Molly and the pup. I don't want to move them unless I have to. Now I know you're coming home, I'll put fresh sheets on your bed and have Mum bring over a few things for the fridge.'

'You don't have to do that.'

'That was part of the deal. Now that you're coming home, you can take over and I can try getting my job back.'

Mick winced. 'I'm really sorry about the job, Kate. If I'd known how badly things would turn out–'

'You wouldn't have done anything differently. You wanted out. I understand your motives. I never liked the idea of you leaving the farm to a manager, but none of this would have happened if you'd talked to Da's friend.'

'I know. Don't rub it in. There's no use in going over this again and again. It won't change any-thing.'

She was right and he was wrong. He knew it. Just as he knew she'd give out to him again once he got home.

'I'm going to leave the pub now and head to the flat. I'll leave the mobile on until I get home, in case you need anything.'

'All right. I'll see you soon.'

Even though he was on his way home to her – no, he was on his way to the farm, he reminded himself – he found he didn't want to hang up yet.

'It'll be all right, Kate,' he said softly.

There was a pause on the line, then, 'It will be once you're home.'

'I'll be there soon, love.'

'Drive carefully.'

'I will.'

Three-and-a-half hours later, Mick pulled into the farmyard. Kate must have seen his lights coming up the drive, as she was at the sitting room window peering through the curtains. He pulled up beside her Mini, grabbed his bag off the passenger seat, and went to meet his fate.

As he stepped through the door, he couldn't help but think how natural it felt to be welcomed home by her. The house was clean and smelled fresh, there was the scent of something warm and tasty coming from the kitchen, and there was Kate looking good enough to eat.

Sweet Kate. She still wore her nurse's uniform, which was badly soiled, no doubt because of what she'd gone through today. Her hair was still pinned up for work, except for the few curly strands that had managed to wriggle free. There were dark circles under her eyes, but her tired smile lit her face and told him she was happy he was finally home.

God help him, but he wanted to take her in his arms and say, 'Honey, I'm home,' and ask after her day. He knew what kind of day she'd had, though, which made him want to take her in his arms all the more. So he did.

He dropped his bag on the floor, kicked the door closed with his foot, and reached for her. She came to him hesitantly and let him wrap his arms around her. She pressed her cheek against his shoulder. He stroked her back with one hand and with the other pulled the few pins from her hair. He ran his fingers through her curls and rested his cheek against her temple, kissing her there gently.

God, this feels so natural. His heart thrummed with the feeling of Kate in his arms again.

A long minute later, she pulled away and looked up at him. 'What was that for?'

'I thought you might need it.'

'That was thoughtful of you. Thank you.' She stepped away from him, looking at him strangely. Reluctantly, he let his arms drop to his sides. He really wanted to haul her back against him. The feeling was overwhelming.

'I brought more with me,' he winked, 'so don't hesitate to take one when you need it.'

187

She rewarded him with a smile and the look on her face told him he was incorrigible.

He caressed her cheek with the backs of his fingers. 'You look as tired as I feel.' His voice was low and soft.

She chuckled under her breath. 'It's been a rather long day.'

'Why don't you introduce me to the newest member of the family then go get some rest? I'm here now.'

To his surprise, she took him by the hand and led him to the other side of the sitting room. Her hand was soft in his and he had the desire to haul her against him again, dogs be damned.

Molly looked up as they neared. The tip of her tail flicked nervously but she didn't move.

'It looks like we've all had a tiring day.'

'More so for Molly. She gave birth to four pups then fought to save them until I arrived. She was so tired earlier, I had to hand feed her to get some nourishment in her.'

He hated to bring it up, but he had to know. 'Has Flann been back to the farm since I spoke with you last? The van is gone.'

Kate shook her head. 'I haven't seen him. I don't know where he is. I didn't even know he'd come back for his van.'

'I don't suppose you have a key for his place, do you? I mean, if he's scarpered off then he would have taken his things with him.'

'Aye, I have a key.' She pulled a small ring of keys from the pocket of her uniform and made sure to lock the farmhouse door before they walked across the yard to Flann's apartment.

The curtains had been drawn over the apartment window, so there was no way of telling if anyone was inside. Mick knocked but there was no answer. He knocked again, louder in case the man was sleeping, and called, 'Flann. Flann, are you in there? It's Mick. Open the door, mate.'

Silence. He took the key from Kate and inserted it in the lock. It wouldn't turn. 'Are you sure this is the right key?'

'Positive. Try again.' So he did. The lock wouldn't budge.

'Seems our man has changed the locks on his place as well.'

'How will we get in?'

'We'll have to break in, but I'll have to call the Gardai first. We'll want an official witness. After everything that's been happening in the last few weeks, I don't want any more problems.'

Back at the house, Mick tried Flann on his mobile first. Getting no answer, he called the guards. When they arrived, he and Kate led them back to the apartment. One of the guards, John, knocked on the door and called out to ascertain Flann wasn't inside. The other guard inspected the yard to see if Flann's van was anywhere on the property.

When it was established the man wasn't on the farm, Mick was given permission to open the door however he saw fit. He'd found an iron bar in the big barn and used it now to pry open the door.

At first, the door refused to give. The jamb split but the bar refused to cooperate. He shifted the bar's position against the jamb and wedged it in, giving it a mighty pull. There was a chilling splintering as the lock pulled away from the jamb. The door flew open, crashing against the wall inside.

For a moment they all stood where they were, unmoving. Then John moved into the room and looked around. Gerry followed, after a last sweeping look across the yard.

'There's no one here. Step inside if you want to look around,' John said.

Mick allowed Kate to enter before him. When he stepped over the threshold, he gaped at the mess of the room. Flann wasn't there, but his things were still strewn around the place.

Kate stepped forward and pointed to a small pile of clothes in a heap on the floor beside the bed. 'Those were your father's things.' She moved to pick them up, but Mick stopped her.

'Leave them, love. They're just clothes.' He knew it was hard for her to think of them that way, but she must have realized he was right when she stepped back.

She looked around the room, and the already tired look on her face was drawn out even more. He reached over and pulled her against him.

'Your man doesn't appear to be here,' said Gerry. 'Do ye want to file a complaint of some kind?'

Kate looked into his eyes expectantly and said, 'Yes, we do. We can do it back at the house.'

'What do you want to do about the broken door?'

'I'll sort it out in the morning. I doubt he'll be back tonight.'

Later, after the guards had left with promises to keep an eye open for Flann, Mick sat in companionable silence across from Kate in the sitting room. She'd made them tea and fixed them a plate of the Irish stew her mother had made, but she hadn't touched hers. Her eyes were on Molly, who now slept with her puppy curled up against her belly.

Mick finally broke the silence. 'She's a natural mother,' he said quietly, as not to wake the dogs.

'Yeah. Seems to be.'

She still wouldn't look at him, and he wondered what was going through her mind.

'You must be tired. I can look after the dogs.' She looked at him then. Was it panic he saw? 'It's all right. Really.'

'I know.' She glanced back to the dogs. 'I just don't want to leave them. It's silly, I know. I don't know why. I just...' She left the last hanging.

His heart squeezed. What an ordeal she'd been through. The horror she must have felt when she realized what she'd found. He certainly hadn't wanted to be in her shoes, and at the same time didn't wish that on anyone else either.

He rose and went to her side. He knelt beside her chair and took her hands in his. Her fingers were chilled, so he took them between the two of his and rubbed them, forcing some warmth into her.

'I know this is going to come out wrong, but I'll say it anyway. Why don't you stay here tonight?' he suggested. 'You can sleep in Mum and Dad's room, or even here on the sofa if you want to be closer to the dogs.'

'Mick, I–'

'I promise to be good.' He grinned to show her he knew what she was thinking. 'Stay the night. You'll be here if the dogs need you. Honestly, I think you're too tired to drive home, anyway. So, stay.'

Kate looked over at the sleeping dogs. He could tell she was thinking. 'I'll have to call Mum.'

'You can use my mobile so you don't have to get up.'

Kate snorted gently and smiled. 'I'm not that tired. I can make it to the phone.'

'Hey, I'm just trying to help.' For a moment, she held his gaze as she tried to understand what he was saying. Then he spoke seriously. 'I know I haven't been very ... cooperative ... over the last few years. But I've done a lot of thinking since I've been back in Dublin. The long drive home gave me a few other things to think about, too.'

'Mick–'

'Really, Kate. Stay. Let me help. You said we could work on this together. Let's start now, eh?'

For the first time since he'd been home, she looked at him. Really looked at him. She stared so hard, he thought she was looking into his soul. Maybe she was. She used to be able to do that when they were young, and he wondered if it were possible to get back some of what they used to have ... their closeness, the intimacy, her ability to know him better than he knew himself.

Finally, she nodded. He smiled and brought her fingers to his lips and kissed them.

Kate got to her feet and went to the kitchen to call her mother. She wasn't gone long.

'Everything sorted out?' he asked, as he collected their cups.

'Mm-hmm. I spoke with her when she brought over the stew and told her then I'd be home, but told her now I've decided to stay so I can keep an eye on the dogs. She understands. She's already in love with the pup.'

'He...' he paused. 'I guess I should ask if it's a he or she, shouldn't I?'

Kate laughed lightly. 'It's a girl.'

'Have you named her yet?

'No. I haven't really thought about it. I haven't thought about much, to be honest.'

'Maybe it'll come to you in the morning. Let's get you upstairs to bed.' He loved the sound of that. He just wished it were under different circumstances.

Once they were sure the dogs were going to be warm enough and the doors were locked, he turned out the lights then escorted Kate upstairs.

She stopped in the middle of the hallway suddenly.

'What's wrong, love?'

'I know I'm just being silly, but–' She turned toward him. 'Can I sleep in your bed? You take your parents'. I've too many memories of that room.'

Her gaze bore into his. It would be strange sleeping in his parents' bed, but he'd do anything for Kate. He'd realized that as he drove home tonight. He'd been a fool, in more ways than one. What had come between them so long ago had caused him to lose more than just time with his parents. It had affected his entire life, including his relationship with the girl he loved. Now that

193

he was home, he wanted to try getting some of what he and Kate had back again. Even if it meant they could only be friends. He'd take that over nothing.

He rubbed her shoulder. 'It's all right. You can sleep in my bed. I'll take the other. If you need anything, just call. I'll leave the door open so I can hear you.'

Kate snorted at that. 'I sound like a spoiled child, don't I?'

He grinned. 'Not at all.' With that, he turned her around and patted her behind as he pushed her into the bedroom. The look she cast over her shoulder made his heart squeeze, and he growled in response.

As he turned toward his parents' room, he stopped at her voice. 'Umm, I don't have anything to wear to bed. Go on, give me one of your jams.'

He chuckled heartily. 'I haven't worn them in years. If you can find a pair in the chest of drawers, you're welcome to them, but I can't vouch for the state of them.' She looked to the chest of drawers in the corner and her face soured.

'Wait here.' He ran downstairs and grabbed his bag before rushing back to her. He tossed it on the bed and unzipped the top.

'I grabbed a few things from the flat.' He handed her a T-shirt. 'This is the best I can offer. It's clean. Don't worry.'

'It'll do. Thanks, Mick.' To his surprise, she reached up and kissed his cheek. He didn't want to make too much of it, so he didn't say anything. Just smiled. He took his bag into his parents' room and undressed for bed.

Chapter Thirteen

Mick woke with a start. Something was wrong. Kate's whimpering from his room drew him. As he passed through the bathroom, he flipped on the light. She twisted and pulled at the covers, fighting some invisible demon. He hurried to her side, sat on the edge of the bed, and put his hand on her shoulder to calm her.

'Kate. Kate, wake up.'

Suddenly, she sat up. When she recognized him, she flew into his arms and snuggled into him. He held her tightly and rubbed her back. 'Sshhh,' he crooned, rocking her. She panted as if she'd been running.

When she was calm, he leaned away from her and studied her. He stroked the hair away from her cheeks and tilted her face to look at him. 'You okay?' She nodded. 'Bad dream?'

'I haven't had a nightmare in a long time.'

'Wanna talk about it?' He kept her in his arms. He didn't want to let her go.

'I don't remember much of it. Just that Flann was chasing me. The air was bitter and I was choking. I couldn't breathe from the smoke and I felt like I was being strangled.'

'It was just a dream. You're safe.'

There was an awkward silence as he gazed into her eyes. The soft light shining from the bathroom highlighted the curves of her face. She was so beautiful.

He smoothed the hair from her face again as an excuse to touch her. His fingers brushed her cheek and he felt her sleepy warmth.

He cupped her cheek and drew her to him. She was so close to him, her breath whispered across his cheek. Her eyes fluttered closed.

His voice was a strangled whisper. 'Ah, Kate. I want so much to kiss you right now.'

'We shouldn't.'

'I know, I know.' He rested his forehead against hers. 'I don't know what it is you do to me. You're all I've been thinking about since I went back to Dublin.' His heart pounded in his chest at his confession.

She leaned back and looked into his eyes. 'You have?'

'Aye.'

'What about?'

'Everything.' He couldn't choose just one thing he'd been thinking about, because there had been so many. 'Just you, mostly.' He stroked her cheek with the backs of his fingers, then ran his thumb along her lower lip.

'I've thought a lot about your lips. About when I kissed you and you kissed me back.'

'You've only thought about kissing me.' Her words came out as a statement more than a question.

'No. Not just kissing you. I've thought about what else I'd like to do to you, given the chance.'

'So, you've been thinking about sex, is that it?' A single delicate eyebrow rose.

She'd misinterpreted him. 'No, love. That's just

part of it. I've been thinking about you, about us, about all the years between us.'

'Yeah?'

'Yeah.' The sleepiness of her eyes had quickly turned sensual, and now serious, as she seemed to focus on what he was saying.

'Is this the part where we say we need to talk?'

He nodded. 'I think so.'

Her next question was wholly expected, but it still stunned him to hear it aloud. He'd asked himself the same question for years.

'What happened to us, Mick?'

He shook his head. 'I don't know. I mean, I do, but – I don't know. It's hard to put into words.' He ran his fingers through his hair.

'Try me. If we don't talk about this now, we never will.'

She was right. She usually was.

'Shove over,' he said, moving her legs out of the way so he could sit against the wall. She pulled the blankets around her and moved to sit beside him. They both sat shoulder-to-shoulder with their legs dangling over the bedside.

Silence filled the tiny room. He pulled one of her hands into his and stroked her fingers. He remembered how she used to like it and would put her head on his shoulder, as she did now. No matter how upset she would get, this simple token would usually calm her. He realized now the gesture also calmed him and gave his own fidgety fingers something to do.

Finally, he spoke. 'Would it help if I said I was sorry?'

'Sorry for what?'

'Everything. I'm sorry for everything I've ever put you through. We used to be such pals, you and me. I screwed it up.'

'It takes two, Mick. I'm sure I'm as much to blame. I could have been more diligent in getting the story out of you, instead of just letting myself be hurt over it. We did the boy-girl thing. You brooded and I hurt; neither of us making the effort to correct the problem,' she told him. 'We just need to figure out what it was that signaled the beginning of the end for us.'

He kissed the back of her fingers as he thought. 'Do you remember Deaman O'Flannery?'

'How could I forget? He and his thugs were the worst of school bullies. How they could call themselves Irish, I'll never know.' She shivered against him.

'Yeah, well–'

'What?' She looked up then. He cupped her cheek and moved her back to his shoulder.

He took a deep breath. 'Deamo cornered me one day at school. He said you were now his girl and that I was to leave you alone–'

'Rubbish!' she spat, looking up at him.

'–or he'd make me regret ever knowing you. I tried ignoring him, but every day his friends would corner me, take a few jabs, and intimidate me. When I still ignored Deamo's threats, his friends gave me a rough going-over.'

'My God. I remember seeing the bruises on your face, but thought it was from sports. I also remember it was about that time you started avoiding me. And I was never his girl. I avoided him as much as possible.'

'That's what I thought. But when I saw you with him up against the schoolhouse wall and kissing him, I was so angry I could have killed him. Instead, I just left. I was still smarting from the beating the day before.'

'What? Wait a minute. I remember that day. It was the last day of school for summer break. Deamo grabbed me coming out of the schoolhouse and dragged me around the building. He had me up against the wall before I realized what was happening. He said some nasty thing before trying to kiss me. I wouldn't let him.' She chuckled then. 'I got away by kneeing him where it would hurt the most.'

'You didn't!'

'I did,' she said matter-of-factly. 'You should have seen the look on his face. He was mighty angry.'

'I'd say he was,' he snorted.

He sat with her for a moment. The silence settled around them like a comfortable blanket. Deamo O'Flannery was someone Mick had thought about a lot over the years. How could he not, when he was the one responsible for tearing apart his relationship with Kate?

Deamo had been a dark character. Evil would have been a good word to describe the little bollocks. His eyes were as black as night, and his overall appearance wasn't much brighter. Mick nearly gagged remembering the smell of the boy. And Deamo seemed to enjoy antagonizing people. Cruel pranks were a specialty, and Mick had fallen for the worst of them.

'I wish I'd known,' she said, breaking the

silence. 'It's been such a waste of time over a misunderstanding.'

'Yes, but back then, I was an easy target for Deamo.' Mick felt the shame as strongly now as he had back then. His skin flushed with it. His hands began shaking and he moved to pull away from Kate.

She must have sensed his shame and grasped his hand firmer. 'Surely you don't blame yourself for what he did to you?'

'How could I not?'

'Mick, you didn't go looking for Deamo. You were a sensitive, good-hearted, and intelligent boy. It was Deamo's own jealousy that made him seek you out. It wasn't your fault, so stop feeling guilty about what happened.'

She was always intuitive about his feelings. 'But I was weak and couldn't fight him.'

'No, Mick. You were strong. You worked hard on the farm. You chose not to fight him because violence isn't in your nature. There's no shame in that. The only person who should be ashamed is Deamo.'

His breath caught in his chest just then and his body stiffened.

'What is it?'

He looked to her and saw concern in her eyes. 'Isn't there something familiar about Flann?'

'What do you mean?'

'Just that. Does he seem familiar to you?' She shook her head. 'Black eyes, black hair, suspicious behavior, easy cruelty.

He could tell she was thinking but couldn't quite get what he was suggesting. 'Deamo O'Flannery

... Flann Flannery?'

Her eyes went wide then. Recognition hit her hard. 'Do you think–'

'I'd almost count on it. Flann's behavior has been too much like Deamo's. I'm sorry I didn't catch the similarity sooner, or at least recognize him.'

She gasped. 'He told me he saw us in the kitchen the last day you were home. He did something then that should have told me who he was, but I haven't thought about Deamo in ten years so didn't put the two together. After school, he seemed to have just disappeared.'

'What did he do?'

'He wiggled his tongue at me like he used to at school.' She shivered again. 'Ick, just the thought of it makes me sick. And he's said things I should have copped to. Like the night of the break-in, he said I didn't want to find myself backed up against a wall again. I can't believe I missed it.'

After a moment, she asked, 'Do you suppose everything that's happened here has been orchestrated by Flann? I mean Deamo?'

'That seems pretty far-fetched. Ten years is a long time to plan something like this. Like you said, he disappeared after school. I moved to Dublin, and you haven't seen him until I brought him home to manage the farm.' He kicked himself mentally. The danger he'd put Kate in was unfathomable.

'I'd say it was just coincidental, love,' Mick continued. 'He may have read the notice of Dad's death in the paper, but I don't think he knew I'd be in An Pucán. But when he realized who I was, he probably figured he'd chance his arm to see what he could get away with.'

'I suppose anything's possible. He was never consistent with anything but his cruelty. This whole issue with the puppies confirms that.'

'Something tells me we haven't seen the last of Deamo, but I don't think he'll be around any time soon. I'll call the guards in the morning and let them know who they're looking for. When they find him, he'll be arrested. I'll file proper charges. He may not get prison time for what he's done, but it could be an incentive to stay away from us.' Mick could go the rest of his life without seeing the bastard again.

Kate surprised him by wrapping her arms through his and resting her head on his shoulder again. He bent to rest his cheek on the top of her head. He closed his eyes and his heart swelled inside him at the intimacy they were sharing. This was something he'd sorely missed since he'd left Connemara.

'We can thank Deamo for one thing.'

'What's that, love?'

'Well, Deamo was responsible for tearing our friendship apart, and now he's responsible for helping us find each other again.'

'Remind me to thank him if we ever see him.' He chuckled at the irony of it all.

'And what are you laughing at?' Humor etched her voice.

'Just that, for once, Deamo's antics have back-fired on him.'

'If he only knew! I wonder if he'd turn a new leaf. Can you imagine the absurdity of it?'

He chuckled again. 'Yeah, Deamo as Cupid.'

His comment halted Kate's laughter instantly. 'I wouldn't go that far, but if it's got us talking again, I'll take it.' She paused, and then added softly, 'I've missed you.'

He stroked her cheek gently and kissed the top of her head before replacing his cheek there. 'I've missed you, too.'

For the first time in ten years, a comfortable silence rested between them. His confession of what had happened so long ago was like a weight lifting off his chest and he could breathe again. He found he could speak honestly with Kate again, he could open up to her as he used to when they were young and foolish.

Kate reveled in Mick's embrace. She'd longed for the old days and to feel his arms around her again. It seemed like a dream, but it was a wonderful reality. While they'd never had a chance to see if anything romantic could develop between them, they had been thick as thieves growing up. Holding each other in their time of need hadn't been unheard of. All those old feelings resurfaced now. She struggled to contain them or she knew she'd break out in a fit of giggles, she was so happy.

Then Mick continued. 'I owe you another apology. I was a real ass about my parents' illnesses. I should have been here.'

She leaned away from him. 'I won't fault you on that account. You should have been.' Just because things were getting smoothed over between them didn't mean she'd let him off the hook with how he'd behaved over the last few years.

'I deserve every tarring you ever wished on me,' he told her. 'To be honest, I've been holding my breath since I got home tonight, waiting for you to let me have it.'

She looked into his eyes and saw he was serious about his apology. There would come a time in his life when he'd realize what a good life he'd had growing up and what loving parents he'd had.

When they were children, it was easy to cast aspersions at parents – they had no idea what it was like to be young. The problems of youth were foreign to them. All Kate and Mick had were each other. More often than not, she would turn to Mick rather than her own mother when something upset her. Parents just didn't know what they were talking about. Or so they'd thought.

Well, she'd learned the hard way, and she suspected Mick would, too. Their parents were far more learned than either of them could ever hope to be.

Looking at him now, it was in her mind to give him that tongue-lashing he expected. What was the use, though? She could see he was sorry. There was no reason to rub his nose in it.

Instead, she said the last thing he expected. 'He forgave you, Mick.'

His eyes shot open. Emotions flashed across his face as he struggled to accept what she'd said.

'He understood why you left. He didn't like it, but he understood. He envied your pursuit of higher education.'

Mick's voice was strained. 'Kate, stop.'

'I think you need to hear this.'

'Maybe I do, but–'

'But what?'

'Now's not the time.'

'Now's the perfect time. You and I are finally talking through things. We're opening up to each other again. Maybe we're getting back a little of what we used to have so long ago.'

'Can't you just take my apology and leave the rest alone?'

'If this rift is to heal properly, you need to hear this. I need to tell it. It's been a long, hard five years for both of us, Mick. We need to get through it. Together,' she told him, keeping her voice calm.

After a moment, he looked away, defeated. She would have her way in this. He only looked back to her when she took his hands in hers. She shifted her body to face him, crossing her legs Indian style under the blankets.

Where to begin? *The beginning, Kate. The beginning.*

'Donal envied you. You were everything he couldn't be. He understood your desire to be something more than a farmer. He'd wanted more, too. Things were different for him, though. He had to stay on the farm.'

'Why? If he wanted it badly enough, he would have found a way to leave.'

'Sometimes it's not that easy. Like you, he was an only child. In his day, there was little career choice. He was a farmer's son and would inherit when his father passed on.'

'And I was supposed to have done the same.'

Kate gave a noncommittal shrug. 'Sometimes

things are meant to happen, or not. We don't always understand why things happen the way they do. We just have to trust there is a reason for it.'

'Like this thing with Deamo?'

'Maybe. There's no understanding his cruelty, but it got you home and we're talking.' Mick seemed to follow what she was saying.

'Did you know your parents met at the Lis-doonvarna Festival?' Kate hoped to lighten the mood. 'I'll bet there are dozens of things about your parents you don't know. Now that we're talking to each other again, I want to tell you everything I can.' Her diary of stories would be a gift to him later.

There was no hiding the surprise in his voice. 'You mean the Matchmaker's Festival?'

'The very one.'

'I'll be.' He chuckled lightly.

'Because Donal spent so much time on the farm, there was little time for courting. Your grandda took him down to Clare for the month-long festival.' Kate snickered, remembering the story Donal had told her. 'He told me he had just regis-tered with the matchmaker, and as he was leaving the pub, Mary walked in with her father to register. It was love at first sight and they were inseparable for the whole festival.

'They very nearly didn't get married, you know. Mary's father didn't have a big enough dowry to satisfy your grandda.'

'How did they get around that?'

Kate grinned. 'Donal told their fathers he'd slept with Mary.'

'I bet that went over well,' he exclaimed, with as much sarcasm as was meant by the statement itself. 'Mum must have been mortified.'

'It was your mum's idea. Donal claimed she was still a virgin on their wedding night. It had all been a ploy, you see.'

Mick chuckled. 'I never knew Mum was so devious.'

'Your da had a lot of stories about your mum. He was quite taken with her.' Her voice grew serious once more. 'She never knew your father was ill. He kept it from her the entire time. Kept it from everyone. He didn't want to give your mum anything else to worry over, since she was ill herself. He loved her and didn't want to add to her suffering, so he suffered in silence.'

'She died not knowing Dad was following her to the grave.' His voice was solemn.

'Your da didn't realize he was dying. When he found out he was terminal, he still kept it to himself until it was obvious to anyone something was wrong.'

'Is that when your dad phoned me?'

''Twas. He was hoping you'd come home. Donal missed you more than ever, Mick.'

'I came home as soon as I could. I was just back from Mum's funeral. I couldn't get more time off so soon.'

'Was the job worth more than caring for your da in his last days? You were his son. You should have been here.'

Anger rose in his voice and in his face. 'I know,' he snapped. 'I didn't think he was that sick. Mum just died. I didn't believe Dad was dying, too. I

207

mean, no one loses both parents so close to each other unless it's an accident. That's why I brought the pup home. I thought it would give him something to care for, and maybe it would be something to live for. I thought he was just putting it on to get my attention.'

'He loved Molly. It was his only connection to you. There were days when I had to take Molly away from him so he didn't stroke the hair off her.' She grinned, but the scowl remained on Mick's face.

Just then, he shot off the bed. He paced the room in nothing more than his jocks. He ran his fingers through his curly hair, then took deep calming breaths, muttering under his breath, 'Jazus, I should have been here,' over and over.

Kate jumped with a start when he balled his fist and punched the bedroom door. She gasped at the sharp crack of splintering wood.

The following silence told her he was more than just angry. He stood with his arms akimbo and stared into the darkened hallway.

'Mick,' she called softly. He wouldn't look at her. It was a moment later when his fist rose to scrub at his eyes.

She untangled herself from the blankets and crossed the room. The chill of the room forced her to pull the hem of the T-shirt down over her hips.

'Mick,' she said again.

She touched his arm, but he jerked away from her. She touched him again. This time she reached up to cup his cheek in the palm of her hand. She felt the heat there, and the dampness. He didn't pull away but he wouldn't look at her, either. She didn't need him to. She stepped closer and insinuated herself against him.

At first, he was unresponsive, but as she wrapped her arms around his waist and laid her cheek against his chest, he finally put his arms around her and buried his face in her hair.

She didn't have the chance to remark on the feel of his hard body against hers, the smell of his skin, nor the heat penetrating the thin T-shirt she wore. One moment she was struggling to embrace him and the next he was crushing her to him.

The one emotion she'd never shared with Mick was grief. His. She'd shared a few of her own emotions with him, but he was her pillar, her strength. His tears now about undid her.

She held him as he cried. His body's heat rose and she felt a fine film of perspiration as she stroked his back. He would eventually come to grips with what had happened, but she had no idea it was going to come so soon, certainly not tonight. At least she was here for him.

Long minutes passed with him sobbing in her arms. When he quieted, he remained against her shoulder and forced himself to take deep breaths.

Finally, he lifted his head, but still wouldn't look her in the eye. She reached up to stroke the tears from his cheeks. He grasped the hand in his and kissed her fingertips softly.

'You all right?'

He nodded. 'Sorry about that. I don't know what came over me.'

'I do. It's called grief. I'd say you were well-due.'

She tried stepping away from him, but he held her firmly. He looked at her now. The moisture in his eyes made them gleam; his brows accentuated his intense gaze.

Her arms were still wrapped around him and his heart pounded heavily beneath her fingertips. His own hands splayed over her back, holding her firmly to him. She couldn't tear her gaze away from him, but was conscious of the fact something had changed between them. He stroked up her back to her shoulder, his palm coming to rest on her cheek. His fingers grazed her scalp, drawing her closer still.

She was pressed against the full length of his near-naked body. His heat flowed through to her marrow and warmed every inch of her.

As she stared into his eyes his erection moved between them. It pressed against the soft mound of her pelvis and grew firmer with each pulse. Mick pressed that hardness into her. Her eyes shot wide at his low groan. His face came closer to hers, his eyelids sliding closed as he neared her. Her breath caught in her throat, her heart pounded in her chest.

He rested his forehead against hers, his breath warm on her lips.

'Kate.' She heard the strain in his voice when he spoke her name. The growl came from deep in his chest. It reverberated across her already sensitive breasts. She didn't move. She couldn't move.

His fingers trailed along her cheek, down her jaw to her throat. Her own pulse jumped. His other hand wouldn't let her move away from him.

Her eyes closed at his touch, but her other

senses switched on full. The lingering scent of his cologne, laced with the pure male smell of him, filled her nostrils and dizzied her.

Her fingertips seemed to tingle where they touched his skin. The light perspiration on his back, slick under her touch, aroused her.

In the silence of the room, Kate only heard the beating of their hearts and the sound of her own breath as she fought to keep it steady.

The feel of skin sliding on skin, as Mick moved his fingers over her, awakened her senses.

In that instant, she wanted to taste him. She wanted to kiss him as he'd kissed her twice before. She wanted to run her tongue brazenly along his shoulder and lick at that bit of skin she'd seen pulsing along his throat.

He drew her closer. His lips were a breath from hers.

'Kate.' His voice was thick with need. 'Let me kiss you. I just want to kiss you. Please.' His voice a deep whisper that made her shiver.

He gazed deeply into her eyes. Dampness glistened on his lashes. Emotion was etched across his face. She knew he strained to control himself, because she fought control, too.

Chapter Fourteen

Mick cupped her face in his palms and drew her to him. The instant their lips touched, lights exploded behind her eyelids. Electricity coursed through her body, and her knees weakened. Every romance novel cliché she could recall became her reality. He threaded his fingers through her hair and tilted her head. His lips slanted over hers possessively, firmly. He drew her lower lip between his and suckled it gently then ran his tongue along her upper lip. She groaned at the feeling. It was all she could do to stay upright.

He took advantage of her parted lips and slipped his tongue between them to rub with hers. She relaxed into him and let him work his magic on her. His carnal kisses woke her own beast and she found herself kissing him back.

He moved his hand beneath the thin T-shirt to cup her breast. She groaned again as he gently massaged her. The warmth of his touch fueled her desire.

Moving lower, he kissed her chin, her throat, and collarbone. He lifted the T-shirt over her breast and started kissing it.

She wove her fingers through his hair and held him against her. He'd be in serious trouble if he tried moving away from her now.

He did, but only to pull the T-shirt over her head. For a moment, he could only stare at her.

The look in his eyes smoldered as he gazed at her breasts. She tried covering herself, but he pulled her arms from in front of her, shaking his head.

'Don't hide yourself, love. You're beautiful.' She thanked the heavens the pale light of the room hid the blush that must have reddened her cheeks.

He kissed her lips again and once more his hands moved over her, pulling her close, stroking her body, caressing her flesh. She gasped when her breasts moved against his chest. The warmth of him tingled and she pressed herself closer, digging her fingers into his hair to hold him to her.

His fingers played across her back ever so lightly, causing gooseflesh to rise all over her. She grasped handfuls of his hair and shivered uncontrollably at the tickling sensation. He chuckled when she wiggled against him to soothe the itch.

Then his hands dipped lower. They slid from her back to her waist then lower to cup her bottom, squeezing as if massaging it. This was a new sensation and she sighed with approval. She rose on her toes as he held her.

Suddenly, she found herself off her feet. Mick wrapped her legs around his waist and carried her to the small bed. His erection pressed into her. The touch was so intimate, her body jerked in response.

Ever so gently, he laid her out then stood back looking at her once more. She wore only her plain white cotton panties, but his penetrating gaze made her feel completely nude. She moved to pull the blanket over her in an effort to hide her embarrassment.

He shook his head, stilling her hand with his own. 'No, love. Let me look at you.'

He lowered himself to sit on the edge of the bed and stroked his hand across her belly. It tickled and her muscles spasmed of their own volition. He smiled and moved his hand higher until he reached her breasts. He cupped one in his hand and rolled the nipple back and forth with his thumb. If she could think straight, she'd ask him what it was he did to her. One touch and she forgot herself.

The bed creaked when he bent over her. He kissed her breast again, his hand hot where he stroked her ribcage and belly. His heat seemed to burn right through her. Her head lolled across the pillow, her eyes squeezing closed at the sensation.

Then he was lying beside her. She tried shifting to make room for him, but her back met the cold wall. He lay on his side propped on his elbow, pulling her legs between his. She couldn't get off the bed now if she tried. He had her pinned between him and the wall. Did she really want to move?

He circled her breasts with the tips of his fingers, one first and then the other, before stroking the cleft between them. He followed the natural line from her sternum down over her belly where he ran his finger along the top edge of her panties.

Then his gaze met hers.

He reached up to run the backs of his fingers along her jaw line. When he spoke, his voice was strained and she could almost feel his apprehension.

'What is it that you do to me, woman?' It was a rhetorical question, but it was the same one she'd had ever since he kissed her so many weeks ago.

'I'd ask the same question of you.'

He looked into her eyes. 'You're all I've thought about since I left.'

'You said that already.'

'Well, I'm saying it again,' he chided playfully. 'I really missed you.'

He ran his finger along the curve of her lower lip then placed a kiss on the very spot he'd just touched, silencing any reply she might have had.

'I'm sorry about the last day,' he said, referring to the day he'd kissed her in the kitchen. 'That's not an apology for kissing you, but for the harsh words we shared.'

'Don't apologize. We both said angry things to each other.'

'You didn't deserve any of it. You've never been anything but good.' He kissed her as he spoke. 'Generous ... beautiful ... exciting...' Once more he kissed her deeply. She wound her arm around his neck.

'Ah, Kate,' he whispered, looking back into her eyes. Moisture welled up in them. 'How does a fool like me go back ten years to correct the past?'

She was taken aback for a moment. What was he asking? 'What do you mean?'

'I mean, I was a fool. I should have known everything Deamo said were lies. When I saw you against the schoolhouse wall with him, I should have known it was against your will. I should have been there for you, just as I should have been here for you and my parents these last few years.'

A drop splashed on her breast. Her gaze met his and she realized how much emotion he had bottled up. He must have suffered as much as she had.

She reached up and brushed a tear from his cheek. 'We were both fools. We were young. I should have pressed you more to talk to me, but I didn't want to nag you. Mum said boys your age were just moody and you'd come around eventually.'

Mick grunted. 'I bet she didn't think it would take this long.'

'Are you coming around?'

'Maybe I am,' he told her. 'You have no idea how much I cared for you. I ruined everything.'

'Maybe you should tell me how much, Mick, because I cared for you a great deal, too. My life hasn't been the same since you left.'

He caressed her cheek. 'I guess this is the night for confessions.'

She tried to shift so she could sit up, but he wouldn't let her move. 'Stay, Kate. I want to look at you.'

She settled back and shifted so she was pressed up against him. His warmth kept the gooseflesh away. And there was something soothing about hearing his heart beating so close to her.

Mick slid his gaze over the length of Kate's body. His chest tightened every time he touched her. He loved how his touch affected her.

His breath caught. The dim bathroom light highlighted her soft curves. Her beauty amazed him. Her goodness oozed from within her to light her face. Her love was more than obvious in her eyes, but she'd never speak of it. He'd treated her badly for so long because of his own pathetic pride. And through it all, he saw she'd loved him before he so thoroughly screwed it all up.

He gently traced the line of her ribcage.

'Stop that. I want to hear what you have to say.'

'Then tell me what you meant by your life not being the same since I left.'

'What is there to tell? I thought there was something between us. When you left, life as I knew it was destroyed. I was destroyed. I cared a great deal for you. You were my best friend. Then you were gone. I've struggled all these years trying to understand what happened. Just when I vowed to put you behind me, you were everywhere but.'

'Would it make you feel better to know my life hasn't been much easier?'

'Hasn't it?'

'No.' He splayed his hand across her belly and stroked her skin. 'It's been a living hell. The more I thought about you, the harder I'd force myself to study, or work, trying to forget you. I was such an ass. I knew it was my fault, but I hurt so much I didn't feel I could come back to you ... to apologize. You deserved better.' His gaze locked with hers. 'I am sorry, Kate. Truly.'

'I'm sorry, too.'

His heart pounded in his chest as he looked at her. Could there be anything between them after all this time?

After a moment's pause, she asked, 'Where does that leave us now?'

He grinned and let his gaze roam over her body. 'It leaves you nearly naked in my arms, and

217

me with a desire to make love to you so strong I'm finding it hard to control myself.'

Her eyes widened, but she didn't say anything.

'I want to make love to you, Kate. I won't deny it. I've wanted to make love to you since that day at the stones. You've been in every fantasy I've ever had.'

'I've dreamed about you, too.'

His gaze shot to hers at her confession. 'Let me make love to you.'

Her voice was so low he almost missed her reply. 'No, Mick.'

'What – no? Why not?'

Softly, she said, 'I told you before, I won't make love with just anyone. It has to be right.'

'You want to love him.'

'Aye, Mick. The man I give myself to must love me. There has to be a future in it.' She moved to pull away from him again, but he held her firmly. 'Please, Mick. Let me up.'

'Stay, Kate. If you won't let me make love to you, at least let me kiss you.' He lowered his lips to hers. He placed delicate kisses on her chin, her lips, her cheek. 'Let me kiss you.'

'Yes,' she whispered, as his lips lowered to devour her again.

It amazed him how quickly she heated. Within moments, she was writhing beside him. He shifted his weight to the edge of the single bed and moved her into the center of the mattress. He hovered over her as he continued kissing her long and slow. Every one of his senses ignited. He fought to control them, but refused to be led by them, even as she wound her arms around him and pulled him down on top of her.

He pressed himself against her hip. He was so hard. She excited him more than any other woman. He'd have to be careful or he'd embarrass himself.

'Ah, Mick,' she sighed, when he finally relaxed beside her, pulling her to spoon with him.

'Whisht, love. Sleep now,' he whispered. He wrapped his arms around her and kissed the back of her neck. She made no motion to leave his side.

With a quick flick of his foot, he grabbed the blanket off the floor and spread it over them. She was already asleep and he was in no mood to leave her alone.

For the first time in a very long time, he felt contentment. Lying with her in his arms felt as natural as breathing. And in this very instant, it seemed as though the last ten years had never happened.

Kate told him she would never have sex with a man who didn't love her. She wanted love. She wanted him to love her. She wanted commitment. Could he commit to her? Could he love her as she deserved?

Who was he kidding? He did love her. Always had. She would be his, even if he had to crawl on his knees begging.

Kate shifted in her sleep, brushing her bottom against his erection. He curled an arm under his head and draped the other protectively over the woman he loved, stilling her.

'This is going to be a long night.'

Chapter Fifteen

Mick jolted awake at the sound of breaking glass, followed by barking. He hadn't slept well with Kate's nightmare waking him in the early hours, their loveplay, and his lingering arousal. It was morning, but he was unsure of the time. Ireland was heading quickly into winter and this time of year, the sun didn't come up until well after 8am.

Kate shifted beside him and moaned. 'What's that?' she asked sleepily.

He leaned down to kiss her cheek. 'Nothing, love. I think Molly wants to go out. Stay put and I'll be back soon.'

He slipped from the bed and went to his parents' room. He found his trousers on the floor and hurried to put them on. He slipped his feet into shoes, then grabbed one of his father's knobby walking sticks from the corner beside the door before heading for the stairs.

Molly was still barking as he descended the stairs. The glow from the kitchen light radiated through the small sitting room and gave Mick just enough light to see by. He tried to be as quiet as possible, but he raised the stick just in case the intruder had a partner who was hiding in the dark corners of the room.

When he reached the sitting room, he saw Molly standing facing the kitchen door. She saw him approach, but continued barking. Whoever had broken the glass was still there.

Nearing the kitchen, he heard fumbling around and someone muttering to himself. He edged closer to the door. That's when he saw Flann standing over the sink with his back to him. Rather, he saw Deamo. He knew it was Deamo now. There could be no denying it. To confirm his suspicion, he called him by name.

'Deamo.'

It was just a name but it was the right name, as the man at the sink turned around. They stared at each other for a long moment.

How could he have missed it before? Now that he knew, it was obvious just by looking at him. This was his childhood nemesis. The curl of Deamo's lip told Mick he was right to use caution with this man. He was dangerous, and the sooner he got him off the farm, the better they'd all be.

Deamo grinned. 'So you figured it out, did ye?'

'I did. And I'll be asking you to leave. Collect your things and leave me an address to forward your pay,' Mick said as calmly as he could.

Deamo seemed taken aback. Mick could tell he'd been drinking. The smell of stale whiskey and cigarette smoke permeated the room and assaulted his nostrils.

'You're firing me? What for? Just because I tricked you with my ident – ident – who I am?' Deamo stuttered.

'No, I'm firing you because of your management techniques. Now clear out.'

'Management techniques?' Deamo's face screwed up. 'What the hell are those when they're at home?'

Mick took a deep breath. He didn't want to get into this with Deamo. He just wanted him gone. 'It doesn't matter. What does is that I want you out of this house and off my farm before I call the Gardai.'

'I'll not be leaving. I'll have me an answer here and now,' Deamo demanded. He swayed on his feet and gripped the countertop to steady himself. 'I'd be obliged if you'd shut that dog up.'

'I don't think you're in any position to tell me what to do in my own home.' Mick made it obvious he knew how to use his chosen weapon by continuing to hold it firmly, but it didn't seem to faze Deamo. 'Now will you be leaving, or do I call the Gardai?'

Kate chose that exact moment to come down the stairs. Damn! He'd hoped to get rid of Deamo before she woke.

Mick didn't dare take his eyes off Deamo, but he felt Kate come to his side and pull Molly away from the doorway.

'She's quite a piece, ain't she?'

'She's no concern of yours. Now, leave this house and get off the farm. I'll not be telling you again. Don't make it hard on yourself. You've done enough damage for one lifetime.'

The man just chuckled.

'I called the guards before coming downstairs. They'll be here directly,' Kate said.

'See now? Make it easy on us all and just leave before they get here and I won't have to press charges,' Mick prodded.

'Press charges for what? I've done nothing wrong.'

Kate stepped up beside Mick. 'You don't call murder wrong?'

'Murder? That's a mighty powerful word, girl-een.' He stepped closer. Mick raised the walking stick higher and pushed Kate back from the doorway. Deamo halted and grinned again.

'You murdered Molly's pups. How can you be so evil?' she spat.

'That weren't murder, love. That were a mercy killing. All them pups were girls. I don't need no bitches to work the flock. They're no good.'

'You call that mercy?'

Mick glanced at her briefly. 'It's over, Kate. Deamo's leaving and you saved one of the puppies. Let's move forward.'

'You're not going to press charges?' she asked, her voice incredulous.

'If he leaves, no. I just want him off the farm.'

'Mick, he broke into your house, twice by the looks of it. He stole from you, he killed Molly's puppies. That's just for starters.'

'You can't prove any of that.'

She glared at Deamo. From the corner of his eye, Mick saw fury flash across her face. 'I can prove everything,' she seethed.

Headlights appeared in the driveway. Kate rushed to the front door and swung it open. 'The guards are here.' She went out to meet them while Mick kept Deamo in his sight.

'Looks like your ride is here, Deamo.'

The man only grunted. 'I'd like to see the day when the likes o' them can get a rise out of the likes o' me.'

Mick wasn't sure what he meant by that, but he

was sure it wasn't anything good.

'Don't you lads ever sleep?' Mick grinned to the two guards as they stepped through the front door.

'We were at the end of the shift when the call came in. We were nearby and decided to check in since we were out yesterday. Is this our man?' John asked.

'Aye. I've asked him to leave, but he doesn't seem to understand what I've told him. I think he's been drinking. He can barely stand.' Deamo proved Mick's point by stumbling as he turned toward the back door.

Both guards approached Deamo, and true to form, he resisted. In their struggle to get hold of him, Gerry slipped on the broken glass on the floor and fell. He cut his arm open and blood began to ooze. He seemed more determined as he got to his feet and removed the baton from his side.

Mick held Kate as the two guards took Deamo down and got the cuffs on him. When he was hauled to his feet, they escorted him out to the patrol car and tossed him in the back.

Kate went to Gerry as soon as Deamo was secured and took him into the house to tend his wound.

'Thank you for coming out so quickly,' Mick told John.

'No worries.' Jerking his head toward the car, he continued, 'I had HQ run a check on your man and nothing came up.'

'Aye, I expected that.' At the guard's look, Mick said, 'We discovered his true identity last night.

His real name is Deaman O'Flannery.'

'Is it, now? That would be a name I'd recognize, all right.'

'I'd be surprised if you didn't. He's been a troublemaker his whole life. He looks a good deal different than the last time I saw him and the name threw me. I mean, how many Flannerys are there in Ireland?' Mick asked.

'Do you want to press charges?'

Mick wasn't sure. What use would it be? As long as the man was off the farm, there was no reason to pursue this. But if Deamo was the same person he was as a child, this wouldn't be over unless Mick pressed charges and Deamo was forced to stay away. Worse, if he didn't press charges, Kate would never forgive him, and everything they'd shared last night would have been for nothing.

'Aye, I'll press charges.'

While Kate tended to Gerry's arm, Mick listed the main items – breaking and entering on at least two occasions, theft of his father's clothes, damages to the private apartment, damages to the farmhouse, the killing of the puppies, animal abuse against Molly, and aggravated assault and lewd behavior against Kate. If he found anything else, he'd call the station and add to it, but both Mick and John believed this was more than enough to open a case against Deamo.

Moments later, the squad car pulled away. Mick stood with an arm wrapped around Kate protectively. She was shivering.

'Come in the house, love. It's over.'

Kate leaned away from him and looked into his eyes. The sky was just lightening, and the porch

225

light cast a warm glow across her face. 'Are you sure?'

Was he? 'He's in custody now and we're pressing charges. I would hope he'd cop on and stay away.'

'What about his things?' she asked, nodding to the van sitting in the middle of the yard.

'I'll clean out the apartment and put everything in the van, then drive it down to the station. The guards can deal with it then.'

He turned Kate to face him, but wouldn't let her step away. He enfolded her in his arms, only to have hers go around him. Her fingers were gentle on his bare back. In all the excitement, he'd never stopped to throw on a shirt.

He tilted her face to his. 'My main concern right now, love, is you.'

'Me?'

Mick smiled at the way her brow lifted.

'Aye, love. You.' He realized too late what his statement sounded like, but continued on. 'I'm hoping last night was a turning point for us. I'd like to see where it could go.'

She remained silent. He'd shocked her. 'What do you say, Kate? Do you think we can get back some of what we lost?'

'I ... I don't know. There's been a lot of water under the bridge.'

'Aye, there has. That's a good thing. We're both different people now. We've grown up. And we'll be more responsible this time around.' He pulled her to him again and rested her cheek on his shoulder. 'Ah, Kate, please say we can try again.'

Her answer was in her arms as she squeezed him tighter. When she sniffled, he leaned away from

226

her and cupped her cheeks in his palms, lifting her to face him. 'What's this all about, love?'

She tried smiling and she couldn't meet his gaze. A flush rose in her cheeks. 'It's nothing. Just a silly girl's dream.'

'Nothing about you is silly. Tell me what's brought tears to your eyes so early in the morning. The only tears I ever want to see there are the ones I give you as you're writhing in ecstasy, like last night.'

Her blush deepened. 'You'll not be saying a word of this to anyone, Michael Spillane,' she sputtered. 'I'll deny every word of it.'

He chuckled and pulled her to him again, squeezing her gently. 'Kate, what you and I share is between the two of us. As it's always been.'

He paused and scanned the horizon beyond the farmyard gates. The sun was just rising, the rays casting a haloed glow over the mountaintops and on the undersides of the rain-heavy clouds hanging overhead. The rain would pass, taking with it the years he'd wasted. The sun awakened the land just as it was waking a new beginning for him and Kate.

He whispered into her ear. 'Please, say yes. Say we can start again.'

His heart squeezed in anticipation of her answer. He'd really messed up in the past. Those years were lost. He wanted to make amends. Wanted to set things straight between them. He wanted Kate just as badly as he had all those years before Deamo so cruelly ruined everything for them. Perhaps he wanted her even more now, knowing what he could do to her body.

Her breath was warm against his skin as she spoke. The feel of it was erotic and he wanted to touch her as he had last night.

'For years I've wondered what it would have been like if things had been left to run their natural course. I never thought one day I'd be given the chance.' She cast her eyes to his. He could see hope in them.

'So, I'll take that as a yes?'

'Aye,' she said, then smiled. 'You can take that as a yes.'

Mick couldn't contain his joy. He lifted her off the ground in a fierce hug and twirled her around. Her long curly hair spun around them as she clung to him.

Without putting her down, his lips found hers and he kissed her within an inch of her life.

Kate and Mick took things slowly while they found their footing with each other. This wasn't about him getting her into bed. This was about him regaining her trust.

'Mick,' she said one night while they were sitting together in the living room, 'add stolen sheep to the list of offenses you gave the Gardai. When your da died, there were one hundred head of sheep. Now, there are only a handful – less than twenty, by my count. How could I have been so blind to Deamo's carry-ons on the farm? He sold the flock out from under my nose and I had no clue.' She wanted to scream at the unfairness of it.

'I'm ringing them now. And while I'm at it, think I'll add the slaughtered chickens for good measure.'

She smiled. For once he hadn't argued.

A deep crease marred his face when he put the phone down. She didn't expect his next words.

'Deamo has been released.'

'I thought he'd remain behind bars until his court date came up.'

'I did, too. The guard said even though this is a criminal case, Deamo has been released on bail until the trial. But he assured me Deamo has been warned to stay off the farm and away from both of us, or he'll face harassment charges and find himself locked up until the trial, as well.'

'Show me how to do that.'

'I thought the farm didn't interest you.'

'So I'm a hypocrite. Sue me.' His grin told her all she needed to know. He was beginning to assimilate back into farm life.

Kate started Mick's lessons on how to work Molly with the flock. In no time at all, the dog responded well to each of his commands. She was pleased how Molly fell back into her old routine. It warmed Kate's heart to know the dog would recover and the weeks with Deamo would hopefully be forgotten.

Suddenly, her life seemed perfect. And things between her and Mick couldn't have been better. He'd been a gentleman at every turn, though they both agreed a few kisses wouldn't do any harm. She loved him and she felt he loved her, too, but she wanted to be in love with him, and he with her, before she crossed a line that could never be crossed again. The man she gave herself to would be the man she'd share the rest of her life with. If Mick were that man, he would wait without question.

Thankfully her parents never questioned her late nights. Conn was the only one who'd commented. 'If he hurts you again, Kate, I'll break his legs.'

She laughed and assured him, 'There'll be none of that happening. Things are different now.'

Yes, things were perfect. There was nothing that could happen to ruin things for her now.

The sun was high in the sky when Mick and Molly crossed the hillside with his flock. Molly circled the flock to keep them together, keeping pace with his rambling stroll. It was a beautiful day and he was enjoying it. The days were chilly and short as Christmas time was approaching, but today was idyllic. And he was a man very happy in himself.

Once the sheep had passed through the gates onto his land, he began to relax. He'd never walked a flock between the farms before, but with Molly's help, the job had been an easy one. Truth, she did most of the work. He just opened and closed the gates and kept the dog company on the walk.

After he'd settled the sheep into the near pasture, he and Molly headed to a small rocky rise to rest. He was beat – after being up most of the night listening to Kate tell more of his father's stories, and the task of moving the flock – and fancied himself a short break. He thought Molly could use one too, but by the looks of her, she was ready and primed to leap into action should even one of her flock wander off without her permission.

He smiled as he pulled the red whistle from his pocket and sat back against the heather and moss-covered stones. Kate had given the whistle to him this morning with instructions on how to make it work. This was the second part of Mick's own training. While Molly worked on voice commands up close, he'd need the whistle if she were far away.

The whistle was a small crescent-shaped, folded-over bit of plastic, with a hole in the center of the top fold. It dangled off a colorful lanyard he now put around his neck. Kate had showed him how to hold it in his mouth and told him to practice until he could make it sing. Then she'd teach him how to create the sounds he'd need to work the dogs.

He slipped the whistle into his mouth and blew, but all he got were bubbles of spit. He tried again with the same result.

'This isn't as easy as it looks.' Molly didn't even look at him. He knew she heard him, though, as her pricked ears rotated like radar antennae focusing on his voice. Her back was to him as she lay on the soft grass; her gaze remained on the sheep.

He tried the whistle again. After about fifteen minutes, he finally got a rasping sound out of it. Molly's head spun around to look at him. He tried it again until he got the raspy sound again. Then, as he slid his tongue around on the plastic, he finally got a real note out of the thing.

Molly jerked her whole body around to face him then. She sat with rapt attention. He was encouraged by her interest, so he kept plugging along.

His efforts went from rasping sound, to a squeak, to something that sounded as if it were dying. It was a sickly sound. He tried again. Molly flopped onto her belly and buried her face under her paws in disgust.

'It's not that bad. Give a guy a break. I'm just a beginner.'

He gave the whistle a mighty puff of air, which caused the whistle to shriek. It sounded nothing like what Kate showed him. Molly told him it wasn't right either by rolling over on her back and whining.

'Okay, Molly. I'll stop. It's hurting my ears, too.'

The dog sat up again and gave a tiny bark to show her agreement.

If someone had told him a year ago he'd be sitting in the heather talking to a dog, he would have called them mad. How could he explain how he was sitting here just the same, and loving every second of it?

As he pulled the lanyard over his head and wound it around his fingers to put back in his pocket, Molly's head shot up. Her nose twitched and she let out a deep growl. Mick spun around, but didn't see anyone.

'What is it, Molly?' Instantly, she started running toward the farmyard. 'What the–' he said under his breath. He got to his feet and looked around, but saw nothing. Instincts told him to follow the dog, so he took off at a brisk trot across the pasture.

As he neared the farmyard, he saw smoke coming from the big barn and started running.

Chapter Sixteen

Kate was in the loft with Jess. In the old days, before bailers and silage barns, the loft would have been used to store hay and keep it dry for the few animals that would have shared the barn in the winter months. But the farm now had proper quarters for the sheep to winter in, and the barn was used for storage more than anything else.

While Donal was alive, Molly had been allowed to sleep in the house, but now the place was just too small for two dogs. The old hayloft in the big barn had gone largely unused over the years, so Mick had cleaned it one day for Molly and Jess. He spread hay around the floor for warmth, but it had to be changed every now and again, which is what Kate was doing. She'd already raked the soiled hay out of the old hay door and was spreading out new hay on the floor. She would clean up the mess below when finished in the loft.

Jess thought this was great fun. She chased the rake while Kate tried to work. She giggled at the puppy's innocent game. It wouldn't be long, though, before she started working Jess alongside Molly in the pasture. She was a sheepdog, after all, and wouldn't be truly happy unless working.

Jess ran circles around Kate and the rake. She moved it out to pull the hay and Jess would run after it thinking it was trying to get away. Kate moved the rake this way and that until the puppy was rolling in the hay trying to keep up. She laughed at the state of the puppy covered with bits of hay. Jess's task was still at hand as her gaze was still on the rake, even as she tumbled upside down.

Suddenly, Jess froze. She was on her feet, her ears rotating, listening for something Kate couldn't hear. The pup's gaze darted around the loft and her nose twitched. She trotted over to the top of the stairs and started growling.

'What is it, Jess?' Kate went over to the doorway and looked down.

She couldn't see the entire barn from where she stood, but Jess's continuing growling worried her. A ridge of hair stood up along the puppy's back, which heightened Kate's nervousness. Was there something, or someone, in the barn the puppy didn't like?

'Hello? Is someone there?' Silence was her only answer. She listened carefully, standing as still as possible. Nothing.

She knelt and took Jess by the collar, stroking her fur. 'Come now, Jess. There's nothing there.' The puppy continued growling deep in her chest. Kate listened again. Jess was obviously agitated by something in the barn.

Then Kate heard it. It sounded like splashing. Had Mick returned already and was in the barn? She couldn't identify the splashing sound, though. There weren't any troughs in the barn.

'Hello? Mick? Is that you?' she called. 'Answer me. Mick?'

Silence.

Then, whoosh.

Jess started barking and lunging. Kate dropped the rake, refusing to release the puppy. Something was truly wrong.

She pulled a soft lead from her pocket and snapped it onto the puppy's collar, moving her away from the doorway. She crossed the loft and looked out through the large hay door. Everything looked normal. Until the barn door slid open and Deamo stood beneath her! 'Deamo!' she gasped, causing him to look up at her. Terror filled her heart. The man could only be up to no good.

Smoke began billowing out through the barn door behind him and very nearly swallowed him. A breeze caught it and his angry scowl glared up at her. He looked around, then went back into the barn. Within seconds, his heavy footfalls sounded on the stairs. He was coming up.

Her heart thundered in her chest. What would he do to her? It was obvious he was trying to burn down the barn, but she doubted he'd expected to see her there. Now that he had, fear ripped through her. She looked around for something to protect herself with, but there was nothing. She'd dropped the rake in order to get Jess under control.

She backed herself into a small corner beside the loft door and hauled Jess against her breast, holding her snout to keep her from barking and giving away their position in the thickening smoke.

Luck wasn't on her side. In a blink, Deamo was at the top of the stairs and scanning the room. She crouched in the corner and hoped he didn't see her. Flames started coming through the gaps in the plank floorboards, licking at the fresh, dry hay.

She counted his steps as he approached. As if time had slowed, her heart seemed to pound with each footfall. Four, five, six, and he was standing in front of her. He grabbed her by the shoulders and hauled her up against him. She dropped Jess to keep her from getting hurt. Instantly, the pup started circling them, barking and growling as she tore at Deamo's pant leg. Kate tried pushing him away, but he was too strong. He pulled her into the middle of the room, her feet skidding across the floorboards as she fought him with all her might.

Deamo seemed oblivious to both the puppy's aggression and her own flying fists as he continued pulling her across the loft.

She screamed. Maybe Mick would hear her.

Deamo clasped his rough hand over her mouth. 'Shut up.'

'Let me go,' she cried, under the weight of his hand. What could she do? Though weaponless, she continued fighting him as he pulled her toward the loft stairs. If he planned to kill her, she'd be damned if she'd give up so easily.

His hands loosened and she took the opportunity to slip from his grasp. She ran toward the big loft door overlooking the farmyard and screamed again.

'Mick, help!' she cried at the top of her voice.

Her heart lodged in her throat at the thought that Deamo had already met up with Mick. Was the demented man really capable of murdering a human? She tried screaming again, but her words were choked back by the thickening smoke.

Below, she saw the pile of soiled straw on the ground and considered jumping out with Jess. She couldn't risk hurting herself or the puppy if she landed wrong. Yet the risks seemed just as high by not jumping, especially if murder was on Deamo's mind. That is, if the smoke didn't kill her first.

The smoke was blinding in the loft now. She couldn't see it at all, between the acrid fumes in the air and the tears streaming down her cheeks, though she heard Deamo shuffling around looking for her. Suddenly, she heard Molly barking. She looked through the thick smoke to the farmyard below and saw Molly race into the barn. Then Deamo was on her again, grabbing her and pulling her through the loft toward the stairs once more.

'For God's sake, Deamo, let me go.' His grasp held firm. 'Why are you doing this? What's wrong with you?'

'I told you to shut up,' he grumbled, choking on the smoke, too. 'You weren't supposed to be here, you damn fool woman. Get over here, or do you want to get us both killed?'

His words stunned her. Had he been watching the farm all along, trying to find a time when neither she nor Mick would be home so he could burn down the barn? Now that he found her, what would he do to her?

'Let me go, Deamo. Get out. I won't tell anyone you were here,' she lied. He knew it was a lie, too, because he just laughed.

'Stop fighting me. Get over here.'

Suddenly, he released her. Through the black smoke, she thought she saw something white flash by her. Deamo was gone and the only sound she heard was the licking fire coming through the floorboards. She leaned out of the loft door. Deamo lay sprawled on the ground. He'd hit the hay and lay on his back. Molly towered over him, growling. She had him pinned down, and he wasn't moving.

She found Jess at the edge of the loft door, no longer barking. The smoke had her lying on the hay near the door, gasping. Kate went to the pup's side and picked her up. She enfolded her inside her coat to keep the smoke at bay as she knelt.

Mick raced through the back gate. 'Mick,' she called, waving her arms frantically. He saw her. 'I can't get down. The flames are already coming through the floor. Jess can't breathe.'

Mick stopped at the bottom of the door, ignoring the prostrate Deamo.

'Get me out of here. The hay is catching fire. The smoke is too thick to see my way down. I can't breathe much longer.' She coughed and tried shielding her face from the smoke hitting her from behind. The breeze shifted, and for a moment, she couldn't see anything.

'Kate,' called Mick. Through the sound of the fire, she heard terror in his voice. 'Kate!'

'Help me,' she croaked, her voice weak from the smoke. She was growing dizzy. 'I can't breathe.'

'Jump, love. I'll try catching you.'

'I can't. I've a dying puppy in my arms. Please, Mick. Find a way to get us down.' A fit of coughing seized her.

She lay down on the loft floor, as close to the opening as she could get. The air wasn't any cleaner there, as the smoke was coming through the floor closer to her now. Flames licked the hay around her and she tried to kick it away. The hay served as kindling and spread the fire more quickly than she realized.

Removing her jacket, she bundled the pup in it. She'd be damned if she'd let Jess die now, not after everything the pup had been through.

'Take Jess.'

She lowered the bundled puppy as low as she could, but Mick was just out of reach.

The wind shifted once more and the ground disappeared.

'I can't see you anymore. Mick, where are you?' The burning in the back of her throat was robbing her of her voice.

'Let Jess drop. I'll catch her.'

She let the bundle drop. She trusted Mick.

The moment she released her grip on the puppy, she heard a loud pop. The fire had reached the tractor! She spun as new terror ripped through her. The tractor had a fuel tank on it. The tires were exploding and it was only a matter of minutes before the tank blew.

'Mick!'

'I've got her,' he hollered up to her.

'The tractor is on fire!' She barely heard his expletive through the sound of the fire. The air cleared briefly in the shifting breeze, but she didn't see Mick. Had he left? 'Mick!' She coughed weakly. 'Mick!'

Then he was back. He had a ladder in his hands and threw it up against the barn. He scrambled up the rungs toward her.

She could barely keep her eyes open and struggled to stay conscious. She reached out to him through the smoke. He grasped her by the wrist and pulled her toward him, hauling her over his shoulder.

'Mick,' she gasped. 'Jess?'

'She's fine, woman. Will you ever worry about yourself first for a change?'

Within moments, they were on the ground. She took gulps of air, but the smoke billowed from the big doors of the barn.

'The tractor is on fire,' she repeated. Her voice raspy and raw from the smoke, she barely got out the words.

She tried standing, but her legs were too weak. Mick hauled her up against him and pulled her across the yard toward the house.

'Wait. Jess.' She moved to pull away from him, but Deamo was on his feet, had grabbed the coat with Jess still wrapped in it, and raced after them.

'Go!' called Deamo.

Just as they rounded the house, the tractor's fuel tank exploded. The force of the blast sent them all flying into Mary's garden, the scent of crushed herbs scarcely coming through that of the smoke. Kate landed on Mick, who'd never let her go.

She was safe. He'd saved her.

On the ground, his arms tightened around her and she heard his fear. 'Kate, oh, Kate.' Mick broke down in her arms. He buried his tear-streaked face in the curve of her neck. 'I was so scared, love.'

He leaned away from her and quickly looked her over. He touched her hair, ran his fingers over her cheeks, then crushed her against him again.

She was speechless. Not that she didn't have anything to say, but because so many emotions spun inside her she couldn't gasp even one of them. All she could do was hold Mick and sob with him.

Deamo stood beside them. He still held the bundled pup. Pulling the jacket from around Jess, he checked her over. Mick pulled the puppy out of the man's hands, handing it to Kate. And in one fluid motion, he swung at Deamo, knocking him out cold.

Sirens wailed in the distance. The fire brigade was on the way.

Mick didn't have to talk Kate into staying over that night. She'd barely let him out of her reach since the fire.

Lying in bed with her in his arms, he held her tenderly, spooning with her. He didn't have any words for her. He hoped his touch told her everything he didn't know how to say. He'd come close to losing her today. He'd also come close to committing murder. He wasn't sure which scared him more.

Kate was his life. He'd be a fool to risk losing her over the likes of Deaman O'Flannery.

She snuggled in his arms and sighed. He placed a kiss on the back of her neck. The scent of smoke still lingered on her, though she'd taken a long, hot bath.

She was lucky to have survived the fire. They were both not only lucky Molly had arrived so quickly, but also that her protective instincts had overridden her fear of Deamo to protect Kate.

Mick's heart squeezed at the thought of losing her. After everything they'd been through, if he lost her now, he didn't know what he'd do. It was too horrific to bear thinking about.

Instead, he pulled her closer.

'You should be in hospital tonight.' The ambulance had taken them there to have her checked out. She'd suffered mild smoke inhalation, but was otherwise fine. But she'd refused to stay.

'I didn't want to be alone.'

He didn't agree, but he had promised to care for her for as long as it took. The doctor argued, but finally signed the release form.

Mick groaned when Kate shifted her hips against him.

'Careful with that, love.' He placed his hand on her hip to still her.

'Have you grown tired of me already?' she teased, but regret came through loud and clear in her voice.

'No, I've not grown tired of you. I never will. I'll crave your body until we're both old and too feeble to do anything about it.' That was the truth.

She wiggled against him again. He groaned deeply. 'Come, love, stop that. You're making it difficult for me to honor my promise.'

She looked over her shoulder and met his gaze. 'I'm sorry.'

'Let's just say you've had a trauma today and aren't thinking clearly.' He shouldn't have been surprised when she purposefully ground her bottom against him. He gave her a single sharp spank to let her know enough was enough. She laughed, but settled back against him.

'You're sorely testing me, love.'

He turned her to face him and hovered over her. He fanned her hair out around the pillow, then leaned down and placed a single, chaste kiss on her forehead. He drew her into his arms and kissed her long and slow. He stroked her with the flat of his hand, feeling her warmth. She was so soft. His entire body pulsed with need of her.

He kissed her throat, the curve of her neck, then her shoulder. She arched against him and sighed, her body relaxing once more. It was his own fault she rubbed against him this time.

She met his gaze, moving up to meet his lips. The energy of her kiss stunned him. She covered his mouth with her own and drove her tongue between his lips. The instant they touched, fire ignited inside him. He growled his approval at her enthusiasm.

Rolling him onto his back, she wove her leg between his and leaned into him. His pride wasn't so strong to admit she kissed him senseless.

His heart pounded, trying to fathom the depth of his affection.

But for a moment, he closed his eyes and quit fathoming anything. He let himself be taken over by every sensation coursing through his body. She moved from his mouth, across his jaw, down his neck to his collarbone, her satiny tongue like butterflies on his skin as her mouth moved over him. Electricity shot through his veins.

Jazus! 'Easy, love. I'm not a saint.'

Had he not made her a promise, given her his solemn vow, they'd both be naked and she'd be well on her way to learning this art of pleasure. But there would be time enough for that.

Instead, he grasped her by the shoulder and pulled her up beside him. Her dark curls spilled around her, her passion-filled eyes gazing up at him. He smoothed the hair away from her face and looked at her for a long minute.

Finally, he said, 'You're an amazing woman. And as tempting as you are, right now, I just want to hold you. I came so close to losing you today. I can't put into words how scared I was. Seeing you in the loft, the smoke billowing around you, knowing I couldn't get to you – my heart ripped apart. I couldn't move. It was like my life had suddenly stopped and the only memory I had was seeing you disappear in the smoke. It kept replaying over and over in my mind.'

His heart squeezed again, but this time at the memory of his panic.

Kate's hand cupped his cheek, her thumb smoothing away the moisture there. 'But you did save me. Look at me.' She tipped his face until his eyes locked with hers. 'You saved me.'

'It was a miracle. I couldn't move, then suddenly I knew where the ladder was and ran for it. I don't think I've ever moved so fast in my life.'

'You were very brave.'

'That wasn't bravery. That was scared shitless.'

She laughed as she pulled him down to her, encircling him with her arms, as if protecting him now. Her fingers wove through his hair as she cradled him. He wrapped his arms around her and savored her comfort.

'You know, I'm sure many knights in shining armor soiled themselves in the heat of battle.'

It was his turn to chuckle. 'Oh, Kate. What you do to me.'

Chapter Seventeen

Mick laughed at the most recent story Kate had told him. It was more of a bawdy joke about a farmer and his sheep that Donal had sworn was a real story. She knew better, though. He had loved teasing her mercilessly when he felt well enough. She felt close enough to Mick now to share his father's sense of humor. Mick, true to form, laughed heartily at the punchline, immoral as it was.

She often told him his father's stories about the farm and their forefathers, while he followed her around the farm. She tried making each story relevant to where they were at the time.

She loved hearing the sound of his laughter and told him as many funny stories as she could remember. When Donal was alive, he'd told her so many she couldn't remember them all. So she'd started putting them into a diary so she'd have them for Mick when he was ready to hear them. Quite often, they spent their evenings on the sofa, where Mick had moved it to face the hearth. He'd put his head in her lap so she could run her fingers through his hair while she read from the diary.

Kate now closed the diary and set it aside. Mick's breathing had slowed and deepened, and she knew he slept. To his credit, he had worked very hard putting the farm back to rights. He really needed the sleep. But it was time for her to go home and she was loathe to wake him. It was becoming increasingly difficult to leave him every night. She felt their bond strengthening every day. And since the fire, the last place she wanted to be was away from him.

Kate walked beside Mick on their way in from the pasture. Molly trotted in front of them with Jess tagging along behind.

Typical for December, dark clouds had come quickly over the mountains, bringing with them a very fine slanting rain. Winter was in the air, with its sharp cloying chill. They clung fast to each other for warmth as they passed through the back gate and into the farmyard.

Regardless of the inclement weather, she was warm in the arms of the man she loved, and who loved her. Should she dare to believe she was in love with him? In her heart, she knew he was 'the one'. The feeling made her almost giddy.

As they crossed the farmyard, Kate saw a small car was parked at the front door of the house. Her sense of all things perfect jolted, as a woman got out of the car. Kate couldn't help notice what a beautiful woman she was, even if her makeup looked as if it had been applied with a trowel.

She felt Mick tense beside her. She didn't know if it were her own instincts or his that separated them, but if he hadn't pulled away, she would have been bowled over by the woman's enthusiasm.

'Mick,' the woman screeched, as she rushed over and hurled herself into his arms.

Kate could only stand back and watch this painted woman plaster herself all over Mick, complete with full mouth kisses and her legs wrapped around his waist. Her choice of undergarment became evident as her mini skirt hitched itself over her bottom to show two rosy cheeks. Cheeks that were now clasped in Mick's hands.

If Kate weren't so instantly upset, she would have found the woman absurdly funny.

But there was nothing funny about the woman or the situation. Kate could only step back and watch her life fall apart.

'Oh, Mick,' the woman said between kisses. 'I've missed yous so.'

Kate's fury simmered when he didn't set the woman away. The sound of their sloppy kisses sickened her.

Kate stepped toward the house. 'I – I'll leave you two to get reacquainted.'

'Kate,' called Mick.

She made the mistake of turning and looking between the man she loved and the woman plastered all over him. His brows creased noticeably. The woman, on the other hand, shot daggers at her.

She looked back to Mick again. He still held this woman, though he'd dropped her feet to the ground. He made no motion to disentangle himself from her arms or her affection, but the look in his eyes was of confusion. Didn't matter. She wasn't about to stick around to see what this was all about.

As she walked back to the house, he called after her again, but she kept walking. Her heart pounded in her chest and she had to force herself to breathe. She'd be damned if she let him see how much this hurt her.

She flung open the front door and grabbed her

248

handbag off the coat hook beside the door. Out of the corner of her eye, she saw Mick coming toward the house. The little hussy was on his heels, her hand in his.

Kate panicked. She couldn't go through the front door, so she made a beeline through the kitchen and escaped through the back door. She rooted through her purse for her car keys as she moved. Before he could discover she'd left by the back door, she was in her Mini and backing out of her space.

She made the mistake of glancing in her rear-view mirror. Mick stood with the woman's arms possessively around him, as he ran his fingers through his hair. He disappeared in the cloud of dirt billowing up behind her car.

How could she have been such a fool? She pounded her fist on the steering wheel as she turned down the connecting lane. Tears threatened, but she fought them back, letting anger rule. She wouldn't be hurt over this. She'd rather be angry. Anger, she could deal with. She'd suffered too much hurt over the years and didn't think she could survive another round.

In a few short minutes, the Mini screamed into the yard at Conneely Farm. She exited the car with it still rocking and stomped toward the barn. She had no control over herself as her feet flew across the yard and through the barn doors.

Inside the junkroom, she found what she'd been looking for and went to it. She picked up her old *camogie* stick and lifted it in the air. Anger so strong shot through her as she lashed out at everything around her. The stick connected with saddles sitting on wall mounts, steel tools on their pegs, old lanterns swinging from the ceiling rafters, horse blankets rolled up and stacked in the corner, a rickety support pole that caused dust and hay from the loft above to rain down on her through the cracks in the boards, and more. She lashed out until her arms were sore. The clatter she made was deafening.

Her old ash stick proved a lethal weapon for anything it came in contact with; the hard wood suffered only minor damage as it connected time and again.

When she was so tired she couldn't lift the stick again, she slumped to the floor and collapsed against the old horse blankets. It wasn't until she stopped focusing on her cries of anger that she realized she was crying tears. That only angered her further. She sucked in long, deep breaths for a long time until she was so exhausted she could hardly breathe.

In a fit of hiccups, she pulled herself up and dragged herself into the house.

Mick hadn't thought things could get any better. He had Kate in his arms, the day was bright despite the dark clouds over the mountains, and he was feeling the best he could ever remember. But everything had exploded in front of him when Gobnait launched herself into his arms. Instantly, Kate released him and moved away. From the look on her face, everything they'd shared in the last few weeks had been ruined by Gobnait's unexpected appearance.

He tried putting the foolish woman aside, but she stuck to him like a bug on flypaper. By the time he'd extricated himself from her grasp, Kate had escaped through the kitchen door and was in her car. She was already speeding down the driveway and turning onto the connecting road before he could stop her.

He ran his fingers through his hair and wondered how his perfect life could have flip-flopped so quickly.

He watched her car speed off to Conneely Farm and the last puff of dirt had floated away before turning to Gobnait, trying to figure out what the hell had just happened.

'Aren't yous even going ta invite me in? I've only jes' got here. It's bleedin' cold. And wet.' She wiped long-nailed fingers across her cheeks with dramatic effect.

'What are you doing here, Gobnait?' He was in no mood to contain his anger. He stood arms akimbo, looking down at her. His anger was lost on her as she stood smiling up at him. Her lipstick was smeared across her face from trying to kiss him. His stomach twisted as he dragged his sleeve across his mouth, her lipstick staining the fabric.

'Yous been gone so long. Everyone's been wonderin' where yous'd got to, so I decided to come bring yous back to Dublin where yous belong.'

'Where I belong? Gob, I don't belong in Dublin anymore than you belong in the west of Ireland.' He turned on his heel and strode back into the house.

He needed to make things right with Kate, and went to the phone in the kitchen. Gobnait teetered along behind him on her ridiculous stilettos. He heard her stumble, but he wasn't about to stop and see if she was okay. His concern was Kate. Gobnait's presence was uninvited and her behavior uncalled for.

He dialed Conneely Farm, but there was no answer. He tried Kate's mobile. It diverted to voicemail. He slammed the phone down on the hook and cursed. Running his fingers through his hair again, he spun around on Gobnait. She smiled hopefully.

'She's not answering.' It was a rhetorical comment and didn't require an answer, certainly not from Gobnait.

'So wha'? I'm here now. Why don't yous show me around, yeah?'

'Show you around? Gobnait–' It was on the tip of his tongue to give her a piece of his mind. He was so angry, he couldn't see straight.

'Look, why don't you go back to wherever it is you're staying. In the morning, you can head back to Dublin. Tell everyone you've seen me and I'm fine. I'll be back to Dublin when things are sorted out here.' He thought he was firm enough with her and his request left nothing to the imagination. Leave it to Gobnait to be oblivious to anyone else's wishes but her own.

'Like I said, I've only jes' got here. I don't have a place to stay.' She stepped closer and touched the shirt buttons at the center of his chest. 'I thought I'd stay with yous, yeah?' she added, softly.

He pulled her hands away. 'I don't think that's a good idea, Gobnait.' He stepped away from her and grabbed the phone book from the kitchen drawer. 'I'll arrange a B&B for you. You can stay there tonight then you can leave in the morning.'

252

'Aw, Mick,' she whined. He cringed at the sound. 'Come on, don't make me leave. Lemme stay here with yous. We can both head back to Dublin in the morning, yeah?'

He spun on her. 'Gobnait, don't you understand? I'm not going back to Dublin. I have things here needing sorting. I can't leave.'

Her head jerked toward the door. 'Are yous talkin' 'bout your wan?' she asked snidely.

'She's part of it.' He forced himself to take deep breaths to calm himself then turned toward the counter. He gripped the edge tightly until his fingertips hurt. He glanced at the back gate and imagined himself and Kate coming through it just minutes before. He'd been so happy. And within a flash – poof – the woman he'd wanted to spend the rest of his life with was gone.

He turned to the phone again and redialed the Conneely house. Still no answer. 'Damn it! I have to go, Gobnait.' He headed into the sitting room to grab his coat and keys.

'And wot about me, like?'

He turned back to her, but couldn't believe what he saw. She was the same woman he'd seen so many other times, but he'd never realized just how unappealing she was. She looked little better than a common streetwalker in her too-short blue skirt and netted tights, her matching blue boob tube top, yellow-dyed rabbit fur bolero jacket, and her yellow stiletto heels. Her hair was the same as before, only now it was tinged blue to match her outfit. His stomach turned. This look was probably sexy for someone, but certainly not for him.

'Look, Gob, I can only deal with one thing at a

time. I need to find Kate.' Probably the wrong option, but he couldn't deal with Gobnait right now. 'Why don't you wait here? Watch the telly. Have some tea. I'll be back later.'

'Mick,' she whined when he tried to leave again. 'I've only just got here. Yous can't be thinkin' to leave me.'

'Gobnait, it's because of you Kate left. I have to go smooth things over.'

'Let her to it. She'll be fiyan when she's stopped steamin'. I can't imagine why she'd'a been so pissed off, like. She knows about me, yeah?' She batted her eyes at him.

'Kate knows nothing of my life in Dublin.'

'Well, then, I'm sure she was quite shocked when she saw me. Never mine then. She'll calm down and then yous can talk to her. Besides, by the look a her, I don't think yous should talk to her until shc calms down. She was right pissed.'

He remembered the look on Kate's face as she sped away. She was upset, all right. Maybe it would be better to let her calm down first. Then he'd go to her and explain about Gobnait.

He pressed his fist against his forehead to quell a building headache and wondered how he was going to do that. How did anyone explain Gobnait?

Her voice was sweet again. 'So, since it looks like yous're staying...'

He looked at her outfit again, his eyes going sore with the sight. 'Do you have anything else to wear?'

Gobnait grinned. 'Tryin ta get me out of my clothes again, Mick?'

His stomach lurched. 'No. And there's no proof I ever have.'

'Wot kine a proof do yous want?' She shifted her hip to the left and put a hand on it.

'You know, the usual. Incriminating photos, witnesses, my actual remembering the event. That sort of thing. Since there aren't any, I'll just work on the assumption you tried to have it on with me, but I was passed out. You took advantage of the situation and slept with me in my bed.' The look on her face told him he was right. At least, he thought he was. Her next question set him off kilter.

'Wot about a baby, Mick? Would dat be proof enough for yous?'

He swayed on his feet. His breath caught in his throat and it felt like his heart stopped beating altogether. What was she suggesting?

'Yeah, Mick. I'm up the duff. Pregnant.'

Silence fell around the room like an anvil. He couldn't move. Couldn't breathe.

'Aren't yous gonna say anything?'

He suddenly sucked in deep gulping breaths of air. He gripped the back of his father's chair to stop the room from spinning. 'What do you want me to say?'

'Hows about "less get married" for starters? A baby needs a father.'

He gasped. 'Father?' He lowered himself into his father's chair and stared into the empty hearth. A father? It couldn't possibly be true. He *knew* he hadn't slept with her. He couldn't have. He'd been too drunk.

She lowered herself to the floor in front of him.

255

Her hands stroked his thighs as she looked up into his eyes. 'Wot do yous say, Mick? Will we get married?'

Hesitantly, he looked into her blue shadowed eyes. 'Is it mine?'

She gasped. 'Hows could yous ask such a question? Of course it's yours. Yous're the only man I want. Haven't I made it obvious?'

He was speechless. What could he say? She'd been persistent with her affections.

He pushed her away and shot out of the chair, pacing back and forth in the small room. What was he going to do? He loved Kate. Wanted to be with Kate. He'd never loved Gobnait. He barely tolerated her. And there was still no proof he'd slept with her. How could he be sure she was pregnant? How could she prove it was his baby, if she were?

'I need some air.' He grabbed his jacket and keys off the peg, slamming the door behind him. He ignored her pleas to stay.

The sun was setting as he sped out of the farmyard. He hit the connecting road to Conneely Farm and debated on which direction to turn. Right would take him to Kate; left, everywhere but.

He couldn't face her. Not yet. So he turned left and sped off for a destination unknown.

When Kate woke, her room was dark. There wasn't so much as a sliver of moon to cast a bit of light into the place. She rolled over and flipped on her bedside light. Her clock read nine pm. She'd slept for the last four hours. Her dreams had been filled with images of Mick and that woman, and her heart pounded at the memory of what she'd seen earlier in the day.

She shook her head to clear the last of the images from her mind. It was better to just forget the last few weeks. She didn't know how she'd do it, but she'd find a way.

Swinging her legs over the edge of the bed, she got to her feet and headed for the bathroom across the hallway.

Downstairs, face washed and a change of clothes on her, she met her mother who was in the kitchen tidying up after dinner.

'Is that yourself?'

'Apparently so. I slept through dinner. Sorry.'

'Aye, and you did. I've saved a plate for you. It's in the oven.' Her mother removed the foil-covered plate from the oven rack.

Kate sat at the table, but she didn't know how she'd get through the meal. She just wasn't hungry.

When the foil was removed, a plate of steaming bacon and cabbage looked up at her. Creamy white mashed potatoes completed the dish. Her favorite! Her mother placed salt, pepper and homemade butter in front of her, handing her a fork and knife. How could she not eat? The scent alone made her salivate.

She went through the ritual of cutting the cabbage into the potatoes then added on a chunk of butter. Once the butter melted, she topped the mixture with salt and the finely ground pepper. It looked perfect. Good enough to eat, she thought, laughing to herself, if only she were hungry.

She scooped up a mouthful of cabbage and

257

mash, making sure to get a buttery bite, and put it in her mouth. The flavors melded perfectly. Her eyes closed and she let out a groan of pleasure. She only swallowed, knowing another bite was waiting to be taken. Okay, so she was a little hungry.

Truth, cabbage and mash were her perfect comfort food. That her mother made it meant she knew Kate was upset again. And no doubt, the rest of the family did as well. She groaned at the thought, the fork half way to her mouth.

'You'll never get rid of those puffy eyes if you don't eat.' She glanced sideways at her mother. 'When I got home and saw your car, I knew something was wrong. You haven't been home this early in weeks. You were sleeping when I went up to you. I'm sure you needed it after so many late nights.'

'It's not what you think, Mam.'

'Isn't it? Maybe you should tell me what it is then.' Deirdre sat across from her and waited for her to speak.

She glanced toward the kitchen door. 'Where are the boys?'

'I sent your father and Conn into the village for a drink.'

'That was thoughtful of you.'

'You'll be owing them an explanation, I suspect. There was a hurling match on tonight your brother wanted to watch, and the village pub's telly is on the blink.'

Kate grimaced.

'So?' Deirdre pressed.

Kate put down her fork and told her mother about the last few weeks. She pushed her plate and cutlery away as she told her about the woman. She was afraid she'd pick up the fork and inadvertently stab herself, as visions of the woman got her ire going again.

'Would you care to explain where the camogie stick and straw came from?'

Kate's face screwed up. She thought she'd pulled the straw from her hair in the bathroom. She felt her hair again to check for loose strands.

'When I went looking for you this afternoon, your door was ajar. I looked in and the stick was still clutched in your hand and your hair was covered in hay.'

'Oh, my.' Remembering the state of the junk room in the barn and how she'd unleashed her anger on it, Kate's face warmed. 'I had a little fit in the junk room.'

Deirdre put her hand up. 'I don't want to know, so long as there's no blood on you, the stick, or anywhere in the room.'

Kate grinned. 'I pictured him a few times, but you can rest soundly tonight. I've killed no one.'

'Now what, Kate?'

She sighed deeply and told her mother what had happened. 'I'm going to sneak over to Fairhill and get Molly and Jess and bring them home. That will be the end of it. Mick can have his wan, and he can deal with the farm on his own.'

'You won't contest if he tries to sell up?'

She shook her head. 'If I have to, I'll hire a solicitor to handle the sale myself and have the money sent to Mick. I'm done with him and the farm.'

Deirdre reached across the table and took Kate's hand. Her eyes met her mother's as she fought the tightening in her chest.

Chapter Eighteen

Half an hour later, Kate was back in her Mini and driving through the gates at Fairhill. She cut her lights and cruised slowly into the yard. She didn't see Mick's car, but she wouldn't take the chance at being discovered when he came home. She drove the car around to the back of the barn which contained the apartment and cut the motor.

She got out of the car, heart pounding, and looked around her. With no moon, it was hard to see, but she knew the farm and made her way around the building to the big door which stood open just enough to move through.

Just inside the door, she stopped to listen. Things were quiet, thankfully. She stepped to the workbench and felt around until she found what she was looking for. The torch.

The instant the light snapped on, she looked around her just to be sure no one was lurking in the dark. She had visions of Deamo hiding in the shadows and shivered. When she was sure she was safe, she continued through the barn. She circled an old, broken-down tractor and walked to the back where the stairs would take her to the first floor.

She stopped suddenly with her foot on the first step. There was a dim glow coming from under the door. Someone was up there – the woman by the sound of her voice. And she was giggling.

Kate had to get this over with. Either she would find the woman up there with the dogs, or with Mick. If she was with the dogs, it should prove easy to get them into the car. If she was with Mick, could she handle seeing him in this woman's arms? He had honored Kate's wishes about sex before marriage, but was his need for sex so great he'd turn to this woman to satisfy himself?

As she moved up the stairs, one creaked and the giggles above stopped instantly. 'Mick?'

Well, there was that mystery solved. The woman was alone. Kate stepped quickly up the stairs until she was standing on the landing. She pushed open the door and saw the woman was sitting on her knees playing with Jess. Molly was nowhere to be seen, but she heard pawing through a door at the end of the room.

'Wot are yous doing here?' The woman's voice was filled with venom.

'I should ask you the same question.'

'My fiancé owns dis farm, which means it's mine, too. I think yous should leave before I call the guards, yeah?' the woman had the nerve to say.

Kate gasped. 'Your fiancé? Since when?' Since Mick wasn't around, she'd have some of her questions answered.

The woman grinned. 'We've been dating for some time now. In fact, I came here to give him the good news. He's going to be a father.'

Kate's head spun. 'A father?'

'Yeah. Exciting, isn't it?' she bubbled. 'Aren't yous gonna congratulate me?'

Kate looked her in the eye. The woman enjoyed

taunting her. 'Congratulations,' she managed, but didn't try to disguise her disgust.

'So, are yous gonna tell me what you're doing here, like? It's da middle of the night.'

Kate looked around, stunned. Mick – a father. She was suddenly confused. What was she doing here?

The pup squealed and the sound of scratching seeped through her muddled thoughts. She looked back at the woman. 'I came to get my dog. Where's Molly?'

'Molly, who?'

'The pup's mother. Where is she?' Kate worried the pup had been away from Molly too long. From its squealing and fussing, that appeared to be the case. The wee thing was probably hungry.

'She's in da room over there.' She pointed. 'She was growling at me so I put her in there so's I could play with the puppy.'

Kate opened the door and Molly rushed out and over to her puppy, now clutched in the woman's arms. The woman screeched and fell onto her bottom as Molly came to a stop in front of her, growling. The woman tried scooting back, but one of her stilettos got stuck between the floorboards. Kate laughed at the sight of her.

'Getter off me, getter off,' the woman pleaded.

'Molly is harmless. She just wants her pup. Come on, Molly, let's go home.' Kate reached down to lift the pup into her arms, but the woman protested. 'Give me the puppy.'

The woman wrapped her arms around Jess and scooted back against the wall. 'I'm keeping dis one, yeah? You can take the others.'

'There are no others. Molly is my dog; the pup is Molly's. I'm taking them both home. Now, hand her over. You don't want to get your pretty outfit dirty, do you?'

The woman's look shot daggers at her. 'You're in no position to glare at me like that,' Kate told her. The woman looked at her outfit and the fact that she was sprawled on the floor with a puppy in her arms.

'I'll look at yous any way I want ta.'

Kate's heart sped up. It was going to become an altercation. 'Why don't you put the puppy down and stand up? We can talk about it on equal terms.' With the puppy out of her grasp, there was little chance it would get hurt if Kate had to get rough.

The woman must have read her mind, though. 'Yous certainly wouldn't hurt a pregnant woman, would yous?'

Kate glared. 'I'll do what it takes to get my dogs home safely. I don't care about you. I just want to be rid of this mess – you, the farm, Mick. All of it.'

She grasped the puppy by the scruff of the neck and pushed the woman away. The pup came away easily. Molly danced around nervously, so she put the pup on the floor to let Molly sniff her.

'Molly, outside,' Kate commanded. Molly lifted Jess gently by the scruff and carried her baby down the stairs to the barn.

Kate turned back to the woman and stared down at her. She was a sight. There was hay in her hair, her netted tights were torn, and her skirt was hiked up around her hips. For the second time today, Kate got a rather rosy view of the woman.

As she turned to leave, she called back over her shoulder, 'Put some knickers on.'

Downstairs in the barn, Kate heard shuffling and was surprised when the woman came down the stairs at her. She grabbed Kate by the hair and yanked her backwards. Kate lost her footing and landed hard on her back. The woman took the opportunity and leapt on top of her. She straddled Kate's middle and started slapping her. All Kate could do was try blocking the blows, since she couldn't move the woman off her. She still felt the woman's claw-like nails rake her face.

'Molly,' Kate cried. 'Molly!'

Suddenly, the dog was there, barking and growling, but the woman seemed oblivious. She continued pummeling at Kate. She only understood every other word, but it was enough that she got the gist of it. She wanted Kate out of their lives. That was the base of it. Mick was hers; Kate was an unfortunate slip-up on his part.

'Then get off me and let me leave.' Kate bucked, trying to get the woman off her, but she wouldn't budge.

Then, as suddenly as the woman was on top of her, she was gone and Kate could breathe again. Molly stood growling at the woman, who was dangling by her arm from Mick's grasp.

'What the hell is going on here?'

'She attacked me.'

Kate could only stare in shock at the woman's bold lie. 'I came to get my dogs,' she corrected, breathless from her battle.

'She came slinkin' in here while yous were gone, Mick. She attacked me when she saw me

264

with the puppy. Aren't yous gonna do anything?' The woman's voice whined at such a pitch that Kate cringed.

Mick looked at her then. She didn't comment. Nothing she said would make him believe her. If he had so boldly lied to her, he certainly couldn't recognize the truth.

Without looking at her, he said, 'Gobnait, go in the house.' When she didn't move, he raised his voice to her. 'Now.'

Gobnait hesitated, then turned and fled through the door. Seconds later, the farmhouse door slammed. Only then did Mick put his hand out to her.

She slapped it away. 'I don't need your help.' She rolled over and slowly lifted herself from the barn floor. She was stiff and sore from the attack.

'I'm sorry, Kate.'

She glared sideways at him as she brushed herself off. 'For what? Not telling me you had a fiancée? For not telling me you were going to be a father? Or that she didn't kill me just then?' Kate brushed her hands across her face. No blood, thank goodness.

'None of it, Kate. I'm sorry I wasn't here when you came back. I'm sorry you didn't stick around earlier so I could explain things. I'm sorry about how things have turned out so badly with us.'

'I'm sorry, too, Mick. Goodbye.' She turned to leave, but Mick stilled her with a hand on her shoulder. He didn't grip her tightly. His touch alone stopped her, but she didn't turn to look at him.

'Will you let me explain?'

'What is there to explain? Are you going to be a father?'

'According to Gobnait, yes.'

She thought her heart had stopped beating that very moment. 'Why didn't you tell me you were seeing someone? Why did we have to go through all this?'

'Believe me when I say I haven't been seeing Gobnait. I had no idea she was pregnant until she turned up today.' His voice was strained as he spoke.

'If you're the father, then you must have slept with her. That tells me you were seeing her.'

Mick sighed deeply. 'Supposedly, I slept with her once. I don't even remember it. I can only go on what she told me. I woke up the morning after a night on a bender and she was naked in my bed. I couldn't dispute anything had happened. I can't prove it, either.'

'When was this, Mick?'

'The night I found out Dad had died. You were right. I should have been here for him. I was so upset, I hit the pub. The gang was there. Gobnait was there. I don't remember anything after a few drinks. I woke up in my bed, she was there, and claiming I'd slept with her. She'd been pressing me for a long time and I guess I caved. I just don't remember it.'

She heard him taking deep breaths behind her. She glanced sideways, but the barn was so dark she couldn't see. Her torch had been flung under the tractor and the light shone the other direction.

'Well–'

'I don't love her, Kate.'

266

'It doesn't matter. You have a child to consider now. Save your love for it.'

'I'm not convinced I'm the father. I'm going back to Dublin to sort this out. I will be back,' he vowed.

'I won't be here.' She slipped from his grasp and rushed out of the barn. She called to Molly, who was already waiting with her puppy beside the Mini. Kate let them in, got behind the wheel, and didn't look back.

Mick was sure if he opened the Irish dictionary, his picture would be there in the description for the word *amadán*. He was every kind of fool ever invented.

It was beyond him how things could have gotten so out of control in his life. His gut twisted at the thought. Since returning to Dublin a fortnight before, Mick's thoughts had been filled with images of Kate. He missed her terribly. He rang her on a number of occasions, but she either hung up on him or her family said she wasn't home. He tried her mobile, but got no luck there, either. His last call was met with a 'no longer in service' message, which meant she'd changed the number.

He couldn't blame her for being upset. If he'd been in her shoes, he'd be angry, too. But he'd stick around to see if the claim was true. Or would he? Hadn't he run without finding out the truth all those years before?

In the last fortnight, he'd run the gamut of emotions. Now, he was just disgusted – mostly with himself. If he'd only stood up to Deamo ten years ago, none of this would have happened. If he'd only come home when Kate asked him to so many times, it would have been possible to make up with her that much sooner. If he'd only forced her to listen to him that last night at the farm, he would have made her understand how important she was to him and that he would be back. He would have told her he loved her. If only...

Gobnait's presence was persistent. Like a cat with a full bowl of cream.

He hadn't moved her into his flat, even at her constant persistence, but she came over nearly every night.

He still wasn't convinced he was the father of her baby, but he had no clues to go on that it was anyone else's, either. She was definitely pregnant. When they returned to Dublin, he had insisted she visit the doctor and get a proper test. He didn't trust those over-the-counter things. He had gone with her to make sure she kept her appointment and didn't try pulling anything with him. He wouldn't put it past her. But the test had come back positive and the estimated date of conception matched the date he'd been told his father died – the night he supposedly slept with Gobnait.

In that instant, he thought it could have been possible he'd had sex with Gobnait, memory or not. If she was telling him the truth, how was he going to survive the rest of his life with her as his wife? The thought sickened him. It was Kate he loved, Kate he wanted to make his wife, Kate he wanted to have children with. Now, that dream would never come true, thanks to Gobnait and her ever-conniving ways.

And his stupidity in not going home long before this.

For the second time this year, the third time in his whole life, Mick headed to the Blues Tavern to drink himself into oblivion. The other two times he'd gone on a booze-up were following the deaths of his parents. While he enjoyed a pint as much as the next man, he wasn't a drunk. He didn't like the way liquor made him feel. Didn't like being out of control.

Right now, none of that mattered. He just wanted to get to a point of forgetfulness, as he had been that night with Gobnait.

And as he sat in a snug in the back of the pub listening to piped-in music, he threw back a measure of Jameson. It went down smoothly. He'd gone long past the stage when the first measure had burned its way to his belly. He was well on his way to Numbsville, but still waiting for the memories to fade.

It was early afternoon, and a weekday to boot. He'd lost his job at the museum, but that was fine with him. He wasn't excited about the work anymore. He wanted to be back at the farm. The irony of that admission wasn't lost on him.

The pub was busy during the lunch hour, but nothing like it would be once the offices closed and later when the live bands took to the stage. He hoped to be gone by then, as he didn't think he could handle the noise. He hoped all memory of Gobnait and the position she'd put him in would be a distant memory, at least for a little while. Ignorant bliss. That's what he hoped to achieve.

As he watched the wait staff and customers

move around the pub, he tried putting his troubles out of his mind.

He caught a flash of red move behind the bar. Kieran's sister, Grainne, seemed to be having an argument with the bartender.

When Mick arrived, the new bartender had introduced himself as JD. He'd been kind enough to give Mick the bottle of Jameson he'd requested and left him alone at the snug in the back of the pub.

The look on Grainne's face reminded him of the anger he'd seen in Kate's face, and his heart lurched. He groaned, then poured out another measure and tossed it back. His trip to Numbsville was a long, slow journey. Too slow.

Just then, Eilis stepped into view. Her belly hung over the table as she stood looking down at him. She had a scowl on her face, but it was only there to mock the one he knew creased his face.

'Join me?' He motioned to a seat in the snug.

'I've gone long past being able to fit into a snug.'

He moved to sit up. 'Let me get you a chair.'

'Keep your seat, lad. I can get my own. I'm pregnant, not helpless.' She winked, dropping the bar towel she carried onto the table before turning to pull a chair from one of the nearby tables.

Once she was seated, she let out a long breath. She glanced down and grinned, rubbing her belly. 'Takes a lot out of a body.'

'You must be carrying twins, Eilis, or one hell of a footie player.'

'I reckon a footie player by the way he, or she, is kicking these days, but I'll be happy whatever

270

it is, as long as it's healthy.'

He nodded his agreement.

After a short pause, she spoke up. 'Why don't you tell me what's bothering you, Mick? I haven't seen you drink like this since your father died.'

'Right to the point.' He spun the glass in his fingers. It was empty, but not for long.

Eilis pulled the bottle from his reach. He glared at her, but the look on her face told him she could play dirty if he didn't talk. He'd known her since university. They were two peas in the same pod. Neither of them had been popular. They were too quiet, spent too much time in the library or class, and didn't fit in with the heavy drinkers who spent most, if not all, of their off time getting jarred. Neither of them had a taste for it. That's what made things so ironic now. Eilis was half owner in the Blues Tavern and Mick was in it getting smashed. Or rather, trying to.

She wove her fingers together over her enormous belly and stared at him.

Small talk. Maybe that would pacify her.

'When are you due?'

'Any day now, actually. I'm ready for it.' She chuckled lightly, grinning. 'You know, back in university I used to think I was fat. I had nothing on this back then.'

Her smile was infectious, but he could only manage a halfhearted one of his own. 'Eilis, you've always been gorgeous. And you were never fat. This,' – he pointed to her belly – is just beyond words.'

She wadded the bar towel and threw it at him. 'Hey!'

'What, hey? Let me finish. This—' he pointed again— 'is beyond words because it's marvelous.'

Her face screwed up. 'Care to explain?'

He fought for the right words through the buzz in his mind. He thought he was completely sober after several measures of whiskey. He'd been thinking clearly, could see straight, therefore he was sober. But now he was forced to look for words and have them make sense, and he realized just how many sheets to the wind he was becoming.

'I'm not sure I can.'

'Try,' she persisted. She was having a go off him and he knew it. Well, he would rise to the occasion.

'It's marvelous that you're having a baby.'

'Uh-huh. G'wan,' she prompted, her eyebrow lifting.

'It's a symbol of your love. You and Kieran were meant for each other.'

'I'd like to think so. But that doesn't explain what this has to do with you drinking like a fish.'

'You and Kieran were meant to be together, just as I was meant to be with Kate.' As he spoke, his gaze shifted from Eilis to his empty glass. Another few words and he wasn't talking to her anymore, but to himself. 'We were meant to be together. We were meant to have babies together. Meant to spend our whole lives together – raising babies, raising puppies, raising sheep...' He looked up, but didn't really see his friend staring at him with a puzzled expression. 'We were meant to have incredible sex, so we were. We were good together. But I ruined it. I'm always ruining everything. I'm

272

such a bollocks.'

He reached for the bottle of Jameson again, but it was out of his reach. 'Be a good girl, Ei. Pass me the bottle.'

'Finish your story first.'

Mick scowled at her. She only grinned.

'I'm a bollocks.'

'You said that already. Tell me something I don't know.' She was a minx to tease him so ruthlessly.

'I'm a bollocks and I screwed everything up. Kate is going to have babies with some other bloke now. She's going to be kissing him when she should be kissing me. Those should be my babies she's having!'

Eilis patted his hand. 'Calm down, Mick. Tell me what you mean. Is Kate pregnant by someone else?'

'No, I am.' By the look on her face, he knew that hadn't come out right and tried again. Hmm, how many sheets was he to the wind? Why was it that he could think so clearly when he couldn't string two sentences together coherently? 'I mean I'm going to be the father.'

'Of Kate's baby?'

'No, no. Pay attention, woman. I'm going to be a father. But I don't love her. I love Kate.'

'Mick, try as I might I don't understand. Tell me who's pregnant.'

'Gobnait.'

'Gobnait's pregnant?' Her face screwed up then. 'Who's the father?'

'She says I am,' he said solemnly.

For a long moment, there was silence at the

273

table. Then Eilis struggled to stand and motioned the new bartender over.

'Help me get him in the office, will you, JD? Then bring in a big plate of chips and a pot of tea.' JD nodded and reached over to pull Mick off the seat.

'Easy, now. I can make it on my own,' he told the barman. Mick slid out of the snug and promptly hit the floor. 'You need to keep the floors a bit cleaner, Ei. A person could get hurt slipping like that.'

'Here, mate,' JD said. 'Let me help you up.'

Once Ellis got him settled in the back office, she thanked JD for his help and shut the door behind him. She turned and waddled over to the sofa where Mick was slouched.

He watched her carefully maneuver herself into a stiff-backed chair JD had set beside the sofa. The chips and tea had been set on a table in front of her.

Mick reached for a chip. 'Oy, those are mine.' Ellis slapped his hand away. 'I'm eating for two now and I'm famished. Get that tea into you, now. You need to be sober for what I'm going to tell you.'

He lifted a brow at her comment. 'A few chips would help the process along.'

'Chancer. Drink your tea.' She grinned as she lifted the basket of salt and vinegar chips to rest on top of her belly. She watched him as he poured the tea. He managed to actually get some into the cup.

'Would you like some tea, Ei?' He motioned to the second cup.

'No, Mick,' she grinned smugly. 'There's only one cup.'

He looked back, trying to focus. He closed one eye and sure enough, there was only one cup. He groaned. He was absolutely pissed. Unfortunately, he was far from forgetting his troubles. Eilis hadn't let him drink enough. Just enough to make him sorry he'd started. Now, he would only have the mother of all hangovers in the morning. He swore he could feel it coming on already.

Carefully, he reached over to lift the cup of tea. Success! He brought it to his lips and took a sip. 'I don't suppose there'd be a drop of the *uisce beatha* to go with this.'

Ellis shook her head, smiling as she stuffed another chip in her mouth. 'You've had enough whiskey already.'

A quarter of an hour later, Ellis put the chips basket back on the table and wiped her mouth on a paper napkin. A little bubble passed between her lips. 'Urp.'

Color spread across her face and Mick chuckled. 'Not quite ladylike, is it?'

'You're still gorgeous, Ellis.'

'Keep talking like that and Kieran might be having a word with you,' she teased.

'You're enjoying my drunk, aren't you?'

She nodded vigorously. 'Immensely.'

'Well, have your laugh. I'll not be doing this again anytime soon.'

'Are you ready to tell me what this is all about?' He only shrugged. 'You said Gobnait is pregnant and you're the father?'

'That's about the whole of it, all right.'

'And who told you that you're the father?'

'Gobnait. She came out to the farm to give me the news. Kate and I were coming off the pasture together. We were really connecting. Finally, after so many years, we were talking and working toward a future together. Then Gobnait was there and everything exploded in front of me.' He rubbed his stomach. 'I think I'm going to be sick.'

'No, you won't. Drink more tea,' she told him. 'What happened next?'

He took deep breaths to calm his roiling stomach. 'Gobnait told me she was pregnant and that I was the father. Kate left. She was really upset, but she wouldn't stay so we could sort things out.'

'Are you the father?'

He shook his head and ran his fingers through his hair. 'I don't know.' He told her about waking up beside Gobnait the morning after his last bender.

'What happened next?'

'I went for a drive. I couldn't think straight with Gobnait in my face. I swear that woman is impossible. I don't know how I'll survive a lifetime with her.' He squeezed his eyes shut and shook his head, trying to erase the memory.

'When I got back I heard Molly barking in the barn. I went to see what was wrong with her. I found Gobnait sitting on top of Kate and beating the shite out of her.'

Eilis gasped.

'I pulled her off and sent her in the house while I tried talking with Kate.'

'Was she hurt?'

'Not as much as I hurt her.'

'So what happened next?'

'Nothing. I told her I wasn't convinced Gobnait was pregnant. And even if she was, I wasn't convinced the baby is mine. Kate wasn't convinced Gobnait was lying, so she left.'

'Wow,' was all Eilis said.

He sighed. 'What am I going to do, Eilis? I love Kate. I can't spend the rest of my life with the likes of Gobnait.'

'What about a paternity test?'

'She won't get the test. They told her about the needle and she almost fainted. We'll have to wait until the baby is born.'

'So why not challenge her?' Eilis suggested.

Mick looked up. 'What do you mean?'

'If Gobnait wants you badly enough, she'll do anything to keep you. She's been persistent about being with you and you've kept her at arm's length. Go a step further.'

'What about the baby? If I'm the father, I intend to do right by it. There's no reason the baby should suffer because I couldn't keep my trousers on.'

'Hmm.' She grinned wickedly.

'What, hmm? I don't like it when you do that thing with your eyebrows. Must drive Kieran around the twist.'

'What would you say if I told you that you might be off the hook?'

'I'd say, tell me more.'

'There was talk amongst that group you hang around. One of the blokes was joking about how they've never seen you with a woman or go on a

277

date. They thought you might be gay, and our Gobnait rose to the challenge to get you into bed.'

'That's probably why she's been so persistent in the last few months. Why didn't you tell me this sooner?'

'Because I know she's not your type and you're not the kind to fall into bed with just anyone. You've been pining over Kate for years. Besides,' she added, 'you're not the kind of person who cares what anyone thinks of you.'

The truth hit Mick hard. She was right, of course. 'I haven't exactly been a saint, you know.'

'No, but you've never committed, either. And you've never dated anyone like Gobnait.'

'So, what's this challenge all about?'

Chapter Nineteen

By the time Mick got home, he was feeling better about the outlook of his future. He regretted all the jars he'd consumed the night before. Fortunately, Eilis had stopped him before he made a complete fool of himself. He didn't relish the thought of his image appearing next to the dictionary description of jerk, too. *Amadán* was bad enough.

Her idea was brilliant and he couldn't wait to put Gobnait to the test. He'd called her as soon as he got home and invited her over for supper. He was now getting things ready and waited for her arrival.

The buzzer sounded. He ran to the intercom. 'Yes?'

'Is me, Mick. Open the door, yeah?' He cringed at the sound of her grating voice. How could he ever have thought it cute? He pushed the button and heard the door click open. 'Be righ' up.'

He looked around. Everything was in place.

While he'd been out that afternoon, he'd stopped to buy a few things for the perfect dinner. Perfect, because he didn't have to cook it, that is. He'd also purchased flowers and wine. Along with dinner, he'd chosen some mood music, set the lights low in the apartment, and lit a few candles.

Everything appeared to be set up for a night of romance. However, if he played his cards right,

Gobnait would be sent running. He hoped Eilis was right, because he hadn't bothered changing the sheets on his bed, not that he intended to get that far with the woman. Ever.

A knock sounded on the door and he went to let Gobnait in. True to form, she was dressed provocatively. The yellow-dyed rabbit fur jacket topped a black miniskirt. Dark black tights replaced the nets she usually wore. Her feet were slipped into a pair of black stilettos. It amazed him how she could walk in shoes like that, but he knew why she wore them. She was damn short otherwise.

Her hair was spiked as usual and dyed, this time jet black. Her skin was pale against the dark color, but her heavy makeup made up for the lack of color in her natural tone.

As she stepped through the door, she shed her jacket and tossed it at him when she walked by, taking in the setting before her. She turned to face him with a grin. He couldn't help but notice her sheer black blouse. Beneath it was a black push-up bra. The blouse was loosely tucked into the waistband of her miniskirt.

'What's this all about, Mick?'

He hung her jacket on the peg beside the door, then went to her. He put on his best face, smiling as he approached her. *God, help me tonight.*

'I've been thinking about this whole baby thing. I thought we could talk about it tonight.' Her face lit up. He strode into the kitchen and popped the cork on the wine to let it breathe, then moved to the oven to check his dinner. Rotisserie chicken, roasted potatoes, and veggies were reheating nicely. He then pulled the large pre-made salad from the fridge and gave it a fluff.

'I'm dead impressed. Yous've never made me dinner before.' Technically, he'd only reheated dinner, but she'd never know the difference.

'It's a special occasion, Gob, so I thought I'd splash out.' He pulled out a tray of carrot and celery sticks and passed them across the bar to her. She'd perched herself on a chair, watching him go about his work.

'Wot's this?' she asked, referring to the bunny food.

'Starters.' He didn't have to force a smile at the look she gave him. 'Dig in. Dinner will be ready in a minute. We've a lot to talk about tonight and I'd like to get started as soon as we're done with dinner.'

A few minutes later, he had the chicken, potatoes and veg dished up and the salad was on the bar between them. He poured them both a glass of wine and took his seat.

Turning to her, he lifted his glass. 'To us, Gob. The three of us.' He clinked her glass and took a sip of the wine.

The moment the wine hit her lips, she sputtered, spitting it back into the glass. 'Wot's this then?' She held up the glass.

'Alcohol-free wine. You're pregnant now, so you have to go off the gargle.'

Her face screwed up and she put the glass down. Inside, he was grinning at the face she'd made. Going off the drink wouldn't sit well with her.

He watched her inspect the meal on her plate – plain, skinless chicken breast, unbuttered potatoes and a selection of unsalted vegetables. 'Where's the skin, Mick? That's me favorite.'

'I took it off. It's not on your new diet. You have to eat right if this baby is going to be healthy,' he said. 'Go on, eat up.'

'Yous forgot the budder and salt.'

'Not on your diet, either.'

Reluctantly, she ate her meal. By the look on her face, the food wasn't sitting well with her.

When dinner was done, he cleared the bar. 'Go into the sitting room and get comfortable. I'll bring your dessert.' She jumped at the chance.

A moment later, he set a tray on the table in front of the sofa and sat beside her. She had the remote in her hand and was flicking through the stations. He took it from her and switched the set off.

'We need to talk, Gob,' he reminded her, setting the remote on the table and moving to pour them tea. He placed a bowl of fresh fruit in her hand and handed her a fork.

'Mick, is this going to go on much longer?' she asked, her voice full of frustration.

'For about five months more, from what the doctor says.' He popped a bit of melon into his mouth and smiled.

She put her bowl on the table and sat back, crossing her arms in front of her, and scowling like a spoiled child who'd been punished. Mick let her stew while he ate his fruit.

Finally, 'I'm really looking forward to the whole parent thing.'

'Are you?' she asked, curiosity in her frown.

He turned to face her and put on an expression

of enthusiasm. 'I am. I went to Hodges Figgis today and bought a couple books. I'll get them.' He went to the bedroom and returned with the books. He opened one of them, as he sat and flipped to the section on diets and showed it to her. 'See? This is where I learned about proper nutrition for expectant mothers. I think you should read it, too.'

'Aren't yous going a little overboard, like?' Her brow rose hopefully.

'Not at all. I want our baby to be healthy. I want you to be healthy, too. The baby's health starts with the mother. I've got a whole dietary plan set up for us.' He smiled to cover his laughter of the situation. She was beginning to squirm.

'Look a'me, Mick. I'm hardly fat. I don't need a diet, right?' She reached over, grabbed her purse off the floor, and pulled out a pack of cigarettes.

'What are you doing, Gob?'

'Havin' a fag.' She shook the pack in his face, but he promptly snatched it from her. 'Wha–'

'No more smoking for you. It's not healthy for the baby.'

'Is my baby, Mick. Yous can't tell me wot to do.' Her voice rose.

'It's my baby, too, Gob, and I *will* tell you how to treat your body while you're carrying my child,' he said firmly. She threw her arms around herself and pouted. 'Oh, come on, Gob, it won't be that bad. It's only a few months.' He reached over, put his arm around her, and pulled her against him. Fortunately, she couldn't see the face he made just touching her. Deep in his heart, he wished it were Kate in his arms and Kate he was talking to about proper diets for her and their baby.

Gobnait relaxed against him. 'I know, but I can't just quit cold turkey, like.'

'You're going to have to. I want our baby to be perfect.'

After a moment, as she got used to the idea of the special diet and giving up her cigarettes, he hit her with the next one.

'Umm, Gob, you're also going to have to lose the makeup and hair coloring for a while.'

She shot off the sofa and glared at him. 'Are you mad or wot?'

Sitting at the edge of the sofa, he said, 'Not at all. Those things aren't healthy–'

'–for the baby,' she finished.

'Right. It's the chemicals, you see.'

'Wot else? Might as well get it over with now, like.' She tapped her foot. The look she gave him was of pure disgust. Inside, he was doing the happy dance.

'You'll also need to take exercise classes.'

'Wot?' she screeched.

'And, you'll have to take prenatal classes,' he added.

'Yous are mad. I'll do no such thing.'

'It's not like you're in this alone. I'm taking the classes with you.'

'I don't care, Mick. I'm not doin' it.'

He stood over her now. 'You will do it if I have to pin you down to eat and haul you off to classes myself. We both got into this mess; we'll both get through it. Parenting is a partnership, Gobnait. We have to do this for our baby.'

She went quiet. When it was obvious he was

284

winning, he stepped up to the next level.

'We'll have to talk about your wardrobe, too.' She shot daggers at him. 'You'll have to start wearing looser clothes for starters. You can't wear such tight skirts, no matter how sexy they are. They're too tight.' He swallowed hard. He no longer thought anything about her was sexy.

'And those shoes have to go. I'll not have you falling over and hurting yourself or our baby.' He sat back beside her and tried to pull her into his arms again. She hesitated, but eventually settled back against him.

'This is going to be so great, Gob,' he lied. 'I've always wanted to be a father and now I have the chance. I'm sorry I didn't believe you when you said we'd slept together. I believe you now. I'm just so excited. I doubted at first, but the test proves it, right? I'm going to be a dad.' He sighed dramatically.

'Yeah, fecking brilliant,' she groaned under her breath. There wasn't a hint of enthusiasm in her voice.

His emotional happy dance turned into a traditional Irish reel. He gave her a squeeze. It was more for him than her. He was so happy things were going the way he and Eilis had planned, he could barely contain himself. He was feeling all tingly inside.

He had to cool it, though, or give the game away. He was so close now he could feel it. Glorious freedom!

A chuckle escaped suddenly and Gobnait stiffened noticeably. 'Yous think is funny wot you're putting me through?' she huffed.

He turned her around to face him. 'No, baby, I don't. I'm just so happy about – everything. Aren't you excited?'

Her face was still screwed up with anger, but softened slightly as she thought about it all. 'I'm not thrilled with the diet and all, but is only a few months, right?'

'Initially. But once this baby is born, you'll have to stick to it. You'll be breastfeeding. Anything you put into your body goes right through the breast milk to the baby.' The look of anger hit her again. He continued his onslaught. 'I'm looking forward to this so much that I think we should get you pregnant again right away. We should have a whole houseful of kids.'

She gasped. 'Yous wot?'

'A houseful of kids. Won't it be great? I think we should try for at least two of each.'

She pulled away and got to her feet. 'I don't know, Mick. I haven't even had the first one, like.'

He reached up and took her hand in his. 'It'll be fine. Really it will.'

'Do you think so? Really?' She started to sound hopeful now. He had her flip-flopping. She was confused. He had a couple more issues to bring up with her, then he'd know exactly where his own future stood.

'I do. Really.' He smiled. 'There are a few other things we need to iron out, but I think in the long run you'll thank me. Everything will be perfect.'

Her hand slipped from his and she sat back. 'Wot other things, Mick?' Her thin, hand-painted eyebrow arched dramatically.

'Well, you'll have to go to elocution.'

'Ela-feckin-wot?'

'Elocution. You'll have to lose that accent. It will never go down well in Connemara.'

'And wot would I be doing in the likes of Conne-feckin-mara?' She was boiling now. Once he turned up the heat another notch, she'd explode for sure.

'The house, of course. The house and land are free and clear. I want my kids raised in the house I was raised in, Gobnait.' The truth was, he really did. Just not kids with her. He wanted kids with Kate, at least a dozen of them.

Mick cringed and plugged his ears as Gobnait suddenly screeched in protest. 'I will not move to Conne-feckin-mara, Mick. Is a godforsaken arsehole of Ar'land. If yous think I'll be moving there, yous've got another think comin', boyo.' She shook a black polish painted nail at him.

He stood and started toward her, but she backed up a step. 'Come on, Gobnait. It won't be that bad. You'll grow to love it. I did. It'll be good for the kids. It'll be good for us. Imagine,' he said enthusiastically, 'all the long, dark winter nights we'll have together, snuggled up in front of the hearth, making more babies.' He reached out for her, but she shot across the room.

'Stay away from me, Mick.'

'What's this?'

'I said, stay away. Don't touch me. I can't believe this is happening.' She grabbed fistfuls of hair and yanked at them in frustration as she paced the floor. 'Wot am I gonna do?' she chanted.

'Leave everything to me, Gob. It'll be great.' He smiled at her to show how much he was looking forward to a future with her.

'I'll not be leaving anything to yous, Mick. If I did, my life'd be ruined. I needa think. This can't be happening.'

Mick genuinely worried about the baby now. He reached out and caught Gobnait mid-stride. 'Sit down now or you'll hurt yourself.' He brought her a glass of the nonalcoholic wine and put it in her hand. 'Drink something. Relax. I'm going to the loo. When I come back, we can finish talking. There are a couple other things we need to discuss.' Her brows were so tightly knit together, they almost touched. Her normally pale skin was rosy under the makeup. And her lips pressed tightly together as she fumed. She wasn't just angry. She was seriously pissed.

The second he was through the bedroom door, he saw her race for the phone. He didn't know who she was calling, but he couldn't wait to see what happened next. Closing the door behind him, he went to his bedside phone and lifted the receiver. He would probably go to Hell for eaves-dropping, but wasn't he in Hell now with the prospect of a future with this woman?

'Wot am I gonna do, Shamie?' She recounted all the things he'd told her about how her life would change and how he was moving her to the west to raise their kids. 'This has gotten out of control. Is not funny anymore, right? Yous have got to bail me out of it, right?'

Shamie was one of the blokes from the group he hung out with – sort of the leader, if he could be called that at their age. Shamie was the loud one, the clown, the one who drank everyone else under the table, the one who caused the most trouble. Gobnait calling him meant he'd put her up to this in the first place. It hadn't been as cut and dried as Eilis made it sound. This wasn't a matter of just getting him to sleep with Gobnait. It was for Shamie's entertainment, pure and simple. Mick's gut twisted how this had gotten so out of control, not only for him, but also for Gobnait.

'You'll have to sort it out yourself, baby. You got yourself into this mess. Figure it out,' he told her.

'Shamie, yous're in this as much as I am. Get over here and get me out of this. Yous gotta come up with something,' she pleaded. 'Please, Shamie.'

'All right, all right. I'll be over later.'

'Yous'll be over now, Shamie. I want outa here.'

'Okay, okay. I'll be right over. Calm down.' Then the line went dead and Gobnait hung up on her end.

Mick sat for a moment after disconnecting. This should be interesting.

Half an hour later, the intercom buzzed. Mick rose to answer it. 'Ya?' he said by way of greeting.

'Mickie.' Mick cringed. 'Shamie.'

'Hey, Shame. What's up, mate? I'm a little busy here.' He winked at Gobnait.

'Don't I know it, man. Lemme up.'

He paused to look at Gobnait. 'I wanted this to be a special night, Gob. Just the two of us. Should I tell Shamie to beat it?'

'No, by all means let him up. I've had enough excitement for one night.'

'Are you sure? We still have a lot to talk about.' She nodded vigorously. 'Come on up, Shamie.'

Mick buzzed the front door and set his own door ajar, before returning to sit beside Gobnait, putting his arm around her. He lifted the remote and flipped on the telly. To anyone else, it looked like a cozy evening at home. But at this point, Mick was sure all parties knew the score and it was time to call an end to the game.

A moment later, Shamie strolled in.

Shamie was a smooth character. He never had a hair out of place, wore his suits starched, and always had a shine on his shoes. The average person on the street would have mistaken him for a banker or some other office exec. In reality, he worked construction and dressed in suits when he went out to impress the ladies.

True to form, the man strutted in fully suited. His brassy hair was perfectly styled and in place, his voice smooth.

'Mickieeeee,' Shamie crooned, stepping through the door. He flashed Mick some hand sign he probably picked up on the telly then strutted into the kitchen. Mick heard him open the fridge. 'Hey, man, no beer?'

'We've a pregnant woman in the house now. No more alcohol,' he said over his shoulder. Shamie spotted the wine bottle on the counter and took a swig from it. Instantly, he turned to the sink and spat it out. The look on his face was priceless. 'Non-alcoholic wine, Shame.'

'Shame is right, man. The stuff tastes like piss.' Shamie tore a bit of chicken off the bird and strolled into the sitting room, bits of it dropping onto the floor as he walked. Mick ignored the mess. It was just amazing to him that a guy who looked and tried to act so suave was such a pig at heart. What had he seen in any of the people he called friends?

Shamie sat in a stuffed chair across from the sofa and flung a leg over the arm. 'What's this about pregnant? You get knocked up, Gob?' His eyes glinted, knowingly.

'Shur-up, Shamie.' She gave Shamie an icy glare.

'Mickie just said there was a pregnant woman in the house. You're the only woman here, so it must be you.'

'Yep, it's Gobnait. Isn't it great? We've just been talking about the new life we're going to start back home.' He gave her a squeeze. 'Isn't that right, dear?'

Gobnait glared at him.

Shamie laughed. 'Oh, man!' He held his belly as he laughed, and almost instantly he was doubled over gasping for air.

Mick furrowed his brows as he looked at Shamie. 'What's so funny, mate?'

'Gobnait pregnant, that's what.' He wiped the tears from his eyes. 'That's great.'

'It's not that funny, Shamie,' she said.

'Love, from where I sit, it's fecking hilarious.'

'Why don't you tell us why you're here, Shamie,' Mick suggested. 'We were just going to turn in.' He winked at Gobnait. Her eyes went wide.

'I'm here because she called me.' Silence filled the room as Mick and Shamie turned to Gobnait.

'Okay, yeah, I called him. Yous freaked me out about all this diet stuff and moving. I'm not ready for this.'

'It's a little late for that, wouldn't you say?'

'Give over, Gob,' said Shamie. 'Game's over. All you're going to do is bury yourself in a hole.'

Mick turned to Gobnait again. 'What's he saying, Gob?' He forced concern into his voice.

She was quiet. She sat staring at Shamie, looking for answers.

'What I'm saying, mate, is that she's not pregnant,' Shamie volunteered.

Mick was still staring at Gobnait. Her face went white.

'Is this true, Gobnait?' She said nothing. 'Look at me, woman. Is this true?'

She shot off the sofa then and stomped across the room to stand behind Shamie. 'Yes.'

'What's this all about then?' He shifted his gaze between Shamie and Gobnait, Shamie with his shit-eating grin, and Gobnait with her pale face and looking as if she'd faint at any moment.

'It was a game, Mickie,' Shamie told him.

'Someone had better explain.' He sat forward with his elbows on his knees and clasped his hands, waiting.

When Gobnait remained quiet, Shamie took it upon himself to explain everything, including her friend in the doctor's surgery who falsified the pregnancy reading when Mick took her in for the test.

He was sure this wasn't what Gobnait had in mind when she'd called Shamie for rescuing.

Half an hour later, the two were walking out of the apartment, her screaming all the way. It was no concern of his at that point. He had his life back. To his way of thinking, Gobnait got everything she deserved.

He whooped aloud, spun a circle where he stood, and punched at the air like a boxer who'd just won a prizefight. He was free! And everything that had happened in the last few days was instantly forgotten as soon as Gobnait and Shamie left his apartment. The only thing on his mind was Kate. He had to win her back. He'd do anything to make things right with her.

Chapter Twenty

Winter Solstice – 21 December

Christmas was usually her favorite time of year. Kate loved the tree in the sitting room, dripping with colorful decorations and flashing lights. She loved the smell of baking from the kitchen – the cinnamon buns and the richness of the roasting turkey. And she loved wrapping the gifts, though she could do without the mayhem of the shopping.

In December, holiday music filled the air, family and friends gathered for good cheer, and everyone ate far too much food.

Galway City would be thronged with people rushing from shop to shop. Lights and decorations would be hanging from anything that would hold them. And Santa would be standing at just about every corner.

And if they were fortunate, a little snow would fall, and children would rush out to have snowball fights before it melted away.

Every year, Kate leapt head first into anything to do with the holiday. Her enthusiasm drove Conn mad, and she loved taunting him. Even while she cared for Donal, and Mary before him, Kate had always found ways to bring the holiday cheer into their home with decorations, music, baking, and a present or two.

She'd always made sure the Spillanes were part of the Conneely holiday. And why not? Wasn't Donal her own father's closest friend? And he'd needed the Conneelys even more with his wife gone and Mick away. Sure, Mick would visit for a day or two, but he was usually absent on the day itself. She understood better now why he'd stayed away, but that still didn't make things any easier for his parents.

Yes, Christmas was usually a joyful time and Kate reveled in the ostentatious, and sometimes atrocious, nature of the season. It was gaudy, too commercial, and aggravating. And she loved it.

Rather, she used to love it. Now, it was like pulling teeth to get her out of her room. According to her mother, if it weren't for Molly and Jess, she was sure her bed would swallow her whole. She only wanted to hide under the covers and hope the world would disappear.

Since Mick left with Gobnait, Kate had forced herself to stay away from Fairhill Farm. There was nothing up there for her now. Donal and Mary were gone, she had Molly and Jess home with her, and Mick was back in Dublin starting a new life with a child on the way. The only person who had gone over to Fairhill was her father to move the remaining sheep back to their farm, since no one knew how long Mick would be gone this time.

The remaining few chickens had come home as well. Now their own coop was filled to bursting. Conn said he would bring the coop over from Fairhill Farm, but as of yet it hadn't appeared. Surely her mother was now thinking of a few extra chicken dinners.

On the lead-up to Christmas Day, Kate forced herself out of her cocoon to help around the house and farm. She pretended she was in the holiday spirit so as not to bring her gloom into a home filled with holiday cheer. She rolled dough for gingerbread men, she mixed the fruit into the batter for the pudding, and she washed the holiday china her mother had taken out of storage for the big day. She even found a recipe to make a few special treats for her dogs.

If there was a job needing doing, Kate was the first to volunteer, anything to keep her mind off how much her broken heart ached.

This suited Conn to a tee, of course. He and Liam were often found sitting in front of the telly watching any sporting match on, once the farm chores were done. She paid them no mind as she went about performing whatever task needed doing that kept her from thinking about Mick.

But how could she keep him from her mind? His kisses still lingered on her lips, and thoughts of the things he had done to her body made her ache with the memory. When she remembered where he was now and with whom, she suffered a deep feeling of loss she could only say was worse than losing both Donal and Mary.

While her days were filled with holiday preparations, her nights were spent alone in her room or outside with Molly and Jess. She preferred being alone with her thoughts, of which Mick seemed to be the central focus, no matter how hard she tried forgetting him. The simple truth was that she'd fallen in love with him all over again while he had been home. And God help her, she still loved him. She always had and feared she always would.

Kate now sat on an old horse blanket in the center of the ancient stone circle she and Mick had once considered their private place. The solstice sky was clear and lit with the full moon. It seemed the perfect time to perform the task.

It had been most of ten years since she'd been here last and she'd struggled to find the old path that wound up the hillside. All of the scratches she'd suffered winding through the prickly gorse would be worth it once her task was done.

Legend told of Druidic rituals here. She remembered when Mick had told her that the thirteen stones in this circle followed each of the thirteen full moons that made up the calendar year. She'd always been impressed by the things he learned in his books.

To her and Mick, visiting the circle had been like stepping back in time to a place where human habitation was sparse and places like the stone circle were sacred. It had been sacred to them because they called it their own. While they could see the rooftops of both farmhouses from here, the circle seemed in another world. Looking between the tall stones, it was easy to picture the Druids going about their work of plotting moon cycles and charting the stars.

She remembered many of the evenings they'd come here during the full moon. With their lantern turned low, they'd lie in the center of the circle and try to determine which stone aligned with the moon.

The circle had 3000 years of history behind it

and untold years ahead, but she and Mick also had their own history here.

It was a special place for both of them, but it was a place she hadn't come back to once she realized he'd left for college. Today was her first trip back, and her last. She was saying goodbye to Mick forever.

Her emotions had been like a roller coaster ride with him, especially over the last few months since Donal's death. She couldn't continue anymore. She needed to bury her childhood dream of a life with Mick. She was twenty-five years old and needed to find a life to call her own. The only way to do that was to put him behind her. All of him.

Together with the old horse blanket and lantern, Kate brought a small wooden box Mick had given her. He had made it in woodworking class and she'd used it to keep all of her most important mementoes. He'd given them to her when they were young—silly things like a lock of his hair tied with a ribbon, wildflowers he'd put in her hair which she had pressed and dried, photos of her and Mick taken for a punt in a kiosk booth, various rocks and feathers, and other trinkets only kids would understand.

She emptied the contents of the box onto the blanket in front of her and sifted through them. She reminisced about each item he'd given her, before replacing it in the box.

Her heart pounded. This would be the last time she'd ever see or touch these things.

When she finished, she closed the box. She'd brought a small camping shovel with her as well and used it to dig the hole, first pulling at the soft moss until she reached dirt.

When the hole was big enough, she placed the box at the bottom. She shuddered at how the box rested there like a casket in the dark earth. She couldn't say goodbye just yet.

She stood and walked over to the edge of the circle and looked out over the valley. The view was spectacular, even more so with the sun sinking behind the mountains on the other side of the valley. The sky was awash in wispy pink and lavender clouds. Dew collected on the stones and grass, immediately turning to frost. The temperature was definitely dropping, and quickly. If it rained, they might have a white Christmas. That would have been a wonderful treat, if only she wasn't so miserable.

As the sun set, deep shadows crossed the circle until it was almost dark. Kate turned to the old lantern she'd brought and set a match to the wick. The flame flickered and cast a soft yellow glow around her.

The sun had finally set, the perfect time to complete her task. She knelt beside the hole. It would be a fitting end to this part of her life. The setting sun signaled the end of the day, just as the sealing of the hole would signal the end of the first twenty-five years of her life. But as she lifted the first handful of dirt, she just couldn't bear to let it drop onto the box.

She stared at the box. What was keeping her from finishing this? She'd prepared all day and said goodbye to each item before digging the hole. What more could she do to move forward?

She drew the lantern closer to the hole and opened the box. It was as if something was speaking to her. She sifted through the items and went right to the small kiosk photos. Lifting them from the box once more, she looked at them to see what about them called to her, but she couldn't figure it out.

She stared at the photos for a long time, oblivious to the growing cold around her. Something was missing. She just couldn't put her finger on it.

Then it hit her. She'd bought Mick a Christmas gift before Gobnait had shown up. She'd meant to give it to him on Christmas morning and tell him how much she loved him. With the woman's appearance and her shocking news, everything had been ruined.

She tossed the pictures back into the box before reaching into her pocket and withdrawing a green velvet box. She unsnapped the tiny button and lifted the lid. The light from the lantern glinted off the gold Claddagh Ring nestled inside. Hands for friendship, heart for love, and crown for loyalty.

The ring had been a symbol of love across Ireland since the seventeenth century. Over time, the symbol had come to be used from a friendship ring to a wedding band, and everything in between. These days, the symbol adorned items from doorknockers to letter openers – all meant for tourists. But the real symbol was in the ring.

It was bad luck to buy a Claddagh Ring for one's self. It must be gifted to bring luck to both the recipient and the giver.

Kate pulled the gold ring out of the box and

turned it in her fingers, letting the dim lantern light catch all of its angles. Once in the box with the rest of her memories, this ring would never again see the light of day.

The thought of that released pent-up tears, which spilled over onto the ring. She tried wiping them away, but only managed to smear them on the gold. She frantically looked for something soft to clean the ring, but came up empty. Desperation crept over her. The ring, never worn by the intended recipient, would go to its grave with the tears of a lover smeared all over it. The thought only made things worse. She hung her head, squeezing her eyes tightly trying to force back the tears.

'That ring looks a lot like this one.'

Kate spun around where she sat, her heart pounding suddenly in her chest. Mick stood behind her, with a matching Claddagh Ring in his hand. He'd scared years off her, on top of the fact he shouldn't have been up here. He was supposed to be in Dublin with ... that woman.

She gasped. 'What are you doing here?' She quickly placed the ring in its velvet box and tossed it into the wooden box in the ground.

'I saw the lantern from the house and came to see what you were up to.' He moved in front of her and knelt.

'What I'm doing is no concern of yours, Michael Spillane. I'll be thanking you to leave me be.' Her eyes darted everywhere but in his direction.

'I can't do that, Kate. We need to talk.'

She started shoveling the dirt in on top of the

box, but his hand stayed her. For a moment, she froze before jerking free of him.

'What's this?' He looked into the hole and extracted her box. She grabbed for it, but he pulled it out of her reach and opened it.

'That's mine. Give it back.'

'I know. I gave it to you.' He sat back, looked at the contents, and smiled. 'Silly trinkets,' he noted, moving his finger through the contents.

'Silly to you maybe, but they mean ... meant ... everything to me.'

'If they mean so much to you, why are you burying them?'

'If you must know, I'm burying my past. I'm moving on. I've let you dominate my life for too long.'

He looked back in the box, looked through the contents once more and extracted two items. He closed the box and put it back in the hole. 'You can bury it now, if you wish'

She looked to see what he had in his hand – the photos and the Claddagh Ring.

'Put them back, Mick.'

He held up the photos. 'These are as much mine as yours, so I'm keeping them.'

'And the ring?'

'I'm guessing this was my Christmas present, which means it's mine as well.' His grin made her want to slap him.

'I didn't give it to you, so it's still mine. Give it to me.' She held out her hand.

'No, it's mine. You can have this one if you wish.' He handed her the Claddagh he'd shown her just moments before. It was similar to the one she'd bought for him, only smaller, and with a heart-shaped emerald in the center. She gasped.

'I'd meant to give it to you as a Christmas gift. I guess great minds think alike. Here, give me your hand. I'll put it on for you.'

She moved away from him, drawing her brows together. 'What are you on about, Mick? Go home to your fiancée and baby.' She moved to stand. To her surprise, he grasped her about the shoulders and hauled her against him. They both knelt on the old horse blanket. The shock forced her to meet his gaze. The lantern lit the planes of his face dramatically.

'It's over, Kate.'

'Aye, it's over all right. Between you and me. Now, let go of me or I'll scream.'

'Scream all you like. There's no one to hear you.'

He was right. She sagged in defeat. There was no getting away from him. Her heart seemed to stop beating. 'What do you want from me, Mick? You've already taken the best of me and tossed it away.'

He smiled. 'Oh, Kate, you haven't given me far enough.'

'I have nothing else to give you. Don't you understand? It's over. Please,' she pleaded. 'Let me go, and let me get on with my own life. Let me say goodbye to you.' Then she was fighting back the tears once more. She hated these female emotions and tried to squeeze them back, but they burst forth anyway. 'Please. Don't make me beg.' Her voice came out a choked whisper.

He looked at her for a long minute, saying nothing. She allowed herself to stare into his mossy eyes. The light from the lantern bounced off the gold flecks. His dark lashes curled sensually. She'd been wrong about her heart before. It still beat, and rather quickly, as she gazed into the eyes she'd loved for as long as she could remember. And now she was telling them goodbye once and for all time.

To her surprise, he relented. 'All right, Kate. I'll let you go. Under one condition.' She nodded quickly. She didn't care what it was; she just wanted it over with. 'Let me kiss you once more. I want something to remember you by.'

'What?' She couldn't believe what she was hearing.

'One kiss. You wouldn't begrudge me that, not after all we've been through. Leave me, but leave me with something to hold onto for all those empty nights when you're not there beside me,' he murmured. And repeating her words, he said, 'Don't make me beg.'

She didn't know what to do. If she didn't kiss him, there was no telling how she'd get away from him. She had to get the box buried and get home. She had a new life to start. If she did kiss him, it would be like throwing salt onto the wound in her heart. It was already deep, and the bleeding from it was like acid coursing through her body.

Maybe he had a point, though. One more kiss – to remember him by. Then it would be over. Yes, she could reason that, anything to get away.

'All right. One kiss – for a memory.'

A gentle smile curved along his lips. She thought she saw something familiar in his gaze. She blinked back the image and waited for him to kiss her.

His hands loosened their grasp on her shoulders and moved up along her neck to cup her cheeks. He stroked the tears from them with his thumbs, before threading his fingers through her hair and pulled her closer. She closed her eyes in anticipation, but he didn't kiss her. His breath felt hot against her cheek. He stroked her nose gently with his own before resting his forehead against hers.

'Ah, Kate,' he sighed. 'Pretend.'

'Pretend what?' Her voice was barely audible, even to her. She looked at him once more through the tears in her eyes.

'Pretend you love me, Kate. Just this one time, pretend you love me and kiss me.' He didn't wait for her reply.

His lips came down on hers fully and possessively, and he took her breath away. This was no gentle kiss. No love play. Stars exploded behind her eyelids and her legs went weak.

There was no pretending.

Chapter Twenty-One

Mick had only meant to warm Kate to the idea of listening to what had happened back in Dublin. But touching her tingled through his fingertips and flashed through his body like an electric shock. The hairs on the back of his neck stood in anticipation of their kiss.

He'd known what kind of reaction he'd have on her the moment their lips met. He'd counted on it. He wanted to kiss her senseless and make her pliant in his hands. He just didn't count on her kissing him back so fully, so thoroughly, so demanding. He tried to control himself, but just her touch made his body ache.

Instead of releasing her, as he knew he should after he'd agreed to only one kiss, he wrapped his arms around her waist and pressed his body to her. He groaned at the intense sensation. She tilted her head and he took this as a sign, slipping his tongue between her lips to rub with hers. He cradled her head in the crook of his arm and kissed her until they were both breathless.

'Ah, Kate.' He took deep breaths to control his desire. 'Beautiful Kate.'

His fingers trembled as he stroked her cheek. He leaned away and watched her passion-filled eyes flutter open. They were still damp with her tears, and he hated that he'd been the cause.

He bent to kiss each eyelid. 'I'm sorry, Kate. I

wish I could make you believe me, but I am sorry.'

'For what?' she asked, breathless.

'To have put you through so much for so long. I really thought we had a chance there.'

'So did I.'

'Will you let me tell you what happened? Maybe it will change your mind about burying me in your past. Maybe it won't. I just don't want to leave things undone between us again.'

After a pause, she finally nodded her consent.

He wanted it to be right when he told her what had happened in Dublin. He wanted the right setting, the right mood, but the top of a hill in the dead of winter with only a pair of lanterns to warm them would have to do.

'Here, love. Let me hold you while I tell you. You're shivering.' He pulled her to him. She didn't fight him, but settled into his side just as she had in his bedroom when the night had been filled with confessions.

He told her everything about his life in Dublin and the people he knew. He started by telling her what he knew about Gobnait and the group of people he'd thought were his friends. He continued telling her about the trip back to Dublin, the doctor's visit, and what Eilis had overheard. Then he told her about the plan he and Eilis hatched to ferret out the truth from Gobnait, and how, when it was all over, he'd felt such a sense of freedom, he couldn't wait to come back to Connemara and Fairhill Farm. 'And back to you, if you'll have me.'

When he was through, Kate remained silent. His heart pounded in his chest through her silence.

He'd given her a lot to digest, but her stillness was killing him. She'd gone from having what amounted to a funeral for him to an opportunity at a future with him, completely unobstructed.

When she didn't say anything right away, he turned her to face him once more. 'Don't you know what this means?'

'She lied to you.'

'Yes, she lied to both of us. It also means she's gone. She's out of my life for good. Out of our lives.' His voice rose in pitch with his excitement.

'What do you want from me, Mick? I'm worn out. I can't go back to the way things were. I just can't.'

'What I want from you, Kate, is you. Just you. I want your love. I want your body, your heart, your soul. I want you to have everything I have to offer you. I'll give you children. I'll give you my life. Be my wife and I'll give you the moon, if you want it,' he vowed, waving his hand at the moon overhead. His confession and proposal must have stunned her, by the look on her face. Her eyes widened and her mouth fell open.

He touched her chin with the tips of his fingers to close her mouth 'Marry me, Kate. I love you more than you'll ever know.'

Still she said nothing. The anticipation of her answer was taking its toll on him. Even in the bitter cold of the hilltop, he began perspiring.

'Kate? Love, please say something?'

'I don't think you kissed me right the last time.' She looked up at him. 'You better try again, just to be sure.'

He took hold of her and squeezed her to him.

His heart beat so furiously in his chest he thought he'd explode.

'Only this time, Mick,' she continued, 'can we not pretend I love you? I'd rather kiss you knowing my love is real.'

He leaned back and took her face in his hands. 'Say it, Kate.' She'd rendered him nearly breathless. His heart leapt into his throat waiting to hear the words.

'I do love you, Mick. I've loved you ever since we were little. I've never stopped and I never will.'

His heart filled to bursting. 'I'll take everything you have to give me and will return it in equal measure. I'll spend every day of my life trying to make you happier than the last.'

He pulled her back into his arms and kissed her again. It wasn't goodbye this time, but hello. They weren't burying their pasts behind them. They were forging a path toward a future – a future together.

He slanted his mouth over hers and their tongues met in an ancient mating ritual that sent sparks flying through his body.

He lowered her onto the old blanket. His lips never left hers for even a moment. Her arms encircled his shoulders and her fingers toyed with the curls at the nape of his neck, sending shivers rippling through him.

He supported himself on one arm as he kissed her. His free hand stroked her side from hip to ribcage. He parted the heavy coat she wore and fingered his way under her bulky jumper until he found skin. She was hot to his touch, and he sighed when his hand found her breast. He loved how her nipple pebbled beneath his thumb's touch.

'Kate,' he whispered between kisses, 'I love you so much. I wish the last ten years had never happened. Tell me how to make it up to you, love.'

'Shut up and kiss me.'

And he did. He kissed her lips, her throat, and her collarbone. When that wasn't enough, he moved lower and lifted the edge of her jumper. She shivered when the cold air hit her skin. He moved down and kissed some heat back into her, blew hot air across her flesh.

He trailed kisses up her belly to her ribcage until he found the edge of her bra. He pushed her jumper higher to kiss the soft swell of her breasts.

She gasped. 'Mick!'

'What, love?'

'Mick, we can't – not here.'

He looked up. 'Is it too cold for you?'

'No. It's just that – we're outside. Someone will see us.' She sounded panicked.

He laughed. 'It's dark, love. No one can see us up here. I can barely see you in the lantern light.'

He slipped her jumper over her head and removed her bra. He removed his heavy jacket and held it while she slipped it on. He planned to take care of warming her from above, but he didn't want her freezing in the evening air.

She was exquisite and alluring nearly nude in his jacket. His gaze dropped to her perfect breasts. He took one in his palm and gently massaged it, toying the nipple with his thumb. She sighed at his touch, her back arching. He leaned down and took

310

the other nipple between his lips. He kissed her until she moaned and no longer worried about making love out in the open.

He slid his hand down her belly to the band of her pants. Quickly, he had them unbuttoned and unzipped. To his surprise, she reached down and slid the pants down her legs. They got stuck on her boots. He laughed with her as he unlaced them, pulled them off, followed by her pants, leaving her in just her panties and socks, and his jacket.

'You next,' she told him. 'If I'm going to freeze, so are you.' She reached up to pull off his jumper, but she moved too slow for his liking.

'After this time, I'll let you help, but I want you too much right now.' He sat back and stripped. In a blink, he covered her with his naked body. His lips found hers instantly, and within moments they were both warm again.

The feeling of Kate's soft skin made his body tingle. He trailed hot kisses down the length of her throat, between her breasts and down her belly. At her panty line, he stopped and looked up at her.

'Are these your favorite pair of knickers?'

Kate's eyes furrowed at the question. 'No, why?'

Mick grinned with mischief. He hooked the elastic with his fingers and ripped them from her hips. She gasped, then broke into a fit of giggles. He did, too, until he touched her at the juncture of her thighs. The moment his finger found her slick folds, she gasped and threw back her head. He growled low in his throat at the sight of her and stroked her until she was gasping. He only released her so he could kiss her where his fingers

311

had been.

She grasped him by the shoulder. 'No, Mick.'

His head shot up. 'What – no? What's wrong? I want to take you to the clouds.'

She pulled him up to meet her. 'Give me the moon instead.'

That was his undoing.

He covered her with his body, wrapping her legs around his hips. The warmth of her skin sent tingles racing through him.

He wouldn't rush this for her. He took his time kissing her and caressing each of her curves until she sighed with pleasure. He sat back and positioned himself at her opening, slipping in just the tip. He stroked her slowly, coating himself in her sweetness, letting her get used to the feel of him. She groaned and spread her knees wider to accommodate him. Her muscles tightened, and he almost lost it.

When he thought she was ready, he drove himself into her. She instantly stiffened. Her eyes widened and her face contorted. He stayed inside her and held her as her body resisted him. Pain filled her eyes, and her body trembled.

'Oh, Kate. Kate, love. It only hurts the first time. I swear.' He held her and stroked her hair until she stopped shaking.

He looked down at her and stroked the tears from her cheeks. 'Ah, love, thank you for giving me such a precious gift. I should have been gentler.'

'I didn't know it would hurt so much. Just hold me, Mick. We can try again another time.'

He held her to keep the warmth from leaving her body. He remained inside her as he kissed her neck, her cheek, and her lips. He cupped her breast and fondled it until she moaned again.

It was when she arched under him that she seemed to realize they were still joined. She looked up at him, her expression a mixture of confusion and pleasure. He pressed into her gently until fully inside her. He rocked slowly until she matched his motion.

When they found a rhythm, he eased out of her, then back in again, slowly. Holding back was killing him but he wanted her first time to be passionate and memorable. He continued tantalizing her until she was writhing beneath him. He lowered his lips to the curve of her neck and nipped her gently before stroking his tongue from her collarbone to her breast.

It wasn't long before his ministrations had her nearing the brink. He pumped into her, picking up the pace, burying himself with each stroke, over and over. Suddenly, she tightened around him and cried his name. Only then did he allow himself to follow her over the edge.

When he could finally focus, he collapsed on top of her, gasping. His heart pounded as if he'd just run a marathon, and his body rocked from the exquisite love he had for her. Never had he experienced such fulfillment. If the rest of their lives were half as joyful as this moment, he would die a happy man. Hopefully, not until they were both very old.

When he regained his breath, he looked into her eyes. 'Are you all right, love?' He brushed the hair from her cheek.

'Oh, aye.' Her jacket-covered arms reached far

above her head when she stretched. When her eyes shot open, she looked right at him.

'What's wrong? I'm not hurting you again, am I?'

Her answer wasn't one he was prepared for. She wrapped her arms around him in a hug and a fistful of snow chilled his spine. Instant shivers coursed through his body and he tensed. He and Kate were still joined, and the spasm forced his penis deep into her heat. He didn't know whether to laugh or not. He was still hard.

He rolled off Kate and grabbed a fistful of snow of his own. She was on her feet like a shot and an all-out snowball fight ensued. The snow fell lightly, but there was enough to make a couple respectable-sized snowballs. They ducked and dodged between the stones of the circle, hurling balls of snow at each other. She still wore his jacket, but she still had plenty of exposed skin – and his aim was dead-on.

The fight was short-lived, the cold having them racing back to the horse blanket and into each other arms. He slid his arms around her under the jacket to steal some of the heat, while they rubbed each other vigorously to get warm. Her breasts pressed against his chest as she shivered uncontrollably.

'You're mad, woman,' he exclaimed.

'Aye, but you knew that already.' She laughed through chattering teeth.

'Aye.' The feeling of her soft skin on his warmed him and aroused him once more. 'I did and all.' He lowered his lips to hers.

Within seconds, Mick had her up against one of

the tall stones, her legs wrapped around his waist. He carefully guided himself into her. He didn't know what she did to him, but just the sight of her naked body, touching her bare flesh, and her own sweet scent made him hard. He'd waited forever for this ... for her.

His tongue mated with hers as he set a rocking rhythm with her until she whispered words of love to him. He'd longed to hear those words from her since they'd shared their first tentative kiss right here in this very stone circle.

Suddenly, her head shot up and she gasped. 'Mick, do you feel it?' She reached up behind her to grasp the edge of the stone he held her against and smiled. 'The stone. Is it vibrating?'

Mick pressed his hands against the stone. There definitely was a vibration. Stories of auld of stones vibrating and granted wishes shot through his consciousness, but he had other things on his mind.

Only a moment later, she found her release. She grasped the stone as he drove into her. He watched the way her breasts swung with each thrust. Only when she cried out his name did he let go, too.

The ground rumbled as Mick released his seed into Kate for a second time tonight.

As the tremors subsided around them, Mick pressed Kate against the stone and caught his breath. Total darkness had crept in around them, but he hadn't noticed. Kate in his arms was the only light he needed. He dropped her legs to the ground before he collapsed. He had never experienced a multiple orgasm and it took away his breath.

No other woman compared to Kate. She was his true love. Realization struck that she always had been. And knowing she'd given him her most precious possession, not her virginity but her trust, made him love her all the more.

He took her by the hand and led her back to the blanket. The lantern was dim in the expiring oil. 'We have to get home before the light goes out, love.'

Kate pulled her clothes on and reached for her box of trinkets, then stepped back and gasped.

'What is it, love?'

He went to her side and she pointed to the spot on the ground where the box sat.

'Kate!' He couldn't believe what he saw. The hole had been filled in as if she'd never touched it. Atop the ground, the box lay open with both velvet ring boxes inside. They sat side-by-side, with their lids open and the rings nestled safely inside. Dim lantern light glinted off the polished gold.

He knelt down and pulled both rings from their boxes and handed her the larger ring she'd bought for him. He took her hand in his and kissed the palm before turning his gaze to her.

'I love you, Kathleen Conneely, soon-to-be Kathleen Spillane.' He grinned. 'I have always loved you, even when I was too stupid to admit it. Marry me. Share my life, my love, my soul. Everything I am or have is yours. Just as it always has been. *Tá tú grá mo chroí. Tá mé chomh mór sin i ngrá leat,*' he whispered in Irish. His words of love came between kisses. 'You are the love of my heart. I love you so much,' he told her. He then slipped

316

the Claddagh Ring with the emerald on her finger. The green gem sparked off the pale light.

She took his hand in hers and brushed the backs of his fingers against her cheek, then splayed his palm across her heart. And as she slid her ring onto his finger, she said, 'You gave me the moon this night. You made all of my dreams come true. And I promise, with every fiber of my being, to give you my trust. You're a man of your word, Michael Spillane, and I'll always love you. *Tá tú mo shaol, mo beatha, agus mo amháin grá,*' she whispered. 'You are my world, my life, and my only love.'

Spring

It had been the longest three months of a man's life. At least, that's what Mick told her about having to wait to marry her.

Marriage in Ireland wasn't taken lightly. Not just for the bride and groom, but for the State. Three months written required notice to the Registrar's Office of a person's intent to marry. That meant the soonest they could marry, once the office reopened after New Year, was the first week in April. Plus, there was the reading of the banns in church. Not to mention all of the preparations. Mick was a bigger bundle of nerves than she'd ever seen him.

Until today.

The church doors had just swung open, and Kate saw Mick at the altar. He stood with his hands fisted at the sides of his dark blue suit. His back was straight, his shoulders thrown back and, had Kieran not put his hand up to steady her fiancé, she was sure he would have passed out from the stress of it all.

It was a small affair. Mick's only guests were Kieran and Eilis from Dublin, with Kieran standing beside him as best man.

Her own family was nearly as small. Her father was beside her, waiting to give her away. Her mother fussed with her train one last time, and when she was satisfied, she rushed up to stand beside the priest, doubling as Kate's matron of honor. They all stood together at the front of the single row of pews. Conn was beside their only guests – Will, and Tighe Lynch, and Eilis beside them. All of them waited for her to walk up the aisle. Expectation shone in their eyes.

As she took her first steps, Kate could never remember feeling so free. She was too superstitious to go as far as saying everything was perfect. But it was pretty damn close. Even if her knees threatened to buckle under her. She didn't know why she was so nervous. She'd waited her whole life for today. And in very short order, she would be married to a man she loved so deeply no words could describe.

She couldn't help remembering the many amazing things that had happened since the solstice at the stone circle. She used to think her life with Mick had been thrown upside down, but in reality, it all seemed to be thrown right side up. At last.

Christmas had been the most joyful one Kate could recall. Mick had walked her home from the stone circle so they could share their news with her family. She had been so happy she could barely contain herself. She wanted to shout it to the world.

To her surprise, her parents took the news of their engagement in their stride. Almost as if they expected it.

Turning to her, Mick had said, 'I came over to talk to you, but your folks wouldn't tell me where you were until I explained everything. It wasn't easy, since I didn't know if I'd receive his blessing or the back side of his fist, but I asked your father for permission to marry you before coming to you at the stone circle. Figured it was about time I came to my senses.'

She could only hug him. Then hugged her father for giving his consent. Her whole family knew the strain she'd been under over the last few months, and that Mick had been at the center of most of it. Somehow, he had regained their trust, too.

While she'd gone back to Conneely Farm every night, she'd spent much of her free time at Fairhill Farm – teaching Mick how to work Molly and train Jess, readying the house to move into after their marriage, cleaning up damage caused by the fire that had almost cost her life, and spending as much time with Mick as possible. That included taking their lanterns up to the stone circle, as they had done as children, to watch the sunset and talk.

Just before Valentine's Day, Kate took three different magazines to Fairhill – one on decorating the traditional Irish farmhouse, one on Irish weddings, and another on parenting.

It was the third magazine she left beside Mick's dinner plate, where he wouldn't miss it.

319

Solstice night at the circle had been the only time they'd made love, so something magical had happened in the circle of stones. Growing up, she'd heard tales of wishes granted and magic happening if the standing stones vibrated, but never once had she thought it would involve her. Yet, as sure as her name was soon to be Kathleen Spillane, she was pregnant.

Mick didn't have to ask if it was true. She'd never tease him about a thing like that. He simply lifted her out of the chair and carried her in his arms upstairs, where they kissed and cuddled the night away. He continued to respect her wishes about waiting until they were married. She wasn't withholding sex from him. She just wanted her wedding night to be as special as solstice night had been. He'd agreed.

Liam Conneely hadn't been shocked by the news of a baby, as Kate had thought he would be. In true fatherly fashion, he exclaimed, 'You're not even married yet.' But there was no disguising the enthusiasm in his voice at the prospect of being a grandfather.

Now, as she came to stand before the priest, the priest blessed everyone in the church and began the preamble to the ceremony.

'Dearly beloved, we are gathered here today...'

Kate stole glances at Mick as the ceremony began. Nervousness was etched across his face, but his gaze never wavered from her. Anxious as he was, she saw love in his eyes and smiled.

'And who gives this woman in marriage to this man?'

She glanced up at her father through her thin

veil. She saw the pride in his eyes, and unshed tears. He squeezed her hand.

'Are you sure, love?'

Her gaze met Mick's once more. She couldn't keep the smile from her lips. 'Aye, Da. Oh, aye.'

Liam placed her hand in Mick's, then stepped away. Kate felt her soon-to-be husband's strength in his grasp, remembered the feel of his fingers on her body, and the heat of them went right to her belly where she felt her baby move. Or was it butterflies?

When the priest came to, 'If any person can show just cause why they may not be joined together, let them speak now or forever hold their peace,' Kate's gaze snapped around the small chapel then back to Mick's handsome face. The love she saw in his eyes told her everything was all right. She trusted him and loved him more than words could say. And she would trust him until her last breath.

Chapter Twenty-Two

Fairhill Farm, Connemara
September

Kate decided she and Mick would enjoy the Indian summer weather and have their lunch in the little patio he'd built for her in Mary's garden, now her garden. He'd also built a short stone wall around the garden to give the plants more shelter in the winter and trap warmth in the summer.

The garden bloomed with a myriad of colors, from the delicate herb flowers to small bedding plants meant to help keep down pests. Apple trees were heavy with fruit. Lavender borders blushed soft purple and mossy green. And trailing vines of honeysuckle and clematis trailed through the stones of the wall.

It wouldn't be long, though, before autumn floated in and turned Ireland's greens to russet, gold, and rich chocolate brown.

As her pregnancy progressed, she could have sworn her senses were more alive than ever. She inhaled deeply and let the warm breeze wash the heady scents over her.

Molly lay in the shade of an apple tree while Jess scrambled over her, trying to get her to play. Jess was almost a year old now, but they seemed more like friends than mother and daughter. It warmed Kate seeing them playing together.

She looked past the garden wall. Sheep dotted the pasture just beyond the back farm gate, and chickens scratched in the side yard. And if one knew where to look, the ancient stone circle over-looked them all.

Today marked the one-year anniversary of Donal's passing, and she couldn't think of any bet-ter way to honor him than a day such as today. In a way, Donal and Mary seemed to be sitting with them in the garden.

She sat back in her chair, which Mick had padded with pillows to support her aching back before going into the house to make lunch.

Footsteps sounded behind her. Turning, she saw Mick with a tray. Food!

She was in the final days of her pregnancy, days when jumping off chairs and heavy housework seemed an appealing method to induce labor. She was ready to have their baby. More than ready! And the persistent cramps she'd been feeling all day were making even sitting uncomfortable. Nothing could deter her from food, however.

A horn sounded in the driveway just as she lifted her sandwich to her lips.

'I'll see who it is, love.' A moment later, he returned with Tighe Lynch on his heels.

'I'm sorry if I'm interrupting.' Tighe bent to kiss her cheek.

'Not at all, Mr Lynch. I'm sorry I can't get up to greet you properly. Mick, grab another chair. And make another sandwich for Mr Lynch.'

She motioned for Tighe to sit. He removed his jacket and draped it on the back of the chair. He loosened his tie and undid the top button of his shirt, the long sleeves of which he rolled to his elbows. He sat with a sigh.

'Lovely day.'

''Tis and all,' she replied, smiling against the glare of the sun.

Mick was back almost instantly, with another sandwich and glass for the lemonade she'd made that morning from fresh lemons.

'What brings you all the way out here from the big city, Mr Lynch?' She carefully navigated a piece of her sandwich over her belly and took a bite. 'You don't mind if we eat while we talk, do you?' He nodded acquiescence, but she couldn't help noticing the odd look Tighe gave her. 'Don't worry. I'm the only one who eats pickle and banana sandwiches in this house. I'm sure Mick has made you something a bit tamer.'

The men laughed and joined her in eating their own sandwiches.

They made small talk about the weather and the hustle and bustle of the city in between bites. When they were done, Mick turned to Tighe and repeated her question. 'What brings you all the way out here from the big city?'

Tighe pulled an envelope out of an inside pocket of his jacket. 'As I'm sure you realize, today is the one year anniversary of Donal's passing.'

'I'm sure we both realized it, but we haven't talked about it.' Mick took her by the hand, stroking the backs of her fingers with his thumb.

Tighe's eyes darted between her and Mick, then to the envelope he held. 'There was a section to your father's will, Michael, that wasn't read.'

Kate shot a look to Mick. His expression matched her own feelings. Something had been withheld? And they were just now hearing about it?

'What are you about, Tighe?' Mick's brows drew together.

Tighe shifted restlessly in his seat. 'You see ... what I mean to say is...'

He cleared his throat. 'The way your father went about his will was highly irregular. Usually, it's straightforward with a will reading and we've had done with it. Donal complicated things with the addendum and a further request. I understand his reasoning, though, and once you see the contents of this envelope, I'm sure you'll understand as well.'

Self-consciously, he cleared his throat again. 'He asked me to save this particular part of the will and give it to you on the anniversary of his death – providing the two of you had married. Since you're obviously together,' – he nodded to Kate's pregnancy – 'and today is the day he specified, I'm delivering this in person.'

Tighe handed the envelope to Mick. Her heart skipped a beat. What could be in the envelope? She rubbed her belly with trembling hands, trying to still her anxiety at Tighe's revelation.

Mick tore open the envelope and extracted two items. Mick read the letter to himself, then exclaimed, 'Jesus, Mary and Joseph!'

'What is it, Mick?' Her voice shook as much as her fingers. Clearly no longer able to speak, he handed the letter to her to read for herself.

'My dearest Michael and Kathleen,

325

If you've received this letter, it's the one-year anniversary of my death.

As I sit here writing this, I'm watching Kate prepare my dinner. The light is missing from her eyes even as she goes about such loving tasks for me.

I can't help but wonder, again, what pulled you two apart so long ago. It hurts me to see two people who care so deeply for each other deny their love. Anyone who looks can see the love you have for each other. The greatest hurts in life come from those based in love.

It's the love Mary and I had for each other that we wanted for you both. But you're both too hard-headed to overcome whatever pulled you apart. Love is strong, stronger than hurt, stronger than pride. Never forget that.

As I sit here, I know I can't let my passing go without trying to correct a wrong done to you both so long ago. If you're reading this letter, then I have succeeded in that task and best explain myself.

Mary and I both knew you two belong together, as did Liam and Deirdre. Since you were both too stubborn to talk to each other, I had this idea to get you back together. Call me a romantic old fool, but it looks like it's worked.

I added the addendum to the will, hoping you would fight for your heritage, son. While I would have been happy to leave the farm to Kate in the first place, it would not have given you the incentive to fight. You've spent so long running away. It was time you remembered what it was like to fight for something you believe in. And if I know our Kate, she's done more than she should have to see your birthright has been passed on.

I admit it. I forced you two together and I won't die regretting what I've done. You're together now and that's all that's important.

I've filled Kate with many stories and, knowing her, she will have already shared some of these with you, son. Your heritage has been waiting for you and I can't think of a more deserving woman for you to share it with.

I suppose, while I'm writing this letter, I should also take the chance to tell you all the things you never let me tell you before.

I know why you went to university, son, and I'm damn proud of you. You were my only child. It hurt when you left your mother and me, but we were also proud you were following your dream of higher education. You are the first Spillane to go onto university. I can't tell you how happy we were on the day of your graduation. Your mother was too ill to attend, but I took the train to Dublin and stood at the back of the audience with tears of joy in my eyes when you stepped up to accept your diploma. I didn't tell you I was there, but I was. I wouldn't have missed it for the world.

Kate, the daughter of our hearts, you weren't meant for work in the hospitals. You're too tender for that. Your training was God's way of preparing you for our time of need. Mary never felt more cared for than in your hands. And in my own final days, with your care and your love, I am able to say goodbye to this world in my own home, in the bed I shared for so many years with my beloved wife. I don't know any better way to thank you than what I've done for you and Mick. Your parents are as proud of you as Mary and I are. You are the most loved woman in all of Ireland, to be sure.

I regret having to close this letter, but you two have a life to get on with – together.

First, I will leave you with some advice Mary and I lived by. That is, love each other with all your hearts. Never go to bed with anger between you; it makes a cold bedfellow. Talk to each other. With these things, you will have as long and happy a marriage as Mary and I had.

I leave you with all of my love. Be sure to give Molly a few pats for me.

Donal'

Kate read and reread the letter before dropping it onto the table. 'Oh, Mick,' was all she could say. She'd fall into his arms if she could get herself out of her chair. Instead, she reached for him and he came to her instantly.

Tighe tactfully cleared his throat to remind them he was still there. She sat back and dabbed her eyes with the napkin in her lap. Her tears were of joy. Donal had been a clever man right up to the end. She chuckled thinking how he'd been scheming, even near death. And they'd fallen right into his plan. How could he have known it would work?

Had her parents suspected what Donal had been up to? Probably. Why else would her father stay out of the issues she had with Mick and the farm? Why else would her mother confess her own pre-marriage stories? And Conn, he'd been suspiciously quiet during it all, too. They were all in on it. She just knew it.

'Go on, then,' she said. 'Open the other envelope.'

Mick tore open the second envelope and withdrew a slip of paper. Mouth open, he just stared at it.

'Mick?' When he didn't look up, she took the paper from his fingers and read it. Her heart pounded in her chest. Her belly tightened. And something deeper inside tensed, taking her breath away.

'A – a million euro?'

'What's this all about, Tighe?' asked Mick. 'I've been over dad's accounts. There's nothing in them saying he had this kind of money.'

Tighe chuckled. 'Your father won the Lotto.'

Kate flashed a look between Mick and Tighe. 'He never said he won the lottery, Mr Lynch.'

'Lottery winnings are tax-free. That's probably why you never saw it on the farm accounts. The money was deposited directly into a special account and has been earning interest. I was instructed to present the check with this letter today if you two had married,' Tighe explained.

'And if we hadn't?' asked Mick.

'Then the money would have gone to charity. The interest on the million will be divided between the charities outlined per Donal's instructions. Oh, and there's a stipend for Molly to keep her in biscuits for the rest of her life.'

Mick laughed. 'Dad thought of everything, didn't he?'

'Indeed he did. I believe Kate should talk to her parents about the rest of the money. Donal and Liam always bought their lottery tickets under the same numbers.'

'I guess that accounts for the new tractor and Mam's new kitchen.'

329

Her belly twisted again. 'Mick, I'm not feeling very well.' She rubbed her belly. Immediately, he was on his feet, a worried expression on his face. 'You're white as a sheet, love. Let me get you upstairs so you can rest. We've had some shocking news today.'

'No, Mick. I think I'm beyond resting. You better get me to the hospital.'

His eyes went wide and he froze.

It was Tighe who leapt into action. 'I'll drive you to the hospital.' Between Mick and Tighe, they managed to get her onto her feet, but as soon as she stood, fluid sluiced onto the pavement. 'On second thoughts, let's get you into the house. Michael, you better call for an ambulance.'

'I've flowers for you, Mrs. Spillane.' Brigit, a pretty young nurse, entered the room.

'Just because I'm married now, Brig, doesn't mean you can't still call me Kate.'

Brigit laughed. When Kate had worked in this hospital, they'd shared a few shifts together and had been quite friendly. Kate once thought they could be friends outside of work.

Kate looked around the room and wondered where this new arrangement would fit. The large private room she had been put into was quickly running out of space. Beside her bed, Mick was slumped in a chair with his daughter resting in his arms. Across the room, Conn held her son.

Twins! Who'd have thought?

With the flowers safely set down, Brig it turned to plump Kate's pillows and check her chart. 'My, this is a sight to behold, isn't it?' Brigit nodded at the men.

''Tis and all. I wish I had a camera.'

'I hate to interrupt them. They look so sweet.'

Kate chuckled sleepily, knowing the nurse referred to the men. 'It's all right. They'll forgive you. Besides, they'll need their rest. When we get home, I've got plenty of chores to keep them busy.' She winked at the nurse when Conn's head shot up.

She thought they'd have to put up a 'Do Not Disturb' sign on the door. No sooner had Conn been ushered out than her parents showed up. As they left, Tighe Lynch stepped in, followed by what seemed like the rest of Connemara. She was tickled by all the attention. She never realized she had so many friends until they all came to wish her, Mick, and the babies well. Even the hospital staff she'd worked with before being fired had come to visit. She was glad no animosity existed.

The room was empty now, save herself and Mick, who sat in the chair across the room, staring at her from behind his unruly curls.

'And what are you staring at? You've such a serious look about you.'

'Having babies is serious business, love.'

'You don't have to tell me that. I'm the one who had those two.'

She closed her eyes and sighed contentedly. She was a married woman now, mother of twins, and in love with the man of her dreams. What more could a girl want?

'You're tired. I should leave you to sleep.' He rose and wound his way through all the flowers.

'You'll do no such thing. Get over here.' She

scooted over on the single bed and motioned for him to lie beside her.

'Are you sure?' He quickly looked at the partially closed door.

'Yes, I'm sure.' She smiled as he stretched out beside her on the bed and pulled her, carefully, against him to spoon – her favorite intimacy position. Even tired and sore, she snuggled deeper into her husband's arms.

'You didn't mean any of those things you said earlier ... did you?' he asked cautiously.

''Twas the pain talking. That's all.'

'Are you sure? What was it you said? Oh yes. I was a bastard for getting you pregnant. And that wasn't the worst of it.'

'I didn't mean any of it, Mick. Truly. I love you, and I can't tell you how happy I am that we have our babies.'

His arms tightened around her. 'And I can't wait to give you more.' He kissed the curve of the neck.

'Mmm. I can't wait until your arms will fit all the way around me again.'

He chuckled. 'I'll take you any way I can get you, love.'

She closed her eyes, reveling in his embrace.

An hour later, it was this very position the nurse found them in when she came in to check Kate's blood pressure and temperature. The door made little more than a whoosh as it closed behind her, leaving them to their rest. Kate smiled as she sank deeper into Mick's embrace.

The phone rang and woke him. Mick looked at

his watch and noticed they'd been sleeping for a couple hours. The sun was just going down and everything was quiet around them.

He reached over to answer the phone, letting Kate sleep. "Lo?' he whispered.

'Mick?' asked a woman's voice.

'Howya, Eilis. What's the craic?' He yawned as he moved off the bed, whispering so he didn't disturb Kate.

'We heard the good news. Twins? My, my.'

'Can you believe it? Me an only child and Kate's family never seeing them.'

'It's all your own fault, you know.'

'What's that supposed to mean?'

'All that teasing about me being big enough for twins, and now you're the one with them.' She laughed outright.

'Maybe so, but I wouldn't trade them for anything.'

'Ah, Mick. I can tell you're in love already. Have you named them yet?' Her sincere excitement came through the phone line.

'Aye. Mary Deirdre and Liam Donal. Original, huh?'

'Ah, such an honor for both of your parents. I bet they're beautiful.'

'They are and all.'

He looked over at his wife who'd woken and turned over to watch him. She smiled invitingly and his groin tightened. He'd have to remind himself they had to wait forty days before they started making more babies. Not that he'd wait so long before he touched her again.

'I won't keep you, Mick. I just wanted to say

333

congratulations. And to say how wonderful it is that everything worked out for you and Kate.'

'Thanks, Eilis. It's hard to say I wish all the other stuff had never happened. But you know, if it hadn't, I probably wouldn't appreciate what I have now.' He reached out to take the hand Kate offered him, gazing at her as he spoke.

'I know exactly what you mean. I'll let you go now. Kieran wants a word before I hang up. Talk to you soon, and give my love to Kate.'

Then Kieran was on the line. 'Hey, mate. I hear you've got twins.'

'Aye, I do.'

'You poor bastard.'

The publishers hope that this book has given you enjoyable reading. Large Print Books are especially designed to be as easy to see and hold as possible. If you wish a complete list of our books please ask at your local library or write directly to:

Magna Large Print Books
Magna House, Long Preston,
Skipton, North Yorkshire.
BD23 4ND

This Large Print Book for the partially sighted, who cannot read normal print, is published under the auspices of

THE ULVERSCROFT FOUNDATION